When he pulled up to the gates of his compound Chopra found himself confronted by yet another crowd. Impromptu crowds, he reflected darkly, were the bane of Mumbai.

A flatbed truck was parked outside the compound, a driver leaning nonchalantly against the tailgate, chewing on a rod of sugarcane.

Chopra paid the rick driver, then entered the compound. Respectfully, the crowd parted, and Chopra found himself standing between his wife, a small man in a string vest and dhoti, and an elephant.

A baby elephant, he corrected himself, and a very small one at that.

The little beast was hunkered down on the dusty ground, apparently oblivious to the fuss going on around it. Its small ears flapped away the occasional fly, while its trunk was curled up under its face. A length of rusted chain was lassoed around its neck, the end of the chain held by the man in the dhoti.

Chopra was tempted to pinch himself. During the hectic day at the station he had all but dismissed the unwelcome news of the elephant from his mind. It had seemed too incredible, perhaps another of the pranks for which his uncle had been notorious throughout his life.

But there was no getting around the fact that a living, breathing pachyderm was now parked on Chopra's doorstep.

By Vaseem Khan

Baby Ganesh Agency Investigations

The Unexpected Inheritance of Inspector Chopra

The Perplexing Theft of the Jewel in the Crown

A Baby Ganesh Agency Investigation

VASEEM KHAN

www.redhookbooks.com

This book is dedicated to my family. To my late mother, Naweeda, whose words inspire me still. To my father, Mohammed. To my sisters and brother, Shabana, Rihana, Irram and Addeel. And to Nirupama Khan who first showed me her Mumbai.

Redhook Books/Orbit
Hachette Book Group
1290 Avenue of the Americas
New York, NY 10104
www.HachetteBookGroup.com

Printed in the United States of America

LSC-C

First U.S. edition: September 2015
Originally published in Great Britain by Mulholland Books

10 9 8 7 6 5 4 3 2

Library of Congress Control Number: 2015907816
ISBN: 978-0-316-38682-1

INSPECTOR CHOPRA RETIRES

On the day that he was due to retire, Inspector Ashwin Chopra discovered that he had inherited an elephant.

'What do you mean he's sending me an *elephant*?' he said, turning in astonishment from the mirror in which he had been adjusting the collar of his uniform to face his wife Archana, who was hovering anxiously in the doorway, and who was known to friends and family alike as Poppy.

'Here, see for yourself,' said Poppy, handing him the letter. But Chopra had no time for that now. It was his final day in office and Sub-Inspector Rangwalla was waiting for him downstairs in the police jeep. He knew that the boys at the station had planned some sort of farewell celebration, and, not wishing to ruin their surprise, he had been feigning ignorance of the preparations going on around him all week.

Chopra stuffed the letter into the pocket of his khaki trousers, then headed for the door with Poppy in tow, her heart-shaped face pulled into a pout. Poppy was annoyed.

Her husband had not even noticed that she had worn a new silk sari for this special day, that fresh lotus flowers garlanded the silky black bun of her hair, that kohl had been expertly applied beneath her almond-shaped brown eyes. A frown now sat above her small nose and two spots of colour glowed on her milkmaid-fair cheeks. But Chopra's thoughts were already at the station.

What he couldn't know then was that the day would hold another, entirely unanticipated surprise – a murder case, the final case of his long and illustrious career, the case that would rock the city of Mumbai to its foundations and herald the birth of its most singular detective agency.

'It will be one hundred and four degrees today,' remarked Rangwalla as they juddered along the potholed access road leading out of the Air Force Colony within which Inspector Chopra lived. Chopra could well believe it. Already his shirt was sticking to his back, a rivulet of sweat snaking down from under his peaked cap to drip onto his nose.

It was the hottest summer in Mumbai for more than twenty years. And for the second year in a row the monsoons had failed to arrive on cue.

As usual the route to the station was clogged with traffic. Auto-rickshaws buzzed through the dusty urban maze, a menace to man and beast alike. A low-lying cloud of pollution curdled the heat, stinging Chopra's nostrils as he leaned out of the rickshaw and squinted up at another of the numerous giant hoardings that had sprung up around the city since the start of the elections. A labourer in shorts and a tattered vest was balanced precariously on bamboo scaffolding painting a moustache onto the grinning face of a well-known politician.

Chopra leaned back as the local market slid by and the air became hazy with spice particles and the smell of rotting vegetables. A line of roadside food sellers added to the noxious miasma: iron-stomached construction workers queued for early-morning rations sizzling on giant frying pans heated by butane cylinders.

Further along they saw an elephant lumbering down the road, a mahout perched on its back, a bamboo sun hat pulled down low over his ears. Chopra watched the beast sway past. 'An elephant!' he muttered to himself, recalling his recent conversation with Poppy. Surely there had to be some mistake!

A crowd had gathered in the station's courtyard. At first Chopra thought that this was the 'surprise' the boys had been planning for him . . . and then he realised that the gaggle of sweating citizenry was of the type that seemed to materialise, as if by magic, at the scene of any altercation on Mumbai's pavementless streets.

A loud voice could be heard emanating from deep within the bovine press of bodies.

In the centre of the crowd Chopra found the plump,

sweating form of young Constable Surat being loudly berated by a short, dumpy woman in a dun-coloured sari.

'My son is dead, and they won't lift a finger!' the woman was shouting. 'They are only here to serve their rich masters! I won't let them get away with it!'

A number of purse-mouthed clones of the woman muttered encouragement from the edges of the circle.

Chopra immediately noted that the woman's eyes were red and swollen as if she had been crying. Her greying hair had escaped her bun, and straggled around her sweating forehead, on which a red bindi had run, adding to the overall impression of derangement. Confronted by Chopra's uniform, and stern expression, the woman momentarily stopped shouting.

Chopra knew that he cut an authoritative figure. A tall, broad-shouldered man with a handsome head of jet-black hair greying only at the sideburns, he had aged well. His brown skin was as yet unlined. Dark soulful eyes beneath thick eyebrows gave him the aura of a serious man. Beneath those eyes sat a nose that his wife assured him had 'character'. Privately, Chopra was proudest of his moustache, a bristling, well-groomed affair like a double-handed salute held steady beneath his nose.

'What is the matter, madam?' asked Chopra, severely.

'Why don't you ask *him*?' She pointed at Rangwalla, who swivelled his eyes away from the woman's accusing finger and towards Chopra.

'Look!' howled the woman to her crowd of followers. 'He hasn't even *told* the inspector sahib! If I came here in a big white Mercedes they would be jumping around me like pye-dogs! But for a poor woman and her poor son, there is no justice!'

'Enough!' barked Chopra. He was pleased to see that everyone, even the woman, fell silent. 'Rangwalla, explain to me what is going on.'

'What will he explain?' exploded the woman. '*I* will explain! My son, my precious boy, has been killed! His body has been lying in your police station since last night. Until now, not even one officer has come to my house to take a report. Whole night I have waited, crying for my dead son.'

'Rangwalla, is this true?'

'It is true that we have a body, sir.'

'Where is it?'

'In the back, sir.'

'Madam, I must ask you to wait here. Rangwalla, come with me.'

Rangwalla followed Chopra into the rear of the station, where the cells and the storage facilities were housed. In the cells a brace of drunks slept fitfully, and a local thief, well known to Chopra, salaamed as he strode past.

In the storeroom, on a stack of banana crates, lay the body.

Chopra pulled aside the white sheet with which it had been covered and looked down at the bloated, greying face. The boy had once been handsome.

'Why didn't you tell me?'

'It was your last day. The boy was dead anyway. Clear case of drowning.'

'The world hasn't stopped because it is Inspector Chopra's last day,' said Chopra sternly, then: 'Where was he found?'

'In Marol, where the pipeline ends. He must have fallen into the sewage creek. He certainly smelled like it.'

'The creek must be almost dry,' frowned Chopra. 'There's been no rain for months.'

'It seems he was drunk. A whisky bottle was found beside his body.'

'Who found him?'

'A local raised the alarm. They sent a boy over to tell us. I had the body brought here, and sent Surat along to ask a few questions, but no one had seen anything.'

It was funny, thought Chopra, how, in a city of twenty million, where it was virtually impossible to enjoy a moment of privacy, his fellow citizens so often managed to see absolutely nothing.

'Why was the body brought *here*?' It was unusual for a corpse to end up at the station. Usually it would be ferried straight to the local hospital.

'We contacted the hospital but there was some trouble going on over there. I believe some lunatics had set up a roadblock and were harassing vehicles going in and out. I thought it would be better to pick up the body ourselves and keep it here until the morning.'

Chopra understood. The ongoing elections were a heated affair. Up and down the country ordinary people – the 'lunatics' Rangwalla referred to – were making their voices heard. It had been a particularly busy time for Mumbai's police officers. Indians, on the whole, did not believe in demonstrating quietly.

'Do you have a panchnama?'

'Yes.' The panchnama was prepared by the first officer at

the scene and countersigned by two local people of 'good standing' who attested to the fact that a body had been discovered and that the police had been duly summoned. Rangwalla had done well. In many areas of Mumbai, finding two citizens of good standing was harder than finding the killer, Chopra had often reflected.

'How was the body identified?'

'The boy was carrying a driving licence. We contacted his family. The mother came in last night and confirmed the identity. She made quite a scene. I had to send her home.'

Losing a son, thought Chopra. What a terrible shock that must have been! No wonder the poor woman seemed unhinged.

'Look, sir, don't take this the wrong way, but . . . this will soon be Inspector Suryavansh's problem. Let him deal with it.'

Suryavansh was his successor at the station. Chopra hesitated, but then realised that Rangwalla was absolutely correct. It was a matter of protocol, after all. In a few short hours he would no longer be a police officer. He would no longer be Inspector Chopra, just plain old Ashwin Chopra, another member of the billion-strong *aam junta* that made India great.

He was suddenly overcome by a deep feeling of melancholy.

The day passed quicker than he could have thought possible.

After Rangwalla had taken the woman's statement, she had finally agreed to be driven home. Chopra had then settled into the well-worn wooden chair behind his desk to complete the various formalities of his last day in office.

Above him the creaking ceiling fan ladled the hot air around the room, while the *Times of India* wall-clock counted down the final moments of his career. To Chopra the clock sounded like a ticking bomb.

At lunchtime he opened his tiffin-box and sniffed his food. It was a ritual. Chopra was fiercely allergic to ginger – in the presence of which he would sneeze uncontrollably – and had made a longstanding habit of authenticating his meals, even though he knew his wife rarely forgot his aversion. Today Poppy had made him a meal of aloo gobi and chapatti, still warm inside the tiered tiffin-box. But he had no appetite.

He pushed the steel containers aside just as Poppy called to remind him to take his pills. Dutifully, Chopra removed the bottle of tablets from his pocket, shook two into the palm of his hand, then gulped them down with a glass of water and a shudder.

The ritual depressed him greatly.

At three o'clock Chopra was surprised by a call from Assistant Commissioner of Police Suresh Rao. Chopra had been reporting to Rao for years – the Sahar station was one of three that lay within ACP Rao's remit. He and Rao had never seen eye to eye. Rao had once run the nearby Chakala station and Chopra had found him to be a mealy-mouthed thug; a round-faced, pot-bellied little dictator known for his cronyism and exuberant use of police force. In the way of things in the Brihanmumbai police, Rao had been promoted whilst Chopra himself remained in post.

Briefly Chopra wondered if Rao had called to gloat. The ACP had been on cloud nine ever since he had discovered that Chopra was being forced into early retirement. But Rao surprised him by launching himself in another direction altogether. 'Chopra, it has come to my attention that a body was discovered in Marol last night.'

'Yes,' Chopra said. 'That is correct.' He could not bring himself to punctuate his sentences with 'sir' when talking to the ACP.

'Can you tell me by whose authority the body was taken to your station, instead of the hospital?'

Chopra hesitated, then said: 'By my authority.' He had no wish to see Rangwalla on the carpet. 'What exactly is the problem?'

'Well, it is not procedure, is it?' the ACP whined. 'At any rate, make sure the body is sent to the hospital right away. Remember, Chopra, this is your last day. Your interest in matters is at an end.'

'My interest in matters ends at precisely 6 p.m. this evening,' Chopra said.

'Always pig-headed!' Rao said, losing his temper. 'Well, let me tell you, Chopra, your days of insubordination are done.' He drew a deep breath. 'Get that body to the hospital. That is an order!'

'And the autopsy?'

'What autopsy?'

'The boy's death may have been the result of foul play. I will be authorising an autopsy.'

'You will be doing no such thing!' Rao exploded. 'The case is open and shut. The boy drowned. There is no need of any autopsy.'

What is going on here? Chopra thought. 'How do *you* know the boy drowned?'

Rao seemed to splutter on the end of the line, then said, 'I make it my business to know. That is why I am an ACP and you are not. Now listen to me very carefully. There is to be no autopsy. The boy drowned. Case closed.'

'Perhaps I will decide for myself,' Chopra said hotly.

'By God, man, who do you think you are!' Rao exploded. 'I'll have your badge—!' He stopped as he realised what he was saying. Then, 'Just get that body to the morgue.'

Rao banged the phone down.

Chopra stared at the wall for a long moment before finally returning the receiver to its cradle.

The end of the day arrived. Inspector Chopra began to clear away his things. He had brought a box with him and into this he neatly emptied the contents of his desk and cupboards. After all these years, there really wasn't much. He had never been the kind to adorn his office with personal bric-a-brac. There were no pictures of Poppy or children; no garlanded photos of his late parents. There was a gold-plated pen stand and inkwell, which his wife had gifted him for one of his birthdays. There were the plaques he had received for completing ten, twenty and thirty years of service. There was his anglepoise desk lamp, by whose light he had written out innumerable reports in the quiet of the station evenings. There was the glassy-eyed stuffed lizard which his old friend, Ashok Kalyan, had given him many years ago as a joke, to remind him of the time he had fallen into a well back in their village of Jarul in the Aurangabad district of Maharashtra. Ashok had had to rescue him, but not before Chopra had screamed himself hoarse in terror of the numerous lizards that had, in their own blind panic, clambered all over him. (Chopra still hated the creatures, and a shudder would pass through him each monsoon, when they tended to slip into Mumbai's apartments and lurk behind curtains, or in bathrooms, scurrying out when you least expected it.)

Chopra was disappointed not to have received a call from Ashok. Ashok was the MLA – Member of the state Legislative Assembly – for the Andheri East constituency of Mumbai, where Chopra lived. Chopra knew that Ashok was extremely busy these days, what with the elections, but had nevertheless hoped he might call. After all, they went back a long way, right back, in fact, to when they had both started out together on the Mumbai police force over thirty years ago.

Chopra hesitated momentarily as he regarded the framed

photograph of himself receiving his Kirti Chakra, a gallantry medal from the Deputy Commissioner of Police. It dated from nine years before, when he had led the raid on a warehouse in the nearby MIDC-SEEPZ industrial quarter, where the notorious gangster Narendra 'Kala' Nayak had been hiding. Nayak had been the target of a Mumbai-wide manhunt, but it was Chopra and his brigade of local officers who had finally taken him down.

Chopra removed the photograph from the wall and put it in with the rest of his possessions.

All in all it was a depressingly meagre hoard.

A curious thing happened as he completed his packing. He discovered a strange sensation arising from the pit of his stomach, and gradually engulfing him. 'It's just another day,' he muttered to himself, but the words sounded hollow, even to his own ears. He had been preparing for this moment for eight months, ever since the doctor's report had confirmed his worst fears; and yet, now that it had finally arrived, he found that he was only mortal after all.

Even Inspector Chopra, who never allowed his emotions to get the better of him, who was always rational and sober, could be overcome by sentimentality.

And finally it was time to leave. 'Rangwalla, please fetch me a rick.'

Rangwalla looked at him, aghast. 'But, sir, I will take you home in the jeep!'

'No,' said Chopra firmly. 'That would not be appropriate. As of this moment I am no longer a police officer. I am a private citizen, therefore I am not entitled to ride home in a police jeep. And you do not have to call me "sir" any more.'

'Yes, sir.'

Chopra could not help but note the diamonds glistening at the corners of Rangwalla's eyes. Twenty years they had served together, a long time in anyone's book. If Chopra considered any of his junior officers to be friends, then Rangwalla came the closest to that description.

Rangwalla, a thin man with a dark face ravaged by childhood acne – the craters now partially hidden beneath a close-cropped black beard – was a devout Muslim and had proven, over the years, to be a more than able lieutenant. His lack of a formal education was compensated for by his tough upbringing on the streets of Bhendi Bazaar, a Muslim enclave of south Mumbai. It was rare for someone entering the force through the constabulary exams to rise to the rank of Sub-Inspector, but Rangwalla had what Ashok Kalyan would call 'street-smarts', a commodity that Chopra felt was fast becoming unfashionable in modern India.

The auto-rickshaw arrived. Constable Surat loaded Chopra's box of possessions onto it and Chopra solemnly shook hands with each of the station personnel, many of whom could not hold back their emotions. Each man had brought him a gift, which they now handed over with due solemnity. Constable Surat, who was young, overweight and impressionable, and hero-worshipped Chopra, gave the inspector a small marble statue of Lord Krishna playing his flute, weeping bitterly all the while.

Chopra, standing by the rick, took one last look at the station, its whitewashed outer wall, the barred windows, the little palm tree in the terracotta-tiled courtyard, the sun-cracked, hand-painted sign above the permanently open saloon-style front doors on which was displayed the station's name . . . Twenty years! he thought. Twenty years in a single posting!

He realised that he knew this place more intimately than he did his own home. The thought brought a lump to his throat.

THE ELEPHANT ARRIVES

When he pulled up to the gates of his compound Chopra found himself confronted by yet another crowd. Impromptu crowds, he reflected darkly, were the bane of Mumbai.

A flatbed truck was parked outside the compound, a driver leaning nonchalantly against the tailgate, chewing on a rod of sugarcane.

Chopra paid the rick driver, then entered the compound.

Respectfully, the crowd parted, and Chopra found himself standing between his wife, a small man in a string vest and dhoti, and an elephant.

A baby elephant, he corrected himself, and a very small one at that.

The little beast was hunkered down on the dusty ground, apparently oblivious to the fuss going on around it. Its small ears flapped away the occasional fly, while its trunk was curled up under its face. A length of rusted chain was lassoed around its neck, the end of the chain held by the man in the dhoti.

Chopra was tempted to pinch himself. During the hectic day at the station he had all but dismissed the unwelcome news of the elephant from his mind. It had seemed too incredible, perhaps another of the pranks for which his uncle had been notorious throughout his life.

But there was no getting around the fact that a living, breathing pachyderm was now parked on Chopra's doorstep.

'Ah, Chopra, it is good that you are here,' frowned Mrs Rupa Subramanium, the president of the Air Force Colony's Managing Committee. 'I was just explaining to your wife that pets are not allowed in the complex. You will find this clearly noted in part 3, subsection 5, clause 15.5.2 of the building regulations, as I am sure you are aware.'

'It is not a pet,' said Poppy heatedly. 'It is a member of the family.'

Mrs Subramanium, a tall, mantis-like presence in a dark sari and a severe coif, did not deign to reply to this ridiculous assertion.

Chopra sighed inwardly. Mrs Subramanium was right, of course. But he knew that his wife would never agree to this fact.

Poppy Chopra had been the first person ever to challenge Mrs Subramanium's longstanding rule over the Air Force Colony apartment complex. When they had first moved into the compound, five years previously, she had quickly discovered that the other tenants lived in terror of the aging widow. Not one of them had ever questioned Mrs Subramanium's edicts; in fact, not one of them had ever even asked for a copy of the legendary building regulations from which she quoted on a regular basis and in which were supposedly enshrined the tenets of her iron diktat.

Poppy, as Chopra had discovered not long after they had been married, was afraid of nothing and no one.

Soon she was instituting committees of her own, and rallying her neighbours in pursuit of various causes of her own making.

Only last year she had managed – much to Mrs Subramanium's chagrin – to persuade the Managing Committee to pass a resolution to open up the rooftop terraces of the three twenty-storey-high towers that made up the complex for celebratory gatherings such as at Diwali or on New Year's Eve. Many buildings in Mumbai did this as a matter of course, but Mrs Subramanium had long vetoed such gatherings on the basis that they occasioned what she considered 'improper behaviour'.

Chopra looked between the two women as they glared at each other. He knew that while his wife was in this mood, there would be no talking to her.

In the end, it was agreed that the elephant would be tethered to a post beside the guard hut at the rear of the compound, and would stay there until Mrs Subramanium convened the Managing Committee to rule on the matter.

Chopra and Poppy lived on the fifteenth floor of the first tower in the complex, Poomalai Apartments. The other two were called Meghdoot and Vijay, the towers collectively named in honour of three famous operations undertaken by the Indian Air Force. Mumbai's lack of space dictated that the bulk of the burgeoning middle class now lived in such high-rise prisons. The city was a hive of construction. If they kept building towers at the current rate, Chopra imagined that Mumbai would soon resemble a giant pincushion. The thought did not please him.

When he opened the door to his apartment, he was immediately engulfed by a thick miasma of burning incense and scented woodsmoke. His senses reeled.

From the floor of the spacious main living area, the face of the person he most disliked in the world turned to look at him with its customary glare of disapproval.

'Where were you?' snapped Poornima Devi, Poppy's mother. 'Couldn't you be on time for this at least?' The old woman – a grey-bunned, spider-like presence in her white widow's sari – glared at him, her black eyepatch radiating hostility.

He and Rao had never gotten along. In part this was literally true, due to the fact that she possessed only one eye, having lost the other in a disagreement with a cockerel many years earlier, but mainly it was because his mother-in-law had never approved of Chopra as a husband for her daughter.

Back when she was busily vetting suitors for her daughter, Poornima Devi had heard that the local landowner, Mohan Vishwanath Deshmukh, had his eye on Poppy. The fact that he was some thirty years older than Poppy and a widower with a reputation for drinking and womanising did not seem to faze her. He was a landowner, and that was all that mattered.

'You could have been a jagirdar's wife,' was a refrain that Chopra often heard falling from the old woman's lips. Usually she waited for him to be in the vicinity before she told her daughter this, more so since she had moved in with them three years ago when her own husband, Dinkar Bhonsle, had passed away.

Once again Chopra reflected on how democratic death was, to take away a man as noble, respected and generous-hearted as his father-in-law, and leave behind the bilious wife whom he had never once heard anyone say anything good about.

On a number of occasions Chopra had tried to convince Poppy that her mother would be better off with her son back in the village. It was, after all, the son's duty to look after his ailing mother, not the son-in-law's. But Poppy wouldn't hear of it.

'You know what a wastrel Vikram is,' she would say. 'He can barely look after himself, how will he look after Mummiji?'

Chopra's brow furrowed in alarm as his mother-in-law advanced upon him. Then he remembered that the old zealot – aided and abetted by his wife – had organised a special religious service to mark the occasion of his retirement.

By nature Chopra was not a religious man. He had long ago decided that organised religion was the number one cause of divisiveness in his great country. He considered himself a devout secularist; he treated all religions with equal respect and personal indifference. This noble sentiment was complicated by the fact that Poppy was a great fan of all things that involved them in what Chopra thought of as the pageantry of their faith.

Take this evening, for instance. A retirement was a matter of fact. What had God to do with it?

Chopra glanced helplessly at his wife. But Poppy was a willing conspirator in his torture and merely smiled encouragingly at him.

He stayed long enough for his mother-in-law to smear holy ash on his forehead and force a stale ladoo into his mouth with such bad grace that she almost chipped one of his teeth, and then he excused himself.

He made his way back downstairs to the courtyard, where he found a gaggle of the building's children gathered around the elephant, which was now tethered by a padlocked chain to a metal pole beside the guard hut at the rear of the towers. This section of the compound was cemented and curved down sharply before flattening out to the brick wall that circled the entire complex. It formed a depression that always flooded during the monsoon, leaving poor Bahadur and Bheem Singh to wade around knee-deep in the swirling rainwater in order to get to and from their guard hut.

The elephant calf was hunkered down on the ground, peering up at the children with doleful eyes. It looked terribly dejected, Chopra thought, and somewhat undernourished. Frail was not a word one usually associated with an elephant, but this one certainly looked as if it needed to build up its strength.

He noted that the children had drawn a series of coloured chalk circles around the calf. As he watched they began circling it and singing, 'Jai, Bal Ganesha! Jai, Bal Ganesha!'

One of the children suddenly bent down and drew a red bindi on the elephant's forehead. The calf immediately flattened its ears and closed its eyes. Its trunk curled further under its mouth. It looked, for all the world, as if it wished to burrow into the earth. Chopra could sense the creature's distress.

'Children, this elephant is not a toy,' he said sternly. 'Go on, now. Go and play somewhere else.'

The children skipped away, casting disappointed looks back at the trembling calf.

At that moment the guard Bahadur wandered up. Chopra gave him a severe look and said: 'Bahadur, I am putting you in charge of this elephant. No one is to harass the poor creature. Do you understand?'

Bahadur pulled himself up to his full unimpressive height, somewhat lost inside his oversized khaki bush shirt and shorts. Bahadur, with his round face and Asian eyes, was descended from the Gurkhas; his real name was something unpronounceable. Bahadur stuck out his pigeon chest. 'Ji, sahib!'

'Has it eaten anything?'

'No, sahib.' Bahadur indicated a pile of bananas and mixed vegetation, both fresh and rotting, which lay untouched beside the calf.

'By the way, is it a boy or a girl?'

Bahadur opened his mouth to speak and then realised that he did not know the answer. 'One minute, sahib.' Without further ado, he scrambled onto the ground, lifted the elephant's tail and attempted to ascertain the creature's sex. 'It is a boy, sahib.'

Chopra crouched down and patted the elephant on the crown of its head. 'Well, young Ganesha, what am I to do with you?'

That night Inspector Chopra awoke with a feathery feeling of spiderwebs passing across his face. He sat up in bed and turned to Poppy who was, as usual, dead to the world. When they had been younger he had worried that there was something unnatural, even unhealthy, in the way his wife seemed to enter an enchanted sleep each night.

In the corner of the bedroom the air-conditioner thrummed away. He wished that for once Poppy might awake so that they could talk.

Eventually, unable to return to sleep, he got up and went into the living room, tiptoeing past his mother-in-law's bedroom.

Chopra went to the windows, pushed aside the curtains and looked out over the city.

From his fifteenth-floor apartment he had an excellent view of Sahar and the adjoining locality of Marol. In the near distance, he could see the blue neon sign of the legendary Leela Kempinski Hotel, and the great glass-faced buildings of the multinational corporations that now lined the Andheri Kurla Road. A little further north was the shanty slum that ran beside the Marol pipeline.

His keen gaze followed the night-time traffic as it sped up the Sahar Road and turned onto the Western Express

Highway, which extended all the way from the suburbs to the furthest edge of the city. Daredevil beggars slept on the ten-inch parapet of the airport flyover, oblivious to the fatal drop on one side and the hurtling traffic on the other.

This was what made Mumbaikers the greatest Indians in the land, Chopra felt. This belief in their own invulnerability.

Chopra loved the city of Mumbai.

When he had first arrived, some three decades ago, the sheer mass of humanity had terrified him. It had been a great shock, coming from the open landscapes of his village. Now he could not imagine living in a place without the noise and sheer energy that powered Mumbai at all times of the day or night.

He would often listen to his colleagues complaining about the many problems that plagued the city: the slums, the pollution, the grinding poverty, the high rates of crime. Chopra thought that this was missing the point. As a famous man had once said, a city was like a woman, and like a woman you could not love only the good bits; you had to love the whole or not at all.

And yet, lately, he would wake up on a bright morning and look out of his window and think that he had awoken in an altogether unknown place. Mumbai's glorious march on destiny was making her unrecognisable to him: the outsourcing bonanza; the advent of hardline Hindutva politics; the westernisation of Bollywood . . . these were all symptoms of a frightening transformation which some were foolish enough to call a 'boom'. And all the time the city grew and grew and grew.

Chopra knew that his nostalgic vision of India was rose-tinted – after all, the universal problems of corruption, caste prejudice and poverty were historical ones. And yet he couldn't help but feel that however untenable his idea of India might seem, it was nevertheless the *real* India, the one that he loved, and the one that was fast disappearing thanks to the mantra of progress.

Yes, thought Inspector Chopra, everything has changed; but I am still the same.

Suddenly, a plaintive mooing came up to him. He leaned out of the window and looked down into the courtyard.

Beside the guard hut he could see the elephant moving around, anxiously circling the pole to which it was chained. The sight of the calf reminded Chopra of the extraordinary fact that he was now the owner of this beast – all thanks to his Uncle Bansi . . . Of course! The letter! Until now he had completely forgotten about it.

Chopra crept back into his bedroom, retrieved the letter from the pocket of his uniform and then retreated to his study.

He switched on his desk lamp, slipped his reading glasses onto his nose, and began to read.

'Dear Krishna,' began Uncle Bansi. (Chopra smiled. His beloved Uncle Bansi had called him Krishna ever since the incident when, as a precocious ten-year-old, Chopra had been caught spying on the village maidens as they bathed in the river. The young Lord Krishna has been renowned for teasing river-frolicking maidens, often making off with their butter churns and breaking their water pots.) 'I know that I have not been in touch with you for many years, but I wish now to ask of you a great boon. I do not have much time left, and must make the necessary arrangements. Soon after you receive this letter, there will arrive at your home an elephant. It is my request that you take in and care for this elephant. It is a newborn, not yet a year old. If I were to tell you the circumstances by which this elephant entered the world you would not believe me, at least not yet. Let me say only this to you: *this is no ordinary elephant*. Remember, what is real and what is *maya*, illusion, is only a matter of perspective. Your Uncle Bansi.'

It was a strange letter, thought Chopra, but then Bansi, his father's elder brother, had always been a strange man.

Chopra's father had loved Bansi dearly, that much he knew, and had taken great enjoyment in regaling the young Chopra with stories of his uncle, each improbable tale only adding to Bansi's legend.

One thing Chopra had established as fact: as an infant, Bansi had fallen into the basket of a travelling snake-charmer. To the astonishment of all he had emerged from the basket completely unscathed.

From that day forth it became a matter of local lore that Bansi shared a special affinity with animals. Perhaps it was a self-fulfilling prophecy, but as time went by Bansi did indeed prove to have a way with the creatures that shared man's world. He even claimed to be able to talk to them, although all but the most credulous of village folk found this hard to believe.

On the morning of his eighteenth birthday Bansi vanished from the village.

He did not return for ten long years, by which time

everyone had decided that he must have long since perished.

When he returned he was almost unrecognisable. His hair had become prematurely white, he had grown a long knotted beard down to his belly, and his eyes seemed to hold things that ordinary men could not begin to imagine.

But beneath this alarming transformation, Bansi's family and friends soon discovered that he was largely the same boy who had left the village all those years ago – a mischievous and intelligent rascal.

This was the period during which Chopra, then a very young boy, had got to know his itinerant uncle.

Bansi had taken him under his wing, and would abscond with him on his frequent walks around the village. They often circled out to the neighbouring hamlets where he was already becoming well known as a sadhu, a man whose blessings were to be sought; in return there would always be a treat, a parcel of jaggery or a rod of sugarcane, which Bansi, ever the generous soul, would share with his nephew.

Chopra recalled now the way his uncle would mutter strange incantations at the behest of some credulous farmer, fluttering his eyelids and hamming it up, much to the awe of his audience. 'They appreciate the theatre,' his uncle would tell him afterwards, with a grin on his face. 'Of course, this doesn't mean that such things don't exist. The great mysteries of the cosmos are everywhere around us, seeded into the land, into the sky, into the air we breathe; all we have to do is open our senses to them.'

They had slept one night under the stars, and Bansi had

told him about his travels to exotic places such as Agra, Lucknow and Benares, the holiest city in the land, and later to the top of the world, the high Himalayas, the great mountains where the Ganga and Brahmaputra rivers are born.

Bansi had told him about Punjab and the village of Goli on the border between India and Pakistan, the place where Chopra's ancestors had lived before they migrated down to Maharashtra, some three generations ago, for a reason that no one could now seem to remember.

Chopra's great-grandfather, a wizened old man who was more fabulously elderly than the eight-year-old Chopra could possibly comprehend, still remembered the move, and told him, in his croaking bullfrog voice, of the trouble they had had settling into the Marathi culture. But settle in they did, and now the Chopra clan were true Maharashtrians: Chopra, like the rest of his family, spoke fluent Marathi to go alongside his native Punjabi and enjoyed Marathi food. There had even been instances of clan members marrying into Marathi households – indeed Chopra's own wife, Poppy, was from a prominent Marathi clan.

Reading Bansi's letter, Chopra found himself struck by mixed emotions. He had had no contact with his uncle for nearly two decades. By now he must be an old man, although, as the years had gone by, Bansi had shown a remarkable resilience to the effects of age. He had continued to live the life of an itinerant, returning from his peripatetic wanderings to his village at ever more infrequent intervals, each time with an ever-more fabulous store of tales.

Chopra hadn't thought of Bansi for years, and now, out of the blue, here was this letter.

Aside from the strange request, the letter seemed to imply that his uncle believed himself to be not long for this world. The thought stirred up emotions in Chopra that he had not felt for a long time. Suddenly, he was a child again, laughing as he skipped along beside his tall, mischievous uncle, the pair of them clambering over the crumbling stone wall of Jagirdar Deshmukh's orchards to steal the ripest hapoos mangoes, gobbling fruit after fruit until the sweet mango nectar dribbled over their chins and clouds of flies came to chase them down from the trees, only moments before the irate mali arrived.

BACK AT THE STATION

The next morning Inspector Chopra awoke for the first time in thirty-four years without the knowledge that he was a police officer.

For a while he lay in bed, staring up at the ceiling. He felt his body urging him to get up, shower, and put on his uniform.

Inertia; wasn't that what people called it? After all, when one has been running, it takes a while for the body to stop even though the finishing line has been crossed.

When he arrived at the breakfast table, dressed in a plain white shirt and cotton trousers, he felt strangely naked.

Poppy was already bustling around the kitchen with the housemaid, Lata, and flashed him a welcoming smile. 'How nice to have you home for breakfast,' she beamed. 'I've made your favourite: masala dosa with sambar.'

Chopra looked down at the steaming dosa on his plate and realised that he had no appetite. He was used to leaving the house precisely at seven. At the station, he would send

Constable Surat to fetch him a vada pao from one of the many street vendors that lined the nearby Sahar Road. In the hurly-burly of the station mornings that was all the breakfast he had needed.

After breakfast, he sat in his study and tried to read; books that he had been meaning to get around to for ever. But then, he suddenly remembered, these books – policing manuals of various descriptions – were of no further use to him. He tidied his study, even though it was, as always, meticulous. Then he rearranged the furniture, even though it had been fine as it was. He tried to watch cricket on the little colour television he had set up in front of his favourite rattan armchair. India was playing abroad and Chopra's favourite player, Sachin Tendulkar, had finished the previous day's play quietly approaching yet another century. But today, though he was usually passionate about following Sachin's batting, he found his mind wandering.

After a while, he went to his desk and took out the calabash pipe that he had purchased many years previously.

Although Chopra would never have admitted it, the truth was that he was a closet Anglophile. He had inherited a healthy respect for the British from his father, who, while not blind to their faults, also understood what the arch-colonialists had brought to the subcontinent during their three-hundred-year reign. Chopra enjoyed all things British and as an impressionable young man had been captivated by Basil Rathbone playing Sherlock Holmes in *Sherlock Holmes Faces Death*. The pipe was an affectation that Chopra exercised only in the privacy of his study. He was not a smoker, but he liked to sit on his balcony and wield the pipe as an accessory to the process of thinking.

On the wall of the study was a portrait of Chopra's other great hero, Gandhi. He was aware that in modern India, Gandhi was considered by many to be irrelevant. Chopra did not agree. He always carried with him a well-thumbed pocketbook of Gandhiisms. He knew, from long experience, that Gandhi had a quote for all occasions.

He took out the book now and thumbed through it . . . What about this one? 'It is the quality of our work which will please God and not the quantity.'

Somehow the words offered him no comfort.

He started to compose a letter to his good friend ACP Ajit Shinde, who had transferred to a posting in the Naxalite-infested jungles of Eastern Maharashtra a few years ago in pursuit of promotion. Chopra himself had been offered the posting before Shinde, but had declined. He had declined a promotion to ACP three times in his career. He hated the politics that came with seniority in the Mumbai police force; he had always preferred the hands-on aspects of policing.

Halfway through the letter he put down his pen and looked at the wall.

He got up and went to the window.

It promised to be another blisteringly hot day. Chopra imagined day after day like this, days stretching out ahead of him for ever . . . Is this what retirement is? he thought. This feeling that you had entered a waiting room, a place that was neither here nor there?

He recalled the visit to the doctor eight months ago,

following the heart attack that had almost cost him his life. Dr Devidikar, an ageing gentleman with tufted ears and a reassuringly wise and indomitable air, had explained to Chopra and a round-eyed Poppy that the inspector was suffering from a condition known as 'unstable angina'. The very words seemed to conjure up the possibility of an unpredictable and calamitous fate. Poppy had almost swooned, as if Devidikar had pronounced sentence on Chopra there and then.

'Not to worry, not to worry,' the doctor had said in his good-humoured voice. 'We're not finished with you yet, sir.' He had told Chopra that the condition was common enough, though not usually for a man in as good a physical shape as Chopra evidently was. 'But these things can be genetic. Body is a great mystery, sir.' The doctor had then delivered the blow that Chopra had been dreading. 'I am afraid that you must desist immediately all activities that may cause anxiety or stress. Next attack may be fatal, sir.'

The doctor had advised that Chopra take early retirement from the police force. This advice had been forwarded to his seniors.

Chopra had resisted, of course, but Poppy had worried him endlessly until in the end he had agreed. The thought of leaving his wife a widow had made him feel selfish and guilty. He could not do that to Poppy. And besides, life was not over just because he was retiring.

'These days life begins at fifty, sir,' Dr Devidikar had said, with a twinkle in his eye.

But what about this supreme sense of . . . of . . . *desolation*?

Why hadn't good old 'life begins at fifty' Dr Devidikar warned him about this? This feeling of bewilderment, listlessness and, if he was being honest with himself, overwhelming terror that Chopra was now experiencing? Devidikar had told Chopra that he should avoid activities that might cause him stress. Did he realise how much stress *that* caused him? To not be able to do the very things that he had spent his whole life doing, the things that gave his life shape and purpose?

Chopra was a practical man and had already begun to plan for a future outside the force. Money was not the issue. A full pension had already been awarded to him, and his needs were simple. No. What was terrifying Chopra was the feeling in his gut that whatever he did now would never be enough, would never be true to the man that he was.

There were no pills that Devidikar could prescribe for that.

After lunch Chopra decided to go out for a walk.

Downstairs in the courtyard he first checked on Ganesha. The little elephant had still not eaten a thing, and, if anything, looked even more despondent than the day before.

Chopra felt a flutter of genuine worry. Ganesha's obvious distress bothered him. The elephant was a child and Chopra had always found the pain of a child the most difficult to bear. It was one of the reasons he had been so tough on those who abused children.

He hoped Ganesha would soon come out of his funk.

Chopra wandered around the Air Force Colony, walking past the flower gardens, which in the prolonged dry spell had been reduced to a display of burnt stalks. He pottered past the deserted badminton courts where he would play the occasional game with his friend and neighbour Captain P.K. Bhadwar, who flew passenger jets and had a devil of a back-hand lob.

For a while he sat on the bench beneath the colossal banyan tree that was a focal point of the complex's grounds. A miniature temple had been built into the trunk of the tree. In the evenings, devout residents would gather to pray and light diyas. One recent disturbing development – it had disturbed Chopra at any rate – was the 'Laughing Club' chapter that now met under the tree each day. It was quite a sight to observe the group of elderly men and women – who, until then, he had regarded as generally staid old types – holding their sides and laughing as if they would expire from it.

Today there was no one.

Outside the Colony Chopra meandered up to the fruit market and bought a kilo of sweet plums for Poppy. Streams of people flowed past. Motorbikes with three or sometimes four individuals precariously balanced like a team of acrobats honked their way through the press of bodies. A thick smell arose from the open sewer on both sides of the road.

A cow had sat down in the middle of the street. Chopra knew that it would stay there for as long as it wished. Cows, with their revered status, were the bane of Mumbai's traffic constables.

As he was buying the fruit, a gaggle of youths from the nearby computing college walked by. They swept past arm in arm, spreading good cheer and laughter as they went. They were the same age, he noted, as the dead boy he had seen at the station.

Chopra recalled the boy's mother, how distressed she had been, how convinced that there would be no help for someone like her in solving the mystery of her child's death. The woman's recriminations had particularly bothered him. Anyone who knew Chopra knew that he prided himself on his integrity. To suggest that he would do less than his duty because the victim was from a poor background, or would somehow do more if the victim had been the son of affluent parents was to suggest that Chopra himself was not an honest man.

Over the years he had maintained a spotless reputation by adhering to the principles his father had taught him as a boy.

'Son,' he had said, on the day that Chopra had left his village as an eighteen-year-old hopeful to begin his training at the police academy in Nashik, 'you must understand that India is a new kind of country. Even though our civilisation stretches back for thousands of years, even though it is all set down there in the Rigveda, the Upanishads, the Puranas, the strange fact is that we are only twenty-three years old and consequently suffer from the afflictions of youth. Since the British cut our country into pieces, we have all felt different. Wouldn't you, if someone chopped off your arms, right and left? In truth, we are still working out what kind of nation we should be. The only way to avoid falling prey to the perils of confusion is to never be confused about what *you* are. If you are an honest man, as I hope you will prove to be, never allow the circumstances of a moment to make you act against your nature. That way lies the ruin of everything you stand for.'

Chopra took a rickshaw to the station, where he was immediately mobbed by his former colleagues. There was a round of good-natured jokes about his casual attire, and a few questions about how his first day as a gentleman of leisure was going.

'It's going,' he mumbled. 'Just don't ask me where.'

In truth, Chopra was taken aback. By nature he was not a sentimental man, and over the years he had maintained a professional distance between himself and the men under his command. Other senior policemen allowed their juniors to become overly friendly, even to the point of drinking with them. But Chopra was not that sort of policeman.

He knew that some of his colleagues considered him to be a bit prickly, but no one could deny his reputation as an excellent and rigidly honest officer of the law. And in the Mumbai police of today this was something to be proud of indeed.

Leaving the men to their work Chopra wandered up to his old office, and discovered Constable Surat installed outside the door.

'Hello, Surat, what are you doing here?'

'Sir! How nice to see you!' Constable Surat seemed positively relieved. 'Sir, new sir has asked me to stand outside the door and check before he receives visitors.'

Chopra frowned. He had operated a far less formal policy. Any of his men could simply walk right up and knock on his door; not that many of them ever did. They knew that Chopra was a stickler for the chain of command. But really, what was the need of wasting a man to act as a glorified porter? 'Well, can you tell the inspector I would like to see him?'

Surat gave a sickly grin. 'So sorry, sir, but new sir is not seeing anyone until two o'clock.'

'Ah, he is in a meeting?'

'No, sir.'

'Then what is the problem? I only wish to have a quick word with him about an important matter.'

'Sir, new sir has given strict instructions.'

Chopra, who had operated throughout his career on the basis of straightforward common sense, decided that he had had enough. Brushing Surat aside, he entered the office.

To his surprise he found the seat behind his old desk empty. He looked around. There was no one in the office. What in the world—? Then his eyes fell on the pair of very large black shoes protruding from behind the desk.

Chopra walked around the desk and discovered Inspector Suryavansh lying on his back on the floor, apparently fast asleep. Erring on the side of caution he knelt down and checked the inspector's pulse. Then, operating on a hunch, he bent his head towards Suryavansh's face; instantly, his nose twitched as the smell of liquor hit him.

Chopra got back to his feet and went out of the office. 'No one is to enter this office until the inspector says so,' he said to a relieved Constable Surat. Then he went looking for Sub-Inspector Rangwalla.

He found Rangwalla sitting in the station's cramped interview room with a very fat man in a grey safari suit who was sweating profusely beneath the wheezing ceiling fan. 'I demand you arrest the scoundrel this very minute!' the man was saying. For emphasis he thumped his knees with both hands. 'Fellow has absconded with my daughter and you sit here and tell me there is nothing you can do! Do you know, he is a Muslim!'

Chopra managed to rescue Rangwalla from the fat man, and they went into one of the back rooms. 'Tell me, has anyone gone to interview the drowned boy's father?' he asked.

'No, sir,' said Rangwalla.

'Why ever not?'

'Inspector Suryavansh's order. He says this is an open-and-shut case. Boy drowned accidentally. End of story.'

'But what about the autopsy?'

'Inspector Suryavansh says no need of autopsy. I am afraid he has countermanded your order.'

Chopra fell silent. 'Where is the body now?'

'It is at the hospital. They will issue a death certificate, then the family can take it for cremation.'

'Show me the panchnama.'

Rangwalla hesitated. 'Sir, please do not be offended, but you are no longer a police officer. Why do you want to be involved in this?'

Chopra hesitated before replying. He had seen many dead bodies over the course of his career. But this was perhaps the last one he would ever see, certainly in his official capacity. That made it significant in some way, he felt. 'Rangwalla, we agreed to be involved the day we took our oath. With or without a uniform, we will always be involved. Besides, I am only making a few enquiries. It is not as if I have anything more pressing to attend to.'

When he left the station, a short while later, it was with a copy of the panchnama tucked away in the pocket of his trousers.

Chopra took a rickshaw into Marol Village. As usual, the Village was bustling with life. This was a poor community, but not a slum. The residents were mainly devout Catholics with Goan roots; the Catholic community of Mumbai was small but vociferous and they prided themselves on their sense of civic order. The houses, though small and cramped together, were well tended and gaudily painted.

Chopra alighted near the address of the first individual listed on the panchnama. When he knocked on the door a short, portly man in blue shorts and white vest stepped onto the porch. He was very dark-skinned, with a black moustache and a telltale tattoo of the Cross on the inside of his wrist. 'Yes?'

'Are you Merwyn De Souza?'

'Yes. What do you want?'

'My name is Inspector Chopra,' said Chopra, showing him the copy of the panchnama. 'I wish you to take me to where the body of the dead boy was discovered two days ago.'

De Souza readily agreed to help. He had nothing else to do anyway, having been recently relieved of his position at the local abattoir where he had worked for ten years. 'You are in plain clothes?' he asked. 'Like CID?'

Chopra did not answer.

They walked along the Marol Pipeline Road, passing the vegetable market and the Mother Mary Convent School. A painting of a blue-eyed, blond Jesus looked down from the convent wall onto the passing traffic with an expression of benign suffering. Two nuns in blue habits conversed by the convent gate. 'Good afternoon, Sisters,' said De Souza, crossing himself.

They passed a man frying banana chips by the side of the road. De Souza insisted on stopping to purchase some. 'Ragu, this is Inspector Chopra, a very good friend of mine. We are currently working on a very important case together. Do you remember that dead body we found the day before yesterday?'

Ragu's eyes rounded with interest as he swirled the frying chips around in the re-used cooking oil of the blackened pan. The pan rested above a butane cylinder housed inside a handcart. 'The boy who drowned in the shit?'

'Yes. Very bad business.'

An emaciated beggar stopped by to scratch himself and stare longingly at the chips. De Souza barked at the man who, in the way of Mumbai's beggars, simply ignored him.

The beggar edged closer. 'Boss, give me some chips. I haven't eaten in three days.'

Ragu raised his ladle threateningly. 'Get out of here. Can't you see I am serving the inspector sahib?'

'The inspector sahib looks as if he has eaten too much already,' said the beggar.

Chopra suppressed a smile. Most beggars in the city were meek, beaten-down specimens, cowed by the relentless assaults of abject poverty. This man seemed to have decided that he would not play the role assigned to him by fate.

Chopra bought the beggar a twist of chips. De Souza stared at him. In Mumbai beggars were so plentiful that they were practically a sub-population in their own right. Feeding a beggar was considered an act of foolhardiness usually committed only by addle-brained tourists.

After a few minutes they walked out of the Village, and into the wasteland beyond.

Amidst a tangle of foliage, they came into the area where the pipeline – a mile-long concrete sewage pipe – ended. The ground was damp with seepage. Chopra's nose twitched at the extraordinarily bad smell in the air. Human excrement, he realised.

'Over here,' said De Souza, leading Chopra around a mound of dumped rubbish to where a shallow pool of water had collected. A number of pigs rooting around in the waste looked up from their foraging to eye Chopra with interest.

He looked around, picked up a nearby stick, then bent down to push it into the pool of stagnant water. Mosquitoes lifted from the surface and buzzed around his face.

He removed the stick and looked at the watermark. 'Six, seven inches,' he muttered. It would be extremely difficult for a man, even a very drunk one, to drown in six inches of water.

'Who discovered the body?'

'I myself,' said De Souza importantly.

'What were you doing here?'

'My lavatory is not working at home.'

'Do many people use this place?'

De Souza shrugged. What was 'many' in Mumbai?

'And you say you found an empty whisky bottle by the body?'

'Nearly empty,' said De Souza. 'Black Label.'

'That is very expensive whisky.'

'Yes,' grinned De Souza. 'Imported.'

How did a poor boy afford such an expensive bottle of liquor? thought Chopra. 'Did you see anything else . . . out of the ordinary?'

'What do you mean "out of the ordinary"?'

Chopra did not know what he meant, but there was a feeling growing inside him that was familiar. It was a feeling that came to him whenever he was working a case and he knew, without being able to put his finger on it, that something was not right.

'*Hutt!*' barked De Souza suddenly as one of the pigs snuffled at his sandal and was rewarded with a stout kick. The pig wandered off, squealing indignantly.

Chopra began to walk around the pool of water in ever-widening concentric circles, his eyes carefully scanning the ground. After a few circuits, he knelt down behind the rotting stump of a tree. The ground was drier here, but there was just enough moisture to reveal the imprint of a pair of tyres. His fingers traced the embedded single track. A motorcycle had parked here.

Who would bring a motorcycle here?

Chopra tried to judge the depth of the imprint. His years as a sub-inspector, when he had been directly involved with the day-to-day business of investigation, told him that there had been two people on the bike, one of them heavyset. Could the boy have been on the bike?

He stood up. There was another mystery here, which no one seemed to have considered. What had the boy been doing here? He was a local of Marol; why did he need to use this place as a latrine? Was there an epidemic of broken lavatories in the area? Chopra filed this under the 'unlikely' heading.

He considered other scenarios that might have brought the boy here.

Perhaps he had been with a friend? Had they been drinking and suddenly needed to go? Had the boy suggested they use this spot, perhaps not wishing to enter his own home in an inebriated state with a drunken friend in tow? And then what? An accidental drowning, Rangwalla had said. But if his friend was drowning, wouldn't the other party have helped? Or was he too drunk himself? But if he was so drunk how did he drive his bike away? And why hadn't he called an ambulance or the police?

Too much conjecture, thought Chopra. Too many unanswerable questions.

HOMI AT THE HOSPITAL

From the Village, Chopra took another rick, this time to the Sahar hospital.

Once there, he plunged his way through the heaving corridors, which always reminded him of the sort of semi-ordered chaos one saw in a riot, and down to the basement level where he found his old friend Homi Contractor, MBBS.

Homi Contractor was the senior police medical examiner stationed at the hospital. In between his duties as a leading heart surgeon, Homi also served in various other capacities in the city of Mumbai. As a scion of the famous Contractor dynasty – whose innumerable philanthropic acts had led to a bronzed statue of Homi's grandfather, Captain Rattanbhai Framji Contractor, being erected in the hospital's recovery garden – Homi had been a shoo-in for the much-coveted position of Chair of the College of Cardiac Physicians and Surgeons of Mumbai, a post that he now ruled with a tyrannical fist.

Outside work Homi was equally industrious, a devoted and domineering father of four, foremost member of the board of the Parsee Cyclists Club – the renowned bastion of Mumbai's oldest cricketing traditions – and a rabidly outspoken critic of the Nehru dynasty.

Chopra had always wondered how his old friend found the time to conduct autopsies for the three police stations under ACP Suresh Rao's command.

Chopra himself had known Homi for more than twenty-five years. He was a grimly cheerful man, with a macabre sense of humour that he often employed whilst elbow-deep inside the internal organs of a corpse.

'You owe me ten bucks, Chopra,' he said gruffly as Chopra walked into his office.

Not for the first time Chopra thought that Homi's thick belly did not sit well with his thin, pale hangdog face. The effect was as if he had stuffed a pillow under his white lab coat. Homi's bulbous nose sat beneath a cap of greying frizzy hair and his grizzled eyebrows were reminiscent of the vultures that ate the Parsee dead in the Towers of Silence on Malabar Hill.

Homi had bet Chopra that Sachin Tendulkar would not complete his century. Sachin had been run out on ninety-nine that very morning. Homi was the only man in India who would dare bet against Sachin. 'And how's the whole retirement business going?' he added.

They exchanged pleasantries, and then Chopra got to the point. 'You had a body come in from my station, a young man found in Marol, possible drowning.'

'What's his name?'

'Santosh. Santosh Achrekar.'

'Achrekar, Achrekar . . . Yes, I know the one. He's down in the morgue. The accidental drowning case. I believe Rohit completed the examination just an hour ago.' Rohit was Homi's youthful assistant. He was a newly qualified examiner, and was usually given the straightforward cases, together with a generous lashing from Homi's acid tongue.

'Have you conducted an autopsy?'

'Autopsy? What for? The station sheet requested no autopsy.'

'*I'm* requesting.'

Homi looked thoughtfully at Chopra's face. 'What's this about, old friend?'

'A hunch.'

Homi shook his grizzled head. 'And who is Homi Contractor, a mere mortal, to question the hunches of the great Inspector Chopra?'

'*Former* Inspector Chopra.' He hesitated. 'You don't have to do it. I would understand.'

'Don't be such a nincompoop. Give me a day. I'll have some results for you tomorrow. The only thing is if I have to send samples to Ranbaxy for analysis, they will charge me. Without a station request, that will leave a hole in the paperwork.'

'I would prefer that the station does not know about this for now.'

'The fees will still have to be paid.'

'I will pay.'

Homi pulled at his cheeks, an old habit of his. For a moment he looked as if he were going to say something, but then he simply nodded. ‘OK. OK. Call me tomorrow. Now, tell me – do you still have time from your busy schedule to go to Wankhede next month for the One Day International with Pakistan?’

‘Homi,’ said Chopra, smiling, ‘time is the one thing I do have now.’

As Chopra walked out of the hospital his thoughts lingered on the parting expression he had seen on Homi’s face. He could practically read his friend’s thoughts. Would this be how it was when Homi himself retired? Like Chopra he was a man devoted to his work. Would he find himself back at the hospital, without his white lab coat, sniffing around the next incumbent of his position, making a nuisance of himself while the juniors laughed at him behind his back?

No, that was not fair, Chopra thought. He was certain that no one had ever laughed at either Homi or himself. He did not think they would start now.

HOW INSPECTOR CHOPRA MET POPPY

When Chopra arrived home, he discovered that the children had ignored his interdiction. The little elephant was still slumped despondently beside the pole to which he had been chained. A garland of lotus flowers had been tied around his tail. Someone had jammed a paper crown onto his knobbly skull; Chopra could see that it was meant to resemble the filigreed gold crown that usually adorned idols of Lord Ganesh. On a silver platter by the elephant's still-uneaten food was a pyramid of coconuts.

'Bahadur!' called Chopra crossly. 'I thought I told you the children were not to interfere with the elephant.'

'Not children, sir!' quavered Bahadur. 'Poppy Madam.'

Chopra felt a surge of irritation. Trust Poppy to turn the poor creature into an object of devotion! And then it occurred to him that it would be a far harder task for Mrs Subramanium to eject a god from the complex than a mere elephant. Poppy had always had a way of being cleverer than he suspected; many times he'd thought he had the better of his wife only to find that she had somehow confounded his intentions.

He shook his head ruefully. Twenty-four years they had been married now. Who would have thought that? Certainly not he, on the day that he had first seen her.

He had been twenty-seven then, already an assistant inspector, returning to his village after a gap of almost three years. As he had been walking past the river, the very river beside which he had been caught as a youth spying on frolicking maidens, he had passed her coming the other way. She had been in the company of her sister, who Chopra recognised as the eldest daughter of Dinkar Bhonsle, sarpanch of the village council.

He had stopped to say hello, and had noted how the beautiful girl had pretended not to be interested in him, even though he was at his dashing best with his hair freshly oiled, his moustache waxed, and wearing his newly pressed khaki uniform. Her sister – a married matron with three children and an eye for a good catch – had been far more impressed, and had insisted that he come to their home for dinner one evening whilst he was in the village.

He had not gone.

Instead, after making enquiries with his family, he had sent his father to arrange for the girl to be married to him. He had discovered that her name was Archana, that she was eighteen, that she was called Poppy by her friends because of her habit of constantly snacking on raw poppy seeds, and that she had passed her elementary school certificate at the second attempt. In fact, like all the children of the village, Chopra's own father had been her tutor.

Shree Premkumar Chopra had graduated from the University of Mumbai in 1947, just a few months before the traumatic upheavals of Partition. Having worked for a number of years in the big city, he had eventually decided to return home and take over the little village school in which he himself had received his junior education. Since then he had been known as Masterji, a term of great affection and respect.

Thus, when Masterji requested the hand of his good friend Dinkar Bhonsle's youngest daughter for marriage to his youngest son, a handsome young police officer living in Bombay city with a monthly income of no less than eleven hundred rupees, there was no question of a refusal. The two old friends were overjoyed to be united as family.

Over the years, Chopra had wondered how his life would have turned out if he hadn't been walking by the river at the precise moment that Poppy and her sister had wandered past. No doubt he would have left the village without meeting her, and, by the time he returned, she would have been married off elsewhere.

He could not imagine his life these past decades without Poppy. He had married for love; this was true, though he would certainly not admit it. He had feared, because of her beauty, and the fact that she was somewhat younger than him, that she might not appreciate a husband with the simple qualities he had to offer, namely, honesty, integrity, thoughtfulness. And when he had discovered that his wife was a fanciful, often flighty romantic, he had feared that perhaps what she had really wished for was a dashing hero like the stars of the Bollywood masala movies she enjoyed so much, an Amitabh Bachchan perhaps, or a handsome Vinod Khanna. But Poppy had proved to be a devoted wife and, in spite of their troubles, they had enjoyed each other's company all these long years.

This thought reminded Chopra of Shalini Sharma, and he felt a sudden pain flower inside his chest.

Chopra had suspected that, following his retirement, he would need something new to inspire him, and this was why he had purchased the run-down old bungalow on Guru Rabindranath Tagore Road. This was why he had employed an architect and a contractor to work on the plot. This was why he was meeting the delectable Miss Shalini Sharma once a fortnight at the Sun-n-Sand Hotel in Juhu. He felt terribly guilty about the whole affair; it made him feel sick to think what would happen if Poppy discovered his secret before he was ready to break the news to her.

'*Subhan'Allah, Chopra Miah, subhan'Allah!*'

Chopra turned to find Feroz Lucknowwallah bearing down on him, with his good friend Vikram 'Vicky' Malhotra in tow.

Feroz and Vicky shared an apartment on the fifteenth floor, making them Chopra's neighbours. Feroz, a lanky beanpole with a goatee and a mop of unruly black hair, was a poet, an aficionado of the Urdu language and devotee of the famous ghazal maestro Mirza Ghalib. He was also a celebrated drunk. Vicky Malhotra, handsome in a debonair way with clean-shaven cheeks and an up-to-the-minute lacquered haircut, was an actor who had a small part in a major serial while he waited for his big break in Bollywood.

Feroz and Vicky were constantly falling foul of Mrs Subramanium's rule book; their raucous parties, which would sometimes go on till the early hours and usually involved Feroz and his friends engaging in drunken poetry competitions whilst Vicky played the tabla as accompaniment, had annoyed Chopra on occasion. But Poppy was very protective of the two young men, insisting that their 'artistic temperaments' be allowed to flourish. They added colour to the building, that much he could agree.

'What a great idea, Chopra Miah!' continued Feroz enthusiastically. 'An elephant in the courtyard! The ghazals are already rushing to my head, I swear absolutely.'

'He looks totally depressed, yaar,' said Vicky. He laughed as if this were the funniest thing in the world.

Chopra knelt down beside the little elephant and removed the paper crown. How long could an elephant go without eating? he thought.

And right there was the problem, whole and soul. He didn't *know*. He knew nothing about elephants. There had been none in his village. The only ones he had seen were in Mumbai. He remembered there had been one on Juhu Beach for many years giving rides to children until that was made illegal. And Byculla Zoo had a pair, male and female. And you saw one now and again wandering down the crowded roads of Mumbai, a mahout on its back, shifting loads around the city. But that was becoming rarer and rarer . . . How could Uncle Bansi do this to him?

The more Chopra thought about it, the more he wondered why his uncle had picked him for this thankless task. Why not his elder brother Jayesh, who, in line with the ancient rules of primogeniture, had stayed in the village to take over their ancestral acreage? Jayesh was a man of the soil; he had bullocks, he had cows; he would know what to do with an elephant. At the very least he would have no problem housing the poor creature, and certainly no Mrs Subramanium to deal with.

The thought of the old battleaxe sharpening her claws gave Chopra heartburn, and he decided to retire to his apartment for a well-earned rest.

After dinner, Chopra went down to check on Ganesha again. The baby elephant still had not eaten anything, and had even turned up his trunk at a sheaf of bamboo shoots which some thoughtful resident had procured for him, and which Chopra had heard were a great pachyderm delicacy. He sat by the little beast and tried to imagine how he must be feeling, displaced from his home, wherever that might be, brought to this strange, clamorous place filled with curious sights, sounds and smells. And people, so many people! No wonder the poor creature seemed shell-shocked.

Chopra re-read his uncle's letter, trying to fathom the mystery of this strange gift. What was Ganesha's story? And why had his uncle claimed that Ganesha was 'no ordinary elephant'?

Inspector Chopra (Retd) went to bed that night no closer to the answers to these troubling questions.

Sleep took some time to arrive. He found his head crowded with thoughts of his retirement. To avoid the unhappiness such thoughts brought with them, he found himself dwelling on the death of Santosh Achrekar. A part of him hoped that Homi's autopsy would end the matter. But another part, the seditious part of his soul that refused to accept that he was no longer a police officer, secretly hoped that Homi's analysis might reveal evidence of foul play.

Chopra had no idea yet what he would do if that proved to be the case.

He finally fell asleep still tossing and turning as he considered the possibilities.

A VISIT TO THE ZOO

The next day Inspector Chopra set off from his home, after forcing down another sizeable breakfast prepared for him by Poppy, in a determined frame of mind. Putting aside all other concerns he had decided that, having been vouchsafed his uncle's trust, he must fulfil his responsibility to the young animal in his care.

'Where are you off to?' said Poppy as Chopra headed for the door.

'I have some errands to run.'

'You are supposed to be retired. You do not have to run errands.' She walked over to him. Taking the tip of her sari she wiped crumbs of toast from his moustache.

'How are you feeling?'

'I feel perfectly fine,' said Chopra. He smiled at his wife. 'What are *you* doing today?'

'I am going to knock on doors. I shall build a support base before the Managing Committee convenes. Remove the ground from beneath Mrs Subramanium's feet before she can make mischief for Ganesha.'

Chopra frowned. 'Poppy, I do not think that is wise. Why don't you let things take their course?'

'Because Mrs Subramanium is wrong. And even if she is right, she is wrong.'

Chopra opened his mouth to reply but was interrupted.

'Well, isn't this a touching scene?'

Poppy and Chopra turned to see Poornima Devi hobbling from her bedroom. 'So much concern for an elephant and a man who looks as healthy as an elephant to me. Why is no one concerned about my health?'

'Because there is nothing wrong with you,' said Chopra.

'Nothing wrong with me?' screeched the old woman. 'I have been at death's door for years.'

'What's stopping you from going through the door?' muttered Chopra under his breath.

'How many times have I asked to be taken to Varanasi so that I can bathe in the pure waters of the Ganges and be cured? But does anyone listen? Does anyone care?'

Chopra reflected that anyone bathing for their health in the waters of Varanasi had clearly not read the government's latest pollution reports. The great river was so filthy there that even holy men had given up immersing themselves.

'We will take you soon, Mother,' promised Poppy. 'Now that Ashwin is retired he has time to plan a trip for all of us.'

Chopra glared at his wife. He noted the mischievous light dancing in her eyes and his glare softened into a reluctant smile. 'I have heard that many old people live for years in Varanasi, just so that they can die in the holy city and attain instant moksha,' he muttered. 'Perhaps we could leave her there.'

'But then you would miss her, dear,' said Poppy sweetly. She gave him another mischievous smile and swished off to get ready for her campaign of guerrilla warfare against Mrs Subramanium.

His first port of call was the new Crossword Bookstore in Juhu.

Juhu was the city's original shining suburb. Even now, all the big movie stars maintained a fancy bungalow in the area, living cheek by jowl with pushy upstarts from the worlds of commerce and cricket. The suburb was home to a plethora of trendy new salad bars and coffee shops of the sort that the young were flocking to.

And yet, Chopra thought, as he looked out from the rickshaw at the eight-storey palace of a famed Bollywood star, even here, beggars still congregated on street corners, stray dogs with patchy fur still roamed in packs, and mounds of trash still collected in the open, a haven for flies and ragpickers.

The Crossword Bookstore, a shining, glass-fronted extravaganza that looked, to Chopra, like a giant yellow chocolate box, was the largest bookstore in the Mumbai suburbs, a five-floor emporium dedicated to the written word. In spite of himself, Chopra was impressed. Yet the sheer scale of the place unnerved him. How was anyone supposed to find anything?

His problem was solved by a very thin young man who appeared behind him like a nervous ghost. Chopra explained what he required and the young assistant, resplendent in his yellow uniform, led him through the labyrinth of the store to the correct section.

Chopra pushed his reading glasses onto his nose, and began to investigate the shelves. *Diseases and Diet of the Asian Elephant*; *The Hidden Life of the Forest Elephant in Northern India*; *Population and Conservation Problems of the Asian Elephant* . . . ah, this had to be the one! *The Definitive Guide to the Life and Habits of the Indian Elephant* by Dr Harpal Singh.

The book was reassuringly weighty, with a glossy cover that showed a magnificent specimen of an Indian elephant surrounded by lush vegetation. On the back cover was a picture of Dr Singh himself, an equally magnificent specimen with a glorious blue turban and a wild, angry beard.

Chopra felt reassured. Here was a man who knew his business.

He opened the book and read the first paragraph. 'The Indian elephant, Elephantus maximus indicus, is the largest land mammal on the Asian subcontinent. The species ranges in size from 2.5 to 3 metres in height, and between 2,000 to 3,000 kilograms in weight. Indian elephants are megaherbivores, and consume up to 150 kilos of plant matter and 100 litres of water daily. They are both grazers and browsers . . .' The chapter continued in this vein, with plenty of factual information and terse, clinical descriptions of every aspect of the biology, genealogy and taxonomy of the Indian elephant that one could wish to know.

After a while Chopra went back to the shelves, walking his fingers along the spines of the other books in the elephant section.

In the middle of the bottom shelf his eye was caught by a very thin volume with a plain brown cover: *Ganesha: Ten Years Living With an Indian Elephant*. The author was a British woman by the name of Harriet Fortinbrass who had come to India as a young girl in the 1920s with her father, Lord Hubert Fortinbrass, the then British liaison to the Nawabs of northern India. Lord Fortinbrass had been an avid hunter, a veritable one-man extinction event by all accounts. On one particular outing he had slaughtered no less than two bull elephants, a tiger and a brace of chinkara gazelles.

One day he had taken his daughter with him on a hunting expedition into the northern interior. That day Lord Fortinbrass had killed a female elephant, who died whilst protecting her newborn calf. Horrified by the senseless massacre of such a gentle creature, Harriet had insisted on taking the young calf back to their palatial mansion in Faizabad, then capital of Oudh.

Over the next ten years an astonishing bond had developed between the young Englishwoman and her ward. 'People speak of the majesty of the elephant [wrote Harriet], its great size and strength; but what I see when I look into Ganesha's eyes is a soul; and a warmth and intelligence that is compellingly human. It is said that elephants, like humans, are self-aware. They understand that they exist, and that they are individuals. An elephant can be taught to recognise itself in a mirror, just as a human child comes to this awareness. Like a human child, Ganesha trusts me implicitly. One must do nothing to betray that trust, for once an elephant's trust is lost it can never be recovered. They *never* forget.'

Chopra was strangely moved by the English noblewoman's words.

Harriet had eventually left India ten years later when Ganesha had contracted a mysterious illness and died. The book said that Harriet herself had passed away at the ripe old age of eighty-two, a lover of elephants and all things Indian until the very end.

He paid for both books and left the store.

Chopra's second errand required him to take a taxi to the southern half of Mumbai. Rickshaws were not allowed beyond the affluent suburb of Bandra. South Mumbai was the territory of the taxi unions, and they defended their turf zealously.

Chopra alighted at the Byculla Zoo.

He hadn't been here for nearly twenty years, back when some of the old British mills were still in operation in the area, dying off slowly like chain smokers, polluting the air as they expired. The Byculla Zoo sat inside the Victoria Gardens, originally built by the wealthy Jewish businessman David Sassoon. At the entrance to the gardens was the statue of Edward VII astride his 'Kala Ghoda', his black horse, moved from its previous posting in the busy Fort area when the Indian government decided that icons of the country's erstwhile rulers should not be so prominently displayed.

He seems happier here, thought Chopra as he entered the gardens.

He made his way to the zoo office. A party of noisy schoolchildren were crowded around the ticket booth, a phalanx of harried-looking teachers attempting to keep them corralled in. Chopra went around the group and entered the door to the office.

'You can't come in here, sir,' said a weary-looking man holding a bucket in one hand and a sheaf of string-tied red folders in the other.

'I am Inspector Chopra,' said Chopra. 'I wish to see the manager right away.'

He was led into the manager's office and asked to wait. Outside, the noise of the schoolchildren dwindled as they moved further into the gardens.

The manager arrived, a small man with dark-circled, sad-looking eyes, like a lemur's, and very thick eyebrows. 'My name is Rawjee. How can I help you, Inspector?'

'I want to know about elephants,' replied Chopra.

Rawjee regarded him morosely, then said: 'They are big. They are dangerous. They do not take kindly to strangers. What else do you wish to know?'

Chopra said nothing. He looked around the office. It was very cramped, with a worn-down look, much like its owner. Filing cabinets took up much of the space, crowned by stacks of precariously leaning paper. The whitewash had peeled in a number of places as if the walls were suffering from a scrofulous infection. There was a general air of neglect.

'The zoo is not as popular as it once was,' said Rawjee, noticing Chopra's scrutiny. 'Nowadays, there are so many other distractions, malls and multiplexes and whatnot. Who wants to come to the zoo?' He sighed. 'Follow me.' He scraped back his chair and led Chopra into the zoo.

They walked past the crocodile pen, the nilgai deer enclosure and the monkey cages where the schoolchildren giggled and made faces at the macaques, who howled and gibbered in incandescent fury. Chopra noticed that the enclosures were generally ill-kept, littered with discarded plastic bottles, gutka pouches and stale food items.

They arrived at the elephant enclosure, where Rawjee instructed him to wait. Then he turned on his heels and slouched away.

Chopra walked up to the rusted bars of the enclosure.

Inside were two fully grown Indian elephants with the characteristic patches of pink pigmentation around the eyes and ears. The plaque on the enclosure stated that they were called Shah Jahan and Mumtaz. They looked rather weary and long in the tooth to be named after the legendary royal lovers, he thought.

'Please stay back, sahib.'

Chopra turned. A small man in khaki shorts and a tattered white vest walked up to the enclosure. 'Last year, this pair killed a man.'

Chopra remembered the fuss. A drunken man had clambered into the enclosure from the lawn behind. Once inside he had begun singing at the top of his voice. The female of the elephant dyad had wrapped its trunk around him, picked him up and bashed him against the wall. After that, both enraged elephants had stomped on the man until he had expired. For good measure, the male had gored the poor man's body with his tusks.

The zoo attendant's name was Mahi. He was a former mahout who now worked on the zookeeper's staff. He was a living testament to the dangers of working with animals. He had lost three fingers on his left hand to a tiger bite; his ear had been chewed off by an enraged langoor; and he walked with a limp having broken his hip when he had been playfully butted, many years ago, by an adolescent elephant.

'They don't know their own strength,' he said, without rancour.

Chopra explained that he wished to know about caring for an elephant. Mahi looked at him with renewed interest. He enquired whether the police were now going to use elephants the way they used dogs. Then Chopra asked him where one would take a baby elephant that needed a home. Could the zoo take in such an animal? Mahi shook his head. 'You would have to ask Manager Sahib. But I think he will say no. Zoo has no money. We cannot afford to look after another elephant. Elephants need too much looking after.'

That night Inspector Chopra locked himself in his study and learned about elephants. Reading from both Dr Harpal Singh's clinical text and the more personal account of

Harriet Fortinbrass, and recalling the advice given to him by Mahi at the zoo, he built up a picture in his mind of what it would mean to care for the creature that had been bequeathed to him by his uncle . . . 'The elephant,' wrote Dr Singh, 'has been given mythical status in certain quarters, largely due to its association with the Indian god Ganesh. This status leads to the erroneous projection of supernatural and anthropomorphic abilities onto this animal. The truth is that elephants are merely very large land mammals. Flesh and blood and bone. Aside from their size there is nothing very special about the elephant.'

'Elephants are unique,' wrote Harriet Fortinbrass. 'When Alexander the Great reached the banks of the Hydaspes to fight the Indian king Porus, his men were astounded and terrified in equal measure by the legion of elephants that thundered into battle against them. They returned to Asia Minor with tales of these legendary beasts. Instinctively, they realised that elephants are something greater than mere animals.'

In particular Chopra was searching for some clue as to what was currently ailing his ward. 'An elephant,' wrote Dr Singh, 'has no natural predators. Consequently one can deduce that elephants do not know the meaning of fear.' 'Elephants,' wrote Harriet Fortinbrass, 'are emotional creatures. They exhibit signs of happiness, contentment, anxiety and fear. One must always be mindful of this fact. The Indians talk of a condition they call "musth", when an elephant becomes uncontrollable, much like a drunken human. The cause for this condition is not known.'

There was an extraordinary range of illnesses and

afflictions that could befall an elephant, Chopra discovered. From terrible-sounding diseases such as foot-and-mouth and elephant pox, to ones more familiar to humans such as anthrax, rabies and tuberculosis. Elephants were susceptible to pneumonia, arthritis, intestinal complications, tusk and nail infections, skin problems of all types, and a host of musculoskeletal injuries occasioned by their massive size. Elephants were plagued by the foot fly, the bot fly, ringworms, screwworms, tapeworms, ticks, ear mites, skin fleas, flukes and nematodes. Chopra learned that listlessness and a lean appearance were signs of poor health. Conversely, constant ear flapping and tail twitching were signs of good health. Chopra learned that an elephant could even suffer from heart complications brought on by old age, exactly like a human!

By the time he went to bed Chopra's head was swimming with images of elephants; elephants trumpeting, elephants eating, elephants bathing, elephants moving in herds through the jungle. Elephants even invaded his dreams. He dreamt of Ganesha, fully grown now, towering above him, wrapping his trunk around Chopra's waist, lifting him up and bashing him repeatedly against the compound wall, while Bahadur watched, clapping, and Poppy sang 'Ganpati bappa morya!'

He woke up bathed in sweat, and spent the rest of the night staring at the ceiling and listening to the thrum of the air-conditioner, which seemed almost as loud as the drumming of his heart.

THE RESULTS OF THE AUTOPSY

'Come and see me. It's better we talk face to face.'

Chopra put down the phone, and tugged thoughtfully at his moustache. It was not like Homi to be so mysterious. He was, after all, known for his blunt and forthright manner. At any rate, the results of the autopsy were in.

Chopra completed his breakfast, another enormous repast. He patted his stomach. 'If this keeps up, you'll soon be married to a very fat man,' he said, only half joking.

'Yes, yes,' said Poppy, as she fiddled with the tea pan on the stove. Chopra felt deflated, like a magician whose best trick has failed to astound the audience. Poppy had been acting strangely ever since she had returned from her cousin Kiran's home yesterday evening. It was not like Poppy to be so distracted around him. She tended to make a fuss of him, had done since the day they had married. Although Chopra had never acknowledged that he enjoyed this attention – he simply didn't have the words to express how he felt, even if he had wished to – he instantly noticed its absence on the rare occasions when Poppy became wrapped up in something else. He wondered if she had found another of her never-ending causes to fight – perhaps her battle against Mrs Subramanium concerning Ganesha.

Before going to see Homi, Chopra checked on the little elephant again. He was encouraged to see that Ganesha had relieved himself during the night. Admittedly, it was a very *small* pile of dung, but it was a sign of progress at least.

However, when he checked with Bahadur, he discovered that the elephant had still not eaten anything.

Chopra bent down next to the pile of dung. He shooed away the flies, got onto his knees and brought his face closer, taking a deep sniff, as had been advised by Dr Harpal Singh's book.

Bahadur looked on with keen interest.

Of all the Colony's residents, Inspector Chopra was the one he most admired.

Sometimes, as he sat idly on his little chair by the compound gates, he would dream of being a police officer himself. A heroic one like Shashi Kapoor in *Deewaar* or Amitabh Bachchan in *Shahenshah*, beating up dozens of villains with his bare hands, and rescuing the heroine, with whom he would then do a romantic dance number.

Chopra straightened. What in God's name was he doing! How ridiculous he must look, a grown man sniffing at a pile of elephant dung! What was that old saying? *Leave the expertise to the experts.*

He reached into his pocket and pulled out his notebook. In it he found the phone number he had obtained from

Mahi at the Byculla Zoo. He took out his mobile phone and dialled the number.

'Yes?' said a gruff voice.

'Am I speaking to Dr Rohit Lala?'

'You are.'

'Dr Lala, my name is Inspector Chopra and I have a very sick elephant that needs your help.'

Chopra arrived at the hospital in a rickshaw, just as an ambulance raced up to the main entrance. Two men leaped out from the back, carrying a gurney on which lay a bloodied and hastily bandaged body. The body appeared to have lost both legs from the knees downwards. 'Poor fool fell under the train,' said one of the orderlies, as they jogged past. Chopra did not ask how it had happened. After all, falling under a train was an everyday occurrence in Mumbai.

He found Homi sitting in his office, his face hidden beneath a dampened handkerchief. 'Forty-two degrees centigrade and the AC decides to pack up!' he complained. 'It's going to be the hottest summer on record. But you mark my words: when the rains come, they're going to be terrible.'

Chopra noted that Homi's eyes were bloodshot. He knew that his old friend had a taste for fine whisky, and often awoke feeling the worse for wear. But he was a thorough professional, and Chopra had never heard of any complaints about his work.

Over the years they had worked together on a number of

high-profile cases. Early in their friendship, they had collaborated on the case of the Cricket Bat Killer, one of their most famous cases, which had led to hysterical headlines in the local papers.

The Cricket Bat Killer had murdered four people in the Sahar area, all of them bludgeoned to death with what turned out to be a cricket bat. The investigation had been led by Chopra, at the time a sub-inspector. Chopra had examined the wood splinters recovered by Homi from the body of one of the victims, and the profile of the blunt-force trauma marks inflicted by the murder weapon, and had been able to identify both that the injuries had been inflicted by a cricket bat, and also narrow down the make of bat. Being an avid cricket enthusiast himself, he had realised that this particular type of bat was rare, and only sold at one shop in the area. From there it had been a relatively simple task to locate the handful of locals who had purchased such a bat. Only one of those men could not produce the bat for inspection, and he quickly buckled under police questioning and confessed his crimes.

The killer's motive for carrying out the gruesome murders had once again convinced Chopra that simple explanations of good and evil did not fit the facts of human behaviour.

The Cricket Bat Killer had been angry, angry at the small suffocations of his life, his marriage, his dead-end job, his unruly, uninspiring children. Chopra, who was an avid reader of criminological textbooks, did not believe in evil as a measurable human concept, certainly not in any moral or religious sense. Men like the Cricket Bat Killer were, to his mind, sociological freaks. Something had gone wrong with the way they processed the world around them. It was not exactly madness, but not sanity either.

Chopra followed Homi to the hospital morgue. They entered the cold unit, where Homi pulled out the body of Santosh Achrekar, lying on its metal tray.

Once again, Chopra found himself strangely moved as he looked at the boy's once handsome face, now a ghastly waxen mask.

'First things first,' began Homi. 'Technically, the boy died of suffocation leading to cerebral hypoxia – or drowning, if you prefer – as indicated by water in the airways, stomach and lungs. Diatom analysis shows that he was alive when he entered the water. We also found blood in his lungs, which indicates he struggled mightily for breath. That is curious, because if the water was only a few inches deep and he had enough wherewithal to struggle, then I would expect him to have lifted himself clear.

'I also had the boy's blood, stomach contents and fluids analysed. There was indeed a high quantity of alcohol in his system. There is no doubt that he would have been drunk at the time of his death.

'Secondly, we also found drugs in his bloodstream. A cocktail of benzodiazepines, in fact. Now, this is not the drug of choice for even desperate users; benzodiazepines have sedative and hypnotic – that is, sleep-inducing – effects.

There are no other indications that the boy was a regular drug user.'

Chopra looked thoughtfully down at Santosh's face. 'So,' continued Homi, 'he was drunk and possibly on drugs . . . and yet, in my opinion, this was no accidental death.'

Chopra looked up.

'Here, help me turn him over.' They turned the body onto its stomach. 'Look here,' said Homi, pointing at the upper part of the boy's neck, just below the hairline. On the greying flesh Chopra could make out a line of discolouration. 'Bruising. A heavy hand around the neck, held there for some time. A strong, right-handed male, I would say . . . and here, another bruise, near the base of the spine. My guess is a knee, a heavy knee.'

Chopra had an image of the boy, face down in the water, a big man holding him there while he struggled, thrashed about until finally his legs stopped moving, and he was still.

'I found something else too, under his fingernails. Some skin – not the boy's – a little blood, and some microscopic fibres.'

'What kind of fibres?'

'Velvet. Red.' They turned the body over again and Homi pulled the sheet back into place, before sliding the body back into its vault.

'Let me paint you a picture. The boy and his friend are out drinking. Maybe they're high, too. They're out on the road when one of them – let's say the friend – says that he needs to relieve himself. The boy is reluctant to take him to his home; he does not want his parents to meet a friend like this. So he takes him to a place close by, a quiet place that he knows will be deserted at this time of night. In that place, they quarrel; there is a struggle. The boy scratches the friend, tears his shirt, a red velvet shirt. But the friend is too powerful. He pushes the boy down into the water. He holds him there until he stops moving. Then he leaves.'

'Why?' whispered Chopra.

'Yes, that is the real question. Why? Was it two friends who had a fight over a girl, a fight that got out of hand? Or work colleagues falling out over some minor slight at the office? Or just two drunks who fought over a drop of piss one sprayed on the other's shoe? I have no idea. I'm afraid that's where my work stops and yours begins. Or would have begun were it not for the fact that you are now retired.'

Chopra realised that Homi was staring at him. 'I can't just drop it, old friend.'

'Yes, you can,' said Homi sternly. 'That is exactly what you must do. I will notify your successor at the station of my findings. He will have to conduct an investigation.'

'He will not. And even if he does, the investigation will fail,' said Chopra.

'You don't think much of the new man, do you?'

Chopra was silent a moment. 'Do you know what Achrekar's mother told me, on the day I left? She said there would be no justice for her. No justice for her son. They are poor. They are unimportant.'

'Come, now, you don't believe that.'

'It doesn't matter what *I* believe any more. As you said, I am retired.'

POPPY HAS AN IDEA

The greatest disappointment of Poppy Chopra's life was that she had never had children. After twenty-four years of marriage she and Inspector Chopra were still childless, and, ostensibly at least, had long since given up the idea of raising a family.

In the beginning they had consulted doctors, some of them even reasonably good at their jobs. To Poppy's horror they had discovered that the problem lay coiled deep within the mysterious and unfathomable workings of her own body. Those same doctors had suggested potential cures, this and that and whatnot. They had shown her complicated diagrams and described important-sounding technical procedures. They had given her hope.

It had turned out to be false hope, after all.

And when the medical men had failed, Poppy had turned to tradition. She had consulted swamis, and sadhus and vedjis. She had made pilgrimages to the tombs of numerous saints. She had followed the advice of her mother, preparing meals heavy with cottage cheese and alfalfa sprouts. She had tried strange potions from glass bottles sold by mysterious women who came highly recommended by those who were said to know about such things. And nothing had worked.

To his credit Chopra himself had never once hinted at any disappointment at the fact that Poppy had not borne him a child, let alone a son. He had never once blamed her or suggested that he had made a mistake in asking for her hand all those years ago. Poppy knew of many men who would have cast her aside in favour of another more fertile wife. But Chopra was not one of those men. It was the reason that she loved him, loved him more deeply than he would ever allow her to express. And it vindicated her belief, formed on the night of their wedding, when Chopra had behaved towards her with such gentle consideration, knowing that in spite of her bravado she was really just a frightened eighteen-year-old girl on the verge of becoming a woman, that she had married a good man.

In a country where thieves and crooks were becoming ever more commonplace, particularly in the highest offices in the land, where people openly applauded those who managed to hoodwink millions and get away with it, Chopra was a man who stood for everything that was right and good about India. It was this unwavering integrity that Poppy admired most. She had heard it said that every man had a price. Not her husband.

In time Poppy had accepted her fate. 'Why do I need children of my own?' she told her friends. 'India is blessed with children. Everywhere you look there are children. Why, in my own building there are so many children that I cannot even remember all their names!'

Briefly they had discussed adoption, but Poppy had sensed that Chopra's heart was not in it. It was the only time that she had become upset with his attitude, but he had never really explained what it was that he found so objectionable about taking in an orphan. She had pursued the matter for a while, but in the end had given up. That had been a decade into their marriage. By then she was no longer a naïve eighteen-year-old girl. She had learned that the easiest way to lose a man was to push him to a place he did not wish to go.

And so Poppy had resigned herself to a life in which no sweet-faced little angel would ever call her 'Mummy'; no little tyke would ever come home with his clothes all dirty from splashing around in the monsoon mud with his friends; no fine young man would bring tears of pride to her eyes by passing his HSC exams as the class topper.

Sometimes, when Chopra was at work, and she was alone at home on a day when she had nothing else to do, she would dream about her unborn children, and she would feel an ache deep inside her, perhaps in the very place the doctors said had been the cause of her childlessness, and tears would roll down her cheeks. She would sit there for hours, just crying, until there were no more tears inside. And then she would get up, wash her face, admonish herself for her silliness, recount her many blessings, and prepare the evening meal in time for Chopra's return from the station.

This was how it had been for more years that she cared to remember. And just as Chopra had refused to condemn her for the lack of children, so she had refused to permit that lack to cast a shadow over their lives.

And then, on the morning that Chopra had set off to learn about elephants, Poppy had received a call from her cousin Kiran Malhotra, who lived nearby in the affluent suburb of Bandra.

Kiran and Poppy had always been close, and their lives had been mirrors of one another.

Both had been marked out in their extended family by their beauty; both had been transplanted from their village to the big city by their husbands. In Kiran's case, her husband had been an enterprising young Panvel man who had received a bank loan to set up a factory in Pune to manufacture ball bearings. As India's industrial sector had taken off in the late eighties and nineties, his business had prospered. Eventually, he had expanded his product line to heavy machinery, opened a swanky new sales office in Mumbai, and purchased a grand bungalow in Khar Danda in Bandra to go with it.

For a while Kiran had been insufferable, putting on airs and crowing about her husband's success and their fancy new home. But Poppy had put up with her cousin because she knew that at heart Kiran was a good soul, and would soon realise what a bore she was becoming.

As the rickshaw puttered along Carter Road, Poppy looked out interestedly at the grand bungalows lining the seafront. The grandest one, she had always thought, had once been the home of her favourite movie star, Shah Rukh Khan, but he had relocated to an even fancier place on the nearby Bandra Bandstand.

Crowds of people moved down the promenade, taking in the salty air. Carter Road was a place where everyone came – obese joggers in sweaty headbands, shy couples romancing under the stars, shanty children playing tag on the giant stone tetrapods piled up under the promenade to blunt the sea's occasional fury. The smell of drying fish was thick in the air and broken coconuts littered the pavement, fallen from the swathe of palm trees that ran along the side of the road. In the tangle of mangrove below the promenade monkeys yawned, while litter pickers examined the rubbish careless people had thrown into the sea, only for it to be washed back into the waiting thickets.

When Poppy arrived at Kiran's bungalow, she found her cousin in a state of some distress. Kiran's face gave away the fact that she had been crying – her usually impeccable make-up was messy and smudged. She was a natural beauty, and her oval face, graceful neck and porcelain skin had long aroused feelings of wistfulness in Poppy. Her cousin could have been a movie star, and with her height and svelte figure, choosing the right outfit for an important function was an irrelevance. Kiran looked good in anything, even the casual slacks and last night's crumpled T-shirt that she presently wore.

Poppy realised that this was an occasion that called for a pot of her famous tamarind tea. She shooed away the bhai, who gave her a hurt look, and made the tea herself, serving it in Kiran's imported china tea set, the one she had shown off at the kitty party she had held just a few weeks ago, when she had been at her insufferable worst.

'Tell me what the trouble is,' said Poppy, briskly.

'Prarthana!' Kiran blubbed. 'It's Prarthana!'

Prarthana Malhotra was sixteen years old and had recently moved to one of the fancy international baccalaureate schools that had opened in Bandra. Kiran had high hopes that her daughter would become a surgeon or, failing that, a fashion model. She was certainly beautiful, having inherited her mother's looks.

'I thought this school would be the best thing for her. All the teachers are foreigners – you know, English and Swiss and French and whatall. It is costing Anand ten lakhs per annum! All the kids there are sons and daughters of big shots. You know, I heard Ambani's son might be enrolled there next year.' For a moment Kiran brightened, as if the prospect of the scion of India's richest dynasty joining her daughter's school was enough to solve all her problems. But then her face darkened again. 'The trouble started a few months ago. Prarthana started requesting to have sleepovers at her friends' houses. I wasn't in favour of it myself, you know, but Prarthana complained to her father. She said she was being ostracised by her classfellows because she wasn't allowed to do the things all the other cool kids did. Well, you know Anand; he won't hear of his kid being second best. And after that, she started going out in the evenings.

This week it was Renoo's birthday, and next week it is Esha's this thing . . . I tell you, it's impossible to keep up with them!

'I suppose that was my mistake. I should have never given her so much freedom, no matter what Anand said. I should have put my foot down.' Kiran stopped, as tears began to roll down her face. 'Oh, Poppy!'

Poppy put an arm around her cousin's shoulder and waited until she had sobbed herself to a standstill. Then Kiran began again: 'A couple of weeks ago, I began to notice a change in her personality. She started to become evasive, and wouldn't meet my eyes. I actually caught her out telling me a direct lie. And then, one morning, I heard her vomiting behind the bathroom door. Her mood began to swing wildly.' Kiran stopped. On the mantelpiece, a fancy Swiss carriage clock ticked away the agonising seconds.

'Perhaps you're wrong,' said Poppy gently.

'A mother knows, Poppy, a mother knows.'

Well! thought Poppy. For once, Kiran had not been making a fuss over nothing.

She felt a surge of sympathy for her cousin . . . What a horrible, terrible situation! India was changing, India was shining, India was now a very modern place – but there were still some things that were sacred and some things that were taboo. And an unmarried, pregnant teenage daughter was the very worst thing that could happen to any respectable Indian family.

'And the . . . father?' Poppy enquired delicately.

'Vanished!' sobbed Kiran, quietly. 'He is some industrialist's son from Juhu. As soon as Prarthana confronted him about the . . . about the fact of his irresponsibility, he went crying to his big-shot daddy. The next thing we knew, he had been taken out from the school and sent to study abroad.

'Of course, I went to see the industrialist, but he told me in no uncertain terms that as far as he was concerned the matter was settled. Do you know what he said to me? "One hand cannot clap by itself"! Oh, Poppy, I was so angry I wanted to give him two tight raps, there and then. But what could I do? If I had told Anand, he would have gone down there and killed the man, you know what a hothead he is.'

'What about . . . ?' Poppy paused, not sure how to phrase the delicate question she wanted to ask.

'No,' said Kiran, reading her mind. 'My wretched daughter won't hear of it. She says she won't let anyone murder an unborn child. I tried to tell her that this happens all the time. And it can be done discreetly, in complete safety. There are so many doctors who will do it, no one would be any the wiser. She looked at me as if I were some sort of serial killer. It's all these western films, Poppy, filling her head with foreign notions.'

'But then, surely she doesn't want to *raise* this child!' Poppy was shocked. The idea of an unwed single mother in her own family was simply too much. The scandal of it!

'No. She has that much sense at least. My daughter has great ambitions, and realises she won't be able to achieve them with a child to look after and a scandal following her around everywhere she goes.'

'But then what does she plan to do?'

'She wants to give the baby up for adoption.'

It was Poppy's turn to sit back in thoughtful silence. 'That means she will have to bear the child. Everyone will know.'

'No!' said Kiran, vehemently. 'No one will know. I have a plan. In a couple of months, when she begins to show, I am going to withdraw her from school. I am going to get a letter from my doctor stating that she is suffering from some rare illness, and that she is advised complete bed rest, in healthy, clean surroundings. Then I will take her to Silvassa with me for a few months. The baby will be born there and we will hand it over to the Sai Baba Orphanage. Next year Prarthana will resume her education, this time at a school of my choosing, an all-girls convent.'

'But what will you tell Anand?'

'Nothing,' said Kiran determinedly. 'Absolutely nothing. And he will not ask. Anand is self-absorbed at the best of times. He works such long hours, I barely see him any more. And this year he is busy establishing his new plant in Delhi. He is hardly home as it is. He won't even notice that Prarthana and I have vanished for six months.'

Poppy detected a note of bitterness in her cousin's voice. So perhaps the perfect life that Kiran always crowed about wasn't so perfect after all. But who was Poppy to judge? Every marriage concealed its own disappointments, its little trials and tribulations.

The Swiss clock suddenly chimed the hour. An alpine maid emerged from the face of the clock, hotly pursued by an eager young man in lederhosen and a bewildered-looking cow . . . and it was at this very instant that the Idea popped into Poppy's head.

For a full minute, she sat there, not daring to breathe, while the Idea sat in her mind, glistening like a newly buttered ball of dough.

'There is another way,' she said finally.

Kiran looked up from her misery. 'What way?'

Poppy looked at her cousin, and wondered if what she was about to say would sound insane or inspired. In the end, she simply said it, just like that. And then she sat back and waited for Kiran's verdict.

A VISIT TO THE VICTIM'S HOME

Following the visit to the hospital, Chopra decided to return to the Sahar police station. The meeting with Homi had affected him greatly. Now that he had proved that the boy's death had not been accidental, he felt compelled to follow up with Inspector Suryavansh.

He found the new commanding officer in his office, loudly berating Sub-Inspector Patil, who Chopra had always found to be a competent, if rather undemonstrative, officer. He discovered Rangwalla waiting outside Suryavansh's office, and a trembling Constable Surat.

'Why is he giving Patil such a firing?' asked Chopra. He himself had never felt the need to shout at his men. When they made mistakes, he had made his displeasure known in no uncertain terms, but he felt that shouting at people was counter-productive. You could never get to the heart of what had caused the mistake if only one person did the talking. Besides, in his experience, being shouted at by your superior officer only made you wary of sharing information with him in the future. Sometimes that could be the difference between solving or not solving a case.

He was also shocked by the expletives that Inspector Suryavansh was directing Patil's way. Suryavansh had insulted not only every member of Patil's family, both living and deceased, but had also accused Patil of unnatural acts with beasts of burden. Chopra wondered how he himself would have reacted if ACP Suresh Rao had ever spoken to him in such a manner.

'Poor Patil,' said Rangwalla. 'He's been working on the Hayat arson case; you know, the man who was accused of burning down his neighbour's shop in Brahman Wadi and then absconding? It seems Patil got a tip-off about where the scoundrel was hiding. This morning he set up a team to make the arrest. They were waiting around for hours. And then Patil felt the call of nature. He was gone for five minutes. When he returned, he discovered that one of his men had spotted the arsonist, but because he'd been sitting around without moving for so long, he suffered cramp when he tried to move and fell off his perch, alerting the fellow. By the time they got themselves organised to chase him, he had vanished back into the street.'

Chopra told Rangwalla about the autopsy. Rangwalla was interested but did not seem enthusiastic. 'Sir, I have to warn you that I do not think the inspector will appreciate your efforts. As far as he is concerned that case is closed. He told me so himself. In fact, he even asked me to inform him when the family had cremated the body, so that the Final Report could be written up.'

Chopra's forehead creased into a frown, but he held his tongue.

The door to Suryavansh's office opened and a glassy-eyed Patil stumbled away.

Chopra did not wait for an invitation.

When he entered the office, the inspector stared at him as if he had no idea who he was. Finally recognition dawned and he ushered Chopra into a seat. His face still looked thunderous. Chopra felt like an unwelcome guest at a bereavement.

Inspector Suryavansh was the largest policeman Chopra had ever met. He was very dark-skinned, with a bristling moustache and extremely white teeth. He looked like a movie star from the South, thought Chopra. His voice seemed to emanate from the region of his belly, travelling up through his chest – where it was amplified by the bellows of his lungs – to emerge from his mouth as a miniature avalanche of sound, ready to roll over anything in its path.

Chopra knew that Suryavansh had come from a plum posting in south Mumbai in the affluent Nariman Point district. He wondered what the man had done to get himself booted out to the suburbs. Perhaps it was the drinking . . .

'However did you manage with these fellows?' barked Suryavansh, shaking his head. 'It's going to take me a while to whip them into shape.'

Chopra bristled inwardly at the implied insult, but held his tongue. He did not want to get into a contest of egos with Inspector Suryavansh. Keeping his irritation from his voice, he quickly explained the results of the autopsy that he had asked Homi Contractor to carry out.

At this point Inspector Suryavansh became decidedly animated. 'By whose authority did you request this autopsy!' he demanded. 'My dear Chopra, you are retired. This is no longer your business. These are now police matters, and you are no longer a policeman. I am most disturbed by these actions, most disturbed.'

Chopra explained that even a simple citizen of the city had a duty to help the police in their investigations.

'But we do not want your help!' protested Suryavansh. 'What would happen if everyone went around trying to *help* the police? My dear sir, I must ask you to stop interfering with this case.'

'I will stop interfering if you assure me that the matter will now be properly investigated,' said Chopra, his voice finally becoming stern.

'I do not have to assure you of anything,' said Suryavansh. It was clear that he was struggling to control his temper. 'In fact, I would be within my rights to report you.' It was not clear whom he could report Chopra to.

'The boy was murdered,' said Chopra resolutely. 'The question is, what are you going to do about it?'

'It is just your theory!' said Suryavansh loudly. 'You said yourself the autopsy proved the boy had been drinking. We have the whisky bottle next to the body. Case is closed.'

'What about all the other evidence? The blood under his fingernails? The marks on his neck?'

'Who knows?' glowered Suryavansh. 'Maybe he had a fight with his girlfriend. Maybe she tried to strangle him, and he tried to fight her off. Maybe that's why he was drinking.'

'If this is so, you can send an officer to his home. You can find out who his girlfriend is and verify this.'

'Do you think my men are sitting around here with nothing better to do than chase wild gooses?'

My men! At this point Chopra had to use all his legendary self-control to stop himself from shouting. His hands gripped the arms of his wooden chair until his knuckles turned white. Finally he got to his feet. 'Am I to take it that you will not be pursuing this investigation further?'

'You can take it that I will pursue this investigation as far as I deem fit,' growled Suryavansh, also getting to his feet. The big policeman towered over Chopra. Then suddenly he seemed to relent. 'Look, I understand what is happening. You have retired. It is a big adjustment. But take one piece of advice from me. Let it go. Forget about the police work. Enjoy your retirement. Take your wife to Shimla. Go and watch cricket. You will live a much happier life. If you do not, you will be seeing crimes in your sleep for the rest of your days, crimes you cannot solve.'

Chopra left the station thoroughly disheartened. He was certain now that Suryavansh would do nothing to find the boy's killer. It was simply not high enough on his list of priorities. What had the boy's mother said? "*For a poor woman and her poor son, there is no justice.*"

And suddenly he realised that he was not going to let this lie. He was not going to simply forget about this case, as Inspector Suryavansh had suggested. He could not.

Chopra had been a meticulous police officer, a man of method and painstaking procedure. Usually all it took to crack a case was this attention to detail that had become legendary amongst his fellow officers. But sometimes one had to rely on that oldest of police tools: intuition. Gut instinct. And Chopra's gut was telling him that this poor boy's murder had to be solved. And if the police were not going to solve it, then someone else had to take the responsibility.

There were twenty million souls living in the city of Mumbai. They were interconnected, Chopra had always felt, like a great hive of bees. And when one of those souls died in a manner that was unnatural, unjust, it was the responsibility of the hive to resolve the matter. Though he was not a religious man, Chopra was convinced that if this did not happen then the boy's soul would not find *moksha*. It would continue to wander in the limbo between death and rebirth, unable to live or die in peace.

It was not difficult to find the Marol Mayavati complex. It was a poor neighbourhood a twenty-minute walk away from the Sahar police station. The houses were clustered around an old disused patch of wasteground, which, in the monsoon season, turned into a series of miniature lakes. In the prolonged heat it had been baked into a cracked and fissured desert.

A thick, curdled stench arose from a pile of rubbish in one corner of the wasteground. Pigs rooted in the rubbish while stray dogs barked at them excitedly. Wild pigs and dogs were so common in Mumbai that Chopra had often thought that they should have been lauded as the city's unofficial mascots.

When he knocked on the door of the dilapidated home Chopra steeled himself to confront the woman he had seen at the police station, the boy's mother. Instead the door was opened by an elderly man wearing a white kurta, black trousers, open-toed sandals and spectacles. The man had a kindly, avuncular face and an air of composure. He was holding a newspaper. 'Yes?'

'My name is Inspector Chopra. I have come to make enquiries about the death of your son.'

The man said nothing for a moment, then nodded. 'Please come in, Inspector.'

The home had only three rooms: a living area, which also doubled up as a bedroom and kitchen; a bathing room and toilet; and a small second bedroom. There were dirty pans on the stove. The man noticed Chopra's gaze. 'My wife is resting,' he apologised. 'She has not been well. You understand.'

Chopra nodded. He understood. He understood the woman's anger. But how could he hope to understand her grief?

'Please sit down. Can I offer you something to drink? Some lemon water? Or Coca-Cola?'

'No, thank you.'

The man's name was Pramod. Pramod Achrekar, the boy's father.

He showed Chopra a photograph, the boy with his parents on the day that he had passed out from his SSC examinations. 'He was in the top three of his class,' said Achrekar proudly. Chopra regarded the picture. His first impression had been correct; Santosh had indeed been a handsome young man. Young and fresh-looking, with that air of self-confidence that the young had nowadays. His whole future laid out before him.

Chopra explained the reason for his visit. He told the boy's father about the autopsy that he had requested, and its results. The man's face seemed to gather an air of deep sadness. 'A policeman telephoned from the station. He told me that my son had died accidentally. That he was a drunk, and that his own foolishness had killed him. I did not want to believe him; if Santosh had been a drunk we would have seen some sign of it before now. But then how well do we really know our children? My wife was not convinced. She said right from the beginning that this could not be an accident. But then, mothers do not see any faults in their sons.'

'Were there?' asked Chopra. 'Faults in your son, I mean?'

Achrekar removed his spectacles and rubbed the bridge of his nose. 'He was not perfect. He was a wilful boy. After his SSCs he stopped listening to my advice. I wanted him to continue studying, to attend university, but he wanted to work, to earn money. It's funny, when they are young they need you for everything; but as soon as they stand on their feet, they don't need you for anything at all.' He smiled ruefully. 'I remember when he was a little boy, he contracted malaria. For a week it was so bad that we thought he would die. Even the doctors had given up on him. I tried to be the strong man of the house, but inside it was as if God were squeezing my heart inside his fist.'

Chopra felt the old man's silent, dignified grief spreading like a deadly gas, filling the little home. 'Where did he work?'

'He joined the organisation of some exporter. A big local businessman. Santosh told us that the businessman was very impressed with his enthusiasm. He was quickly promoted and worked directly for the head office.'

'Who was this businessman?' asked Chopra, taking out his notebook. 'I would like to talk to him.'

'His name is Jaitley, Mr Arun Jaitley,' said Achrekar. 'The head office is nearby, on Andheri Kurla Road, near the Kohinoor Continental hotel. I don't know much more about him than that, except that Santosh told me he was local to this area. I asked Santosh many times for more information, but he always said that his boss had instructed his staff to guard his privacy.'

'What is *he* doing here?'

Chopra turned. In the doorway of the adjoining bedroom was the boy's mother. Her face was puffy with grief, and there was a vacant expression in her eyes.

Achrekar got up and moved towards his wife. He stood between them and explained to her why Chopra had come. Chopra expected that she would begin to rail at him, as she had done the other day. But instead her legs seemed to buckle under her and she collapsed into a chair by the stove. Her head fell into her hands and her body shook with silent sobs.

Achrekar returned to Chopra. 'You must excuse her,' he said. 'She was always very close to him. He was our only son. We have two daughters, elder to Santosh. They have both married and moved away. Now we are alone.'

'Do not apologise,' said Chopra. He could not imagine what it would be like, to raise a child, to love that child more than anything in the world, and then to light the funeral pyre of that child. A child should never die before its parents: that was a rule of nature. 'Please excuse me, but I would like to see the place where Santosh slept, where he kept his clothes, any wardrobe or almirah.'

'Yes, of course.'

Achrekar led Chopra into the room from which his wife had emerged. 'This was Santosh's room.'

It was a tiny room with a single small cot and a grey steel wardrobe. On the wall was a picture of Salman Khan, Bollywood superstar, in his trademark white vest sitting astride a Hero Honda motorbike. 'May I examine his things?'

'Of course,' said Achrekar. 'I will leave you to do your work.'

Chopra opened the wardrobe. On the shelves, neatly stacked, were the boy's clothes. Shirts, trousers, jeans, socks, underwear.

One by one Chopra took out each item of clothing and searched through the pockets. He did not find anything.

He opened a small drawer built into the wardrobe. Inside were pens, a handful of coins, a stack of visiting cards wrapped in a rubber band, and a diary.

Chopra sat down on the cot and thumbed through the visiting cards. Nothing leaped out at him, at first, and then he went back through the cards and took out a white, gilt-edged one. He looked at it. It said:

Suresh Solanki *Senior Executive* Ram Leela International Export Company, Near Kohinoor Continental, Andheri Kurla Rd, J.B. Nagar, Andheri East, Mumbai, 400059

This had to be the office where Santosh had worked. Chopra put the card into his pocket. Then, on second thoughts, he slipped the entire bundle of visiting cards into his pocket. He suspected there would be other useful information to be gleaned from them.

Next he leafed through the diary. There was very little in it; Santosh had not used it to record his private thoughts, merely as a planner, noting the dates of meetings and other important events. These were written in a cramped scrawl, which Chopra found hard to decipher. Santosh also had a habit of writing in abbreviations. In the past month there was an increasing number of references to 'SNBO'. The most intriguing entry said: '*SNBO – how to expose them?*'

What could SNBO be? Who was this 'them', and what was Santosh trying to expose?

The last entry was made on the day that Santosh had died. It was the only entry that day. 'Meet S. at Moti's, 9 p.m.'

Chopra wondered if Moti's was the residence of a friend, or perhaps a regular haunt such as a bar or a liquor shop. Perhaps that was where the boy went to drink with his friends. Perhaps that was where he had met the friend (this 'S.', perhaps) he had been drinking with that evening.

This was a vital clue, Chopra felt.

If he could find Moti's, he might be able to find someone who had seen Santosh with his friend; and from there he might identify the friend.

He returned to the living area, where Pramod Achrekar was still comforting his wife. 'There is something else,' he said. 'Do you know if Santosh had a girlfriend?'

Mrs Achrekar raised her head sharply. 'Santosh was a good boy,' she croaked, her voice sunken by grief. 'He would have married the girl I chose for him.' This thought brought fresh tears to her eyes, and she sank her face into her hands once again. Achrekar squeezed her shoulder and stood up to accompany Chopra out of the little house.

Outside Chopra felt the full force of the sun; but he knew that at this moment not a single ray of light would penetrate inside the Achrekars' home.

'Santosh was a handsome boy,' said Achrekar, taking off his spectacles and wiping them with the edge of his kurta. 'I would hear him joking sometimes on his mobile phone about all his girlfriends. More girlfriends than Salman Khan, he used to say.' He shook his head as a smile spread across his face. 'Youngsters never think we old people could possibly understand what they are talking about, so they don't bother to keep their voices down. Because of this I don't believe that my son had a serious girlfriend at this time. He was very committed to making something of himself. He wanted to stand on his own two feet before he began thinking about a wife, a family.'

'Did he have many friends? I might need to talk to those closest to him.'

'He used to have a large circle. But over the past six months he has been completely occupied with his work. Many of them have stopped coming to see him.'

Chopra wondered if this had perhaps been a source of tension. Could a friend have taken offence at being ignored? He had seen murder committed for lesser reasons than that.

'Does "SNBO" mean anything to you? Or "Moti's"?'

Achrekar shook his head.

'Did Santosh own a motorbike?'

'No. He had passed his driving test, and he was saving up to buy one. But he never got the chance.' Achrekar looked directly at him. 'There is one more thing I wish to tell you about my son,' he said. 'Santosh had a very strong sense of integrity and fairness. He believed wholeheartedly in the new India as a land of opportunity for everyone, not just the rich. He believed we could make this country truly great if we got rid of all the crime, corruption and complacency; if each individual took responsibility for shaping the future.'

Chopra gathered his thoughts before speaking. 'Sir, I want to assure you that your son's death is not insignificant, not to me. Whatever it takes, I will find his killers.'

Chopra left the grief-stricken father on the porch of his home, staring into the distance along the now vanished road that had once marked the glistening future of his murdered son.

THE RAM LEELA INTERNATIONAL EXPORT COMPANY

It had already been a very productive day, but Chopra was not finished yet. He was energised by that old feeling, the feeling of getting to grips with a case. It was the feeling he always got when the initial impenetrability of a crime began to unravel and things started to become clear. His was a logical mind, uncluttered by irrelevant distractions. In this clean, rational environment he would often lay out the pieces of an investigation, and gradually begin fitting them together as if they were pieces of a jigsaw. He had an unerring sense for where the gaps in the jigsaw lay, and where particular sections fitted together to reveal an insight.

So excited was he by his progress on the Achrekar case that he decided not to return home for lunch. He knew Poppy would be annoyed – she had said she was going to prepare a special chicken makhani curry for him, together with her much-feted boondi raita. But food would have to wait.

The rick dropped Chopra off right outside the building in which the Ram Leela International Export Company maintained their offices.

It was a good-looking building, he saw, faced by imported white marble; the rent here would not be cheap.

In the lobby there was more marble and a pair of bored TOPS security guards. The Ram Leela International Export Company leased the upper four floors of the ten-storey building.

Chopra took the lift upstairs to the company's reception on the tenth floor. Behind a black granite counter, a pretty young woman with long painted fingernails and a surfeit of lipstick tapped away on a computer. She looked up, spotted him and smiled. 'Sir, may I help you?'

'Yes,' said Chopra. 'My name is Inspector Chopra and I wish to see Mr Arun Jaitley.'

'Oh,' said the girl, an expression of puzzlement passing across her face. 'Sir, do you have an appointment to meet Jaitley Sir?'

'No,' said Chopra. 'But I wish to see him all the same.'

'But Jaitley Sir is not here, sir.'

'Where can I find him?'

'Sir, Jaitley Sir has gone abroad.'

'Abroad? Where?'

The girl hesitated. 'Sir, we are not allowed to give details of Jaitley Sir's movements.'

'It is all right,' he said. 'I am a police officer.'

The girl chewed her lip. Chopra could see that he was putting her in a very uncomfortable position. 'I tell you what,' he said gently, 'why don't you get whoever is in charge in Mr Jaitley's absence.'

The girl brightened. 'Sir, this must be Kulkarni Sir.'

'Please tell him that Inspector Chopra wishes to meet with him.'

'Oh.' The girl looked despondent again. 'But sir, even Kulkarni Sir is not here.'

Chopra frowned. 'And where is he? Or are his whereabouts also a national secret?' He could not prevent the note of sarcasm creeping into his voice.

The girl giggled. 'No, sir. Kulkarni Sir is in Chennai on business. He will be back next week.'

'I see,' he said. 'Well then, is there any way I can talk to Jaitley or Kulkarni on the telephone?'

'No sir,' said the girl firmly. 'We have strict instructions never to give out mobile numbers of Jaitley Sir or Kulkarni Sir.'

Chopra was about to give the girl a piece of his mind, but then decided that would not be the wisest course of action. After all, he wasn't actually a police officer any more, and if he over-exercised his dubious authority, he could put himself in line for serious consequences later on, particularly if Inspector Suryavansh got wind of things. 'Look,' he said through gritted teeth, 'I am investigating the death of Santosh Achrekar. I was told that he worked here. Did you know him?'

The girl's face immediately crumpled into an expression of tearful sorrow. He was beginning to think she would have made a fine dramatic actress. 'Sir, yes, of course! Santosh was a very nice boy. So kind and handsome. He always brought me treats. You know, like chocolate éclairs and Marie biscuits. I was too shocked when I heard he had died in an accident, really too shocked.'

'Is there someone here that Santosh worked particularly closely with? Maybe this person?' Chopra held out the visiting card he had found at Santosh's home.

The girl broke into another smile, her sorrow evaporating as swiftly as it had arrived. 'Oh yes, sir. Solanki Sir worked very closely with Santosh.'

'Don't tell me,' said Chopra. 'Solanki Sir is out of town.'

The girl looked puzzled. 'No, sir,' she said, oblivious to his irony, 'why would you think this? Solanki Sir is in his office. I shall let him know you are here.'

Suresh Solanki entered the meeting room in which Inspector Chopra had been parked by the flighty receptionist. He was a tall, thin man with a sallow face, and deep circles etched around his eyes, as if he had not slept well for a very long time. He was dressed in a crisp white shirt and tie, and shiny black shoes. Chopra judged him to be in his mid-thirties.

Solanki did not greet him with a handshake. Instead, he regarded him with an expression of deep displeasure and mistrust. 'Seema tells me you are a police officer. You have some questions about Santosh?'

'Yes,' said Chopra.

'Then I must first tell you that Santosh was not any longer employed by our organisation at the time of his death.'

'Well,' said Chopra, 'this is the first I am hearing of this. I have recently met with his family. If he had left his job, I am sure they would have known about it.'

'Perhaps he didn't tell them. Perhaps he was too embarrassed.'

'What would he be embarrassed about?'

'Well, the fact that he was sacked from his position.'

'I see,' said Chopra. 'And why was he sacked?'

'He was not very good at his work.'

'His father seemed to believe that he had been singled out for special praise by Mr Jaitley, the owner of this business. Why would he say this?'

Solanki shrugged. 'How would I know? Fathers are proud of their sons even when they have nothing to be proud of.'

Chopra bristled but kept quiet. He had taken an instant disliking to this man. Solanki was arrogant and abrasive. There was also something furtive about his manner. 'Tell me, what did Santosh do here, and what was your relationship with him?'

'Santosh was an administrative assistant. He worked for me, doing data entry work; you know, entering accounting records into our computer system. He also went out to our network of suppliers, following up on the processing of purchase orders.'

'What exactly is it that you export?'

'Garments, mainly. We buy from little suppliers all around the country and export to the Middle East and near Asian countries like Malaysia. We even export to Kenya and South Africa.'

'You must do a lot of business to be able to export to so many countries.'

'We are a very large organisation. This is just our head office. We have other offices in Delhi, Bangalore, Chennai and Kolkata.' This was said with unabashed pride.

Chopra considered this information. 'Did you notice anything unusual about Santosh's behaviour recently?' he asked.

Solanki blinked. There was a slight hesitation before he replied. 'Only that he was drinking a lot. That was one of the reasons we sacked him. We don't like our employees to turn up late for work and drunk.'

'This does not sound like the Santosh that his parents described to me.' Chopra looked directly at Solanki's hooded eyes; Solanki tried to hold his gaze but quickly looked away.

Chopra took out his notebook and pretended to peruse it intently. 'Tell me,' he said eventually, 'do you know what "SNBO" means?'

Solanki's face was impassive. 'No,' he said.

'What about "Moti's"?'

'No.'

He could not tell if Solanki was lying. He remembered the entry in Santosh's diary: 'Meet S. at Moti's, 9 p.m.' Could Solanki be 'S.'? He looked carefully at Solanki's face, but could not see any scratch marks. His scrutiny was obviously making the tall man uncomfortable – Solanki looked down at his watch to cover his discomfort.

Chopra was certain he was not telling him everything that he knew. 'Just out of interest, where were you four nights ago?'

'I was at home with my family,' said Solanki, a little too quickly.

'Do you own a motorbike?'

'What has that got to do with anything?'

Chopra did not reply.

'Yes, I own a motorbike,' said Solanki angrily. 'Along with a few million other people in the city.'

He looked down at his notebook again. 'I suppose you have some paperwork to document Santosh's dismissal?' he said finally.

'When we are legally required to produce such paperwork, it will be available,' said Solanki curtly.

Chopra knew that he would get nothing more out of this man.

He left the building with more questions than answers. His earlier optimism had vanished, and he was confronted with the possibility that perhaps he had bitten off more than he could chew. He did not have the resources or the mandate to follow up on the various lines of enquiry that he had uncovered. There was nothing he could do to squeeze more information out of Suresh Solanki.

There was really nothing more he could do at all.

INSPECTOR CHOPRA VISITS A VET

The next morning Inspector Chopra turned his attention back to the problem of Ganesha. The appointment that he had made with Dr Lala was at eleven o'clock, but the doctor did not make house calls. Realising that the veterinary clinic was only a short walk away, on a plot halfway between Sahar and M.V. Road, he decided that he would simply take his ailing charge with him. The walk might even do the little elephant some good.

When Chopra reached the guard hut he found his mother-in-law Poornima Devi and two other grey-haired ladies from the building surrounding the elephant. One of them was Mrs Subramanium.

'What is going on here?'

Mrs Subramanium turned and addressed Chopra with an arch of her eyebrows. 'It has come to my attention that your elephant has been polluting the complex, Chopra.'

'Polluting?'

'He has been doing his business all over the place, it seems.'

'Who told you that?' said Chopra, glaring at Poornima Devi.

The one-eyed harridan merely glared back. '*I* told her. I slipped on the creature's mess this morning,' she said.

'Is this true, Bahadur?' said Chopra.

The guard grinned uneasily. He was caught between opposing forces, and knew, instinctively, that the best thing he could do was to keep his mouth shut.

'Of course it is true,' said Poornima. She raised a sandal from under her white widow's sari. 'What do you think that is? Chocolate?'

'Perhaps you should look where you are going.'

The old woman looked incensed. 'Perhaps your elephant should not be leaving gifts for us all over the compound.'

'He has hardly eaten. I do not think his bowels have been as active as you seem to think.'

'Then who is responsible for *this*?' She shook her sandal at him again. 'Do you think Bahadur did this?'

Chopra decided that arguing with his mother-in-law was futile. 'Very well. I will take care of it.'

He watched the women walk away, trailing a chorus of grumbling.

As they vanished into the stairwell Bahadur emerged from his bunker of silence. 'I am sorry, sahib.'

'What are you sorry about?' said Chopra. He knelt down beside Ganesha. 'Ignore those old crones, boy,' he muttered. 'They have nothing better to do. Now . . . we are going on a trip. Come on.'

It took quite a bit of coaxing to get Ganesha to his feet, and in the end both Chopra and Bahadur had to tug on the chain around the little elephant's neck.

It was no easy task. A baby elephant, even one as frail as Ganesha, weighed in excess of two hundred kilos. However, once he was on his feet, the elephant seemed resigned to his fate. He followed Chopra without protest, plodding along behind him with downcast eyes, trunk dangling listlessly, looking for all the world like a convicted prisoner being escorted to begin his sentence.

The walk proved to be quite eventful. It had been many years since Chopra had had to patrol the beat, but he still maintained a network of contacts throughout the area. This was the real secret of good police work, he knew. He had been lucky in having an able deputy like Rangwalla who, having grown up on the streets himself, understood instinctively the value of an army of watching eyes and listening ears that could be called upon when needed. Of course, it was a two-way arrangement.

It was an unwritten rule of the city that no one did anything for anyone else in Mumbai without asking for something in return. It was not a rule that Chopra was always comfortable with, but he was a practical man. In order to achieve the greatest good, he was willing to occasionally pay informants for information, or allow some minor indiscretion to pass unnoticed. But there was a line he would not cross. And that was what set him apart from many of his colleagues.

A recent Central Bureau of Investigation report had once again confirmed that the Mumbai police force was only marginally less corrupt than the Inland Revenue Service. The report had caused quite a stir and more than a little embarrassment for Chopra's seniors. But it was a matter of fact. Instead of being embarrassed, his seniors should be enraged, he felt. Instead, they had done what they always did and accused the whistleblowers of a conspiracy.

It was another exceptionally hot morning, and Chopra soon found his shirt sticking to his back. They made an odd pair, he knew: the middle-aged gentleman with the greying sideburns, and the despondent-looking undernourished elephant calf. Children followed them along the dusty, crowded streets. One little rascal jumped onto Ganesha's back and rode along pretending to be a hero from the latest Bollywood blockbuster, until Chopra turned around and shooed him away. Ganesha did not even appear to notice.

They stopped by to see Chanakiya, who ran a little hole-in-the-wall shop repairing clocks and watches. 'Ram ram, Inspector Sahib,' the wizened little watchmaker nodded from inside the booth, sitting cross-legged on the narrow counter in his white lunghi and vest.

Chopra picked up a watch he had left with Chanakiya some days previously. The watch had lasted him twenty-four years, and had been a gift from his father on the occasion of his wedding. Poppy was always encouraging him to get a new one, but he wouldn't hear of it. It was the only memento he had of his dear departed father. He paid Chanakiya twenty rupees for the repair, and moved on.

As they passed the Al-Noor mosque on Lalit Modi Marg, Imam Haider called out to him: 'Salaam, Inspector babu, salaam!' Imam Haider was a robust presence, a bear-like man with the fiery red beard of a Mecca-returned haji and eyebrows like cutlasses. He wore a voluminous white kurta-pajama and a tasselled skullcap that Chopra could not remember ever seeing parted from the imam's head.

Chopra had a great deal of respect for Imam Haider. They had known each other for many years, having become friends during the riots back in 1993. The riots had flared up after the demolition of the Babri Mosque in Ayodhya by Hindus who claimed that the mosque had been built over the ancient birthplace of Lord Ram. Incensed Muslims had then retaliated by protesting in the streets; some of the protests had spilled over into violence. Violence had bred more violence, and soon, before anyone knew what was happening, mobs had taken to the streets, rampaging through the city, indiscriminately seeking blood.

It had been a terrifying time for ordinary citizens in the city. But amidst the chaos and horror, Imam Haider had kept his head and coolly hidden hundreds of terrified local Muslims in the basement of the Al Noor mosque, and ridden out the worst of the rioting.

Chopra had been the first man on the scene afterwards

and, together with Rangwalla and his trusty revolver, had held at bay the last of the vigilantes.

The two men chatted for a while, exchanging news. Imam Haider expressed great disappointment upon hearing that he had retired. He commented that with the recent rise of hardliners in the local area – on both sides of the Hindu–Muslim fence – a man like Chopra was needed more than ever.

'These are difficult days, Chopra,' said Haider. 'On the one hand we have more and more firebrands and on the other we have a growing apathy. There is no middle ground any more. No room for moderation. The hotheads won't listen and the others listen but don't care. I don't know which is worse.'

'How are your sons?' enquired Chopra, wishing to change the subject. He knew that once the iman got going on this topic he took a long time to wind down.

'I am *talking* about my sons,' intoned Haider mournfully. 'The older one spends his evening studying his faith, which is good. But then, at other times, he takes it into his head to make incendiary speeches. The younger is interested only in cricket and movies. I tell you, Chopra, the world is changing, and not for the better.' Haider looked down at Chopra's companion. 'Who is your young friend?'

'His name is Ganesha. I am looking after him.'

'I have heard of people taking up strange hobbies when they retire, old friend, but rearing elephants is a new one on me.'

In between the Swapnadeep buffalo sheds and Gokaldas's copperware shop, a large dark-skinned man wearing oil-blackened clothes hailed Chopra from the entrance of a tiny garage. 'Ho, Inspector Sahib, have you thought about my offer?'

Chopra shook his head. 'Kapil, old friend, as I have told you many times, Basanti is not for sale.'

'You're a strange man, Inspector,' Kapil laughed. The towering quiff of gelled black hair sitting atop his head quivered, and the pirate's earrings dangling from his lobes bounced up and down. Kapil's overalls had the sleeves cut off to reveal thick wrestler's arms. He folded those arms now and looked down at Chopra from above a squashed nose. 'For ten years you have had her tuned up every month, regular as clockwork. But you've never even taken her out from my garage. If you weren't paying me so much money to store her, I would tell you you are a madman!'

'What you have here, sir, is a classic case of a suicidal elephant.'

Chopra looked at the veterinary doctor's face in frank astonishment . . . and then Dr Lala burst out laughing. 'I am just pulling your leg, Inspector.'

The good doctor, he was discovering, was a quite different person to the one he had pictured on the telephone.

Dr Rohit Lala was an overweight Marwadi whose wealthy family, as he had informed Chopra, had been horrified when he had refused to take over the chain of family jewellery shops and instead had gone off to study animal medicine.

His father had passed away still bemoaning the fact that his only son spent his days rummaging around in the back passages of buffaloes instead of making money like a decent Marwadi boy.

The veterinary clinic was located on the premises of an old, defunct textile factory, which lay behind the Sakinaka Telephone Exchange.

Stepping through the run-down façade Chopra had discovered a small, unkempt office, manned by an enthusiastic-looking young man with bad skin and a comical moustache. From a room behind the office came the barking of a number of dogs kept in pens.

The young man had led him, with Ganesha in tow, along a side alley to an open plot at the rear of the premises where a number of horses, buffalo and goats were corralled in chicken-wire pens. He had discovered Dr Lala examining a small bear whose fur appeared to be falling out in patches. The bear was extremely undernourished, and looked terribly ill even to Chopra's untrained eye.

'A good-hearted woman rescued it from a travelling circus,' explained Lala. 'I can't save it, but maybe I can give it a dignified death. To be a vet one must first be a *humani*tarian. In a country where we are willing to make a god of every animal under the sun we have no word to describe what it means to put their welfare first. Now, let's take a look at your young elephant here.'

Chopra waited while Dr Lala carried out his examination.

The doctor shone a light into Ganesha's eyes, and examined his ears. He prised open his mouth with the help of his assistant and peered deep inside, paying particular attention to the tongue, teeth and gums. He looked inside the nostrils of the trunk. He lifted up the tail and examined Ganesha's behind. He put a stethoscope to his steaming flank and listened intently. All the while he asked Chopra questions about the little elephant's history, which revealed only that Ganesha's reluctant guardian knew next to nothing.

'Well,' the doctor said finally, puffing out his cheeks, 'I must confess that I am not sure exactly what is wrong with your elephant here. Aside from a certain laxness in growth – he is small for his age, which, by my estimate, is perhaps eight months – he seems to be in fair physical condition. He is not eating, you say, but the question is why not? I will have to take a sample of his blood and saliva and send it for analysis, if you wish for a more detailed diagnosis.'

Chopra agreed to this.

'Of course,' continued Lala, 'we may be dealing with a completely non-physical cause here. Elephants are highly emotional creatures. Perhaps something happened to this poor beast before you took charge of him, and that is at the root of this obstinate behaviour.' Lala scratched his chin. 'In this respect an elephant is no different to you or I, Inspector. When we suffer, we become despondent, listless, emotionally unbalanced. Perhaps our young calf is pining for his mother, his herd – elephants are very social animals, you know; perhaps the mere fact that he has been removed to this new environment has upset him. Once he adjusts, he may begin to settle. Let us hope this does not take too long.'

'If he does not adjust?'

'I have seen elephants simply lie down and die,' said Dr Lala. 'Like humans, they have the capacity to give up on life.'

Chopra looked down at Ganesha, who had collapsed onto his belly and was staring intently at a patch of dirt under his nose, looking every inch the picture of misery that Dr Lala had ascertained him to be.

Chopra was overcome by a sudden feeling of helplessness.

What business did he have trying to nursemaid this poor creature! If his Uncle Bansi had thought that he would be a good friend to the little calf he had been sorely mistaken.

'Dr Lala,' Chopra said, 'is there a place where a calf such as this might find a home? A good home?'

Dr Lala looked thoughtfully at him. 'An elephant is a great responsibility, is it not?'

Chopra said nothing.

Lala pursed his lips. 'There is a sanctuary in Visakhapatnam. An old friend of mine runs it. We attended veterinary school together. I will give him a call. Give me a couple of days.'

Visakhapatnam, thought Chopra. That was on the other side of the country, a thousand miles away on the eastern coast.

He wondered what Uncle Bansi would say. But then, Bansi had requested that Chopra take care of the little elephant. Surely this was the best solution. A sanctuary would look after Ganesha's needs far better than he possibly could.

Chopra looked down at the calf. Flies had settled on Ganesha's eyes and a column of ants were marching resolutely up his trunk as if on military manoeuvres. Ganesha seemed oblivious or simply too despondent to care. He exuded an overwhelming sense of defeat.

Chopra knew that he must do the right thing . . . and at that moment he felt a weight lift from his shoulders. He felt sure that the Visakhapatnam sanctuary would know what to do with the dispirited baby elephant.

Outside the vet's premises, Chopra stopped to wipe the sweat from his brow. He reached into his trousers for his handkerchief. As he pulled it out, he accidentally spilled from his pocket the bundle of visiting cards that he had taken from Santosh Achrekar's home the day before. The cards scattered over the dusty ground. He cursed and dropped to his knees to begin gathering them up. Behind him Ganesha waited patiently, his trunk dangling below his sombre face.

Chopra shuffled across the parched earth, collecting the cards. Suddenly, he froze. He picked up the card that had caught his attention and straightened to his feet. He read the card again:

MOTILAL'S LEATHER EMPORIUM

Shop No. 5, Gold Field Arcade,
Kala Qila, Dharavi, Mumbai, 400017

Motilal's. Moti's. Chopra felt the sudden thrill of a connection made. Why hadn't he seen it before! He felt certain that this must be the place that Santosh Achrekar had visited on his last day on earth. This was the place where he had met the enigmatic 'S.', perhaps the man who had killed him. The investigation that Chopra had concluded only the night before had met an impenetrable brick wall, had opened up before him again. It was an opportunity he did not intend to pass up.

THE GREATEST SLUM ON EARTH

The Kala Qila section of Dharavi lay six kilometres away, a long walk in the hot sun. But Chopra was determined to follow up his newly acquired lead.

The route to Kala Qila lay along the M.V. Road, which meandered southwards around the sprawling eastern perimeter of the Chhatrapati Shivaji airport until it met the bustling Lal Bahadur Shastri Road. From there he could follow LBS all the way past Chunabhatti and into the Dharavi slum proper.

Chopra decided that he would take Ganesha with him; if he walked back home first, he would lose a good hour of time. And he did not wish to waste another minute.

He knew that the course he had embarked upon was reckless. He knew that if Suryavansh discovered that he was snooping around on the case, then he might well have to cross swords with him again.

Chopra was not afraid of Suryavansh, but he did not wish complications to be placed in the path of his investigation. And then there was Poppy to think of. What would she say if she knew that within days of his retirement he was back to his old tricks? The whole point of retiring had been to get away from this sort of thing, so that his ailing heart might be spared potentially fatal excitement.

Well, thought Chopra, I have made up my mind. And once a man does that, everything else should be left to fate.

Halfway along the route, Chopra's belly began to rumble. He decided to stop at a roadside Chinese restaurant.

He watched the passing traffic on LBS Road as he ate his plate of egg fried rice. Across the street a small crowd had gathered to watch a shoot for a low-budget Bollywood potboiler. An overweight and aging leading man in a tight string vest and black wig was serenading a youthful heroine dressed in a skimpy miniskirt, who seemed oblivious to the constant wolf-whistling and suggestive commentary from the gathered crowd. A fat director was bellowing through a loudhailer at various lackeys.

The leading man suddenly tripped over his feet and fell down, crashing into a table and spilling hot tea over a handsome dog panting beneath it, who was playing the part of the hero's sidekick. The fall dislodged the hero's wig, which landed over the dog's eyes. The dog, blind and mad with pain, shot off along the street, barking at the top of his lungs. The crowd roared with laughter, thinking this was all part of the scene.

Chopra thought again of the poor parents of Santosh Achrekar. Once again he imagined himself in the role of bereaved father. What would it be like to know that your child's future had been taken away, not by accident, but by the evil designs of another human being?

Chopra had never talked openly to Poppy of his feelings about the lack of children in their lives. Many times he had wanted to share his own pain and frustration with someone, but he had known instinctively that were he to give Poppy even an inkling of the disappointment he felt, it would for ever undermine the trust that existed between them. And so he had swallowed his tears, and pretended that the whole business of an heir really did not mean that much to him. When his colleagues brought in sweets to celebrate a new addition to their families, he would offer his congratulations and then quickly return to his desk, making no further fuss over the matter.

But sometimes, in the depths of the night, when Poppy was dead to the world, he would lie awake in bed and wonder what it would be like to teach his own son the fundamentals of a proper forward defensive stroke, or how to pop the clutch on a new Hero Honda as Chopra Junior learned to ride his first motorcycle.

Or a daughter, perhaps; he would imagine a line of potential suitors for her hand standing before him, trembling with fear, scared stiff of his uniform. He would imagine, with a chuckle, threatening to arrest them and have them beaten in the cells all night, so that in their fright they might reveal their true characters.

He bought a bunch of bananas from a passing handcart

for Ganesha, but the elephant was not yet willing to break his self-imposed fast.

It had been two years since Chopra had last entered the Dharavi slum of Mumbai. At the time he had been pursuing enquiries on a kidnapping case, a case which had ultimately gone unsolved. It had been only his second foray into the slum and he had found, as on his first visit, that Dharavi was simply unlike anything that he had previously experienced.

In essence the slum was a city within a city, albeit one whose true population had always eluded the census takers. Nevertheless, it was estimated that almost one million individuals lived within its narrow, choking, maze-like districts, all sandwiched in between the city's two principal suburban rail lines, the Western and Central Railways.

What had instantly struck Chopra on both the occasions that he had ventured here was how the residents of Dharavi remained steadfastly unembarrassed by their poverty. They lived in one of the most congested places on earth, an unsanitary, poorly equipped demesne where disease flourished and hardship was a way of life. And yet the slum was home to thousands of successful businesses. If one wished to see the true face of Indian entrepreneurialism, he had often reflected, then one had only to come to the slum-city. Here, without the benefit of foreign capital, or MBA-qualified ex-pats, micro-businesses thrived: little one-man – or one-woman – operations producing and selling everything from enamelled pots, tourist curios, Barbie dolls, blue jeans, cocktail dresses and carbolic soap through to a recycling operation that was the largest in the country. Chopra recalled a recent article he had read which suggested that Dharavi generated upwards of six hundred million dollars in hard currency each year. For this reason Dharavi had often been labelled 'the world's greatest slum' by the newspaper-wallahs.

Chopra could not disagree. There was something both magical and mysterious about the place. In the twilight zone of Dharavi, where even auto-rickshaws could not enter; where houses were constructed from anything available to hand – corrugated tin, plywood, pukkah bricks, asbestos and cardboard sheets – where a billion cockroaches played tag with a million rats; where black smoke from the potters' kilns created an artificial cloudbank overhead; where hundreds of thousands of shopkeepers, street vendors, ragpickers, tinkers, tailors, black marketeers and miniature moguls operated beyond the reach of the municipal authorities; where the sound of hammering from the metalworkers' smithies was a constant background noise . . . the human spirit still flourished.

The Kala Qila area of the slum, Chopra knew, was famed for its leather shops. Leatherwork – from the tanning of hides to the production of beautiful leather garments for sale and export – was one of the oldest industries in Dharavi.

As he walked through the district he was astounded, as always, by the closeness of everything. Dharavi was Mumbai compressed into a smaller-scale version of itself; and yet the same things still mattered. The thousands of little one-room dwellings sprouted aerials for TV connections; posters of the latest Bollywood releases were plastered on every paint-peeled wall; old men discussed the elections while smoking beedis and defecating into the open sewers; women gossiped about their neighbours' husbands as they filled buckets from the communal spigots. There were even beggars here. Life was life, after all.

Chopra stopped outside a small shop that was one of a number of such establishments crowded along either side of a dusty parade. The shops along the arcade had names such as NUMBER ONE LEATHER, ITALIANO LEATHER EXPORTS and ULTIMATE FASHIONS LEATHER HOUSE. He looked at the sign above the shop in front of which he had stopped. MOTILAL'S LEATHER EMPORIUM. The shop was glass-fronted, like most of the premises on the arcade. In the window a number of leather purses could be seen displayed on a series of floating shelves. Beside them, a headless mannequin modelled a brown leather coat.

He looked around. A palm tree grew on the edge of the parade. A raucous gaggle of street children were playing a game of cricket, and had chalked a set of stumps onto the tree's trunk. They were playing the game with a balding tennis ball and an ancient bat held together with tape. When the children spotted him with Ganesha in tow they abandoned their game and clustered around, wanting to touch the baby elephant. Chopra noticed that Ganesha automatically drew closer to him. 'Leave the poor animal alone!' he admonished the children.

He chained Ganesha around the tree's trunk, then once more warned the kids against interfering with him. Then in a flash of inspiration, he realised there was a better way: he removed his wallet and showed them a twenty-rupee note. 'This is for you,' he said. 'I am Inspector Chopra and you are now my deputies and must look after this elephant. He is vital to a very important case.'

The kids looked at Ganesha with renewed interest. One of them, a floppy-haired boy in a string vest and torn shorts, said: 'These days you can't buy anything for twenty chips, sahib.'

What a cheeky rascal! thought Chopra, but he couldn't help smiling. 'Twenty is all you will get,' he said. 'Take it or leave it.'

He left Ganesha nervously peeking out from behind the tree as he watched the children resume their game of cricket, and entered the shop.

Inside, there were more mannequins, racks of coats and jackets, and shelves crammed with leather goods: bags, wallets, belts, knife sheaths, wine casks. The air was pregnant with the heady musk of new leather. Decorating the walls were framed pictures of customers of the shop, minor Mumbai celebrities and a few foreigners who had ventured into Dharavi in search of a bargain. Many of the goods in the shop carried the emblems of famous Italian brands. But he was not here to make a dent in the sea of counterfeit merchandise produced in Dharavi each year.

At the rear of the shop there was a counter, before which a peon dozed fitfully on a stool.

Chopra moved towards the peon, who, as if activated by a hidden alarm, awoke with a start and leaped to his feet, toppling the stool with a clatter.

'Where is the owner of the shop?' asked Chopra.

'Sahib, I will fetch him right away!' The peon lifted a

hatch in the counter and disappeared through a door in the wall behind it.

Moments later, a fat man with a bulbous nose, heavy jowls and a thicket of curly black hair emerged from the doorway. He too looked as if he had been awoken from sleep. 'Hello, sir, hello!' he said enthusiastically, practically rubbing his chubby hands. 'What can I do for you today? You look like a man who needs a new jacket! Yes, with your height, and those impressive shoulders, I have just the piece for you! It is an Italian cut, the very latest design!'

'I do not want a jacket,' said Chopra sternly. 'My name is Inspector Chopra and I am here to make enquiries about a boy that you knew.'

'Boy? What boy?' The man's face had darkened. He was no longer the bustling proprietor of a successful leather emporium eager to conclude a sale. Chopra sensed a note of fear in the man's voice. He removed the photograph that Achrekar had given him and showed it to the man, who he assumed was Motilal.

Motilal examined the photograph in his chubby hands. His fingers were encrusted with rings, and gold chains jangled on both wrists. 'Sir, I have never seen this boy before,' he said eventually.

Chopra had heard many men lie. Some were masters at it, and even a police officer with years of experience could not be sure when they were being deceitful. And then there were others, like Motilal, whose lies were as plain as the nose on their face.

'Let me warn you,' he said sternly, 'we know that this boy knew you. He kept a written record of meetings that he had with you. The boy was murdered five days ago. If you do not cooperate with me I will haul you to the station for questioning. And then we will see what you know.'

Motilal blanched. 'Murdered! Dear Shiva! Sir, I have nothing to do with any murder, nothing at all. I am just a humble leather merchant.'

Chopra looked expansively around the shop. 'Perhaps a raid by the IRS will jog your memory,' he said.

Motilal turned an even whiter shade of pale. There was a type of person in Mumbai more terrified of a raid by the tax authorities than the thought of being implicated in a murder. 'Let me see that picture again . . .' He pretended to re-examine the photo. 'Ah, yes, now that you mention it, I think this boy came here a few times recently. He was simply an administrative clerk, you know. No one important.'

No one important, thought Chopra. A sudden surge of anger welled inside him. But before he could give the sweating shop owner a piece of his mind, the door jangled open behind him.

A tall bald man with a pitted skull entered. He wore a half-sleeved shirt, open at the chest, revealing thick curls of hair and a tangle of gold chains. In the cramped space he loomed like a giant.

Chopra looked at the man's face. The forehead was corrugated above thick eyebrows and narrow eyes. Thick lips sat below a fleshy nose. The man had a heavy, muscular build, and a nasty look. *Goonda* . . . that was the word that rose unbidden to his lips. A hired thug. A goon. He had seen many of them in his time.

The man returned Chopra's look with a belligerent one

of his own. Then he transferred his gaze to Motilal, and the photograph still clutched in his sweating hand. 'What is going on here?'

'Oh, nothing, nothing,' said Motilal a little too quickly. 'The inspector here was simply asking about some boy.'

'What boy?'

'Some boy who was murdered.'

'Murdered? People are murdered in Mumbai every day. It's practically our main line of business. If we started worrying about every person who was murdered in this city no one would do any other work.' He turned to Chopra. 'If you're looking for witnesses, Inspector, you're wasting your time. This is Dharavi. People understand about minding their own business here.'

'Yes, yes,' sang Motilal. 'Minding my own business is practically my religion! Ha ha!' The man glared at him and he turned a sickly yellow. Chopra noted real terror in the merchant's eyes. He understood now where the power lay in the room. But how was Motilal mixed up with this thug? Was it simply a case of extortion, of weekly protection money? Or was it bigger than that? Did the thug represent some local outfit exporting counterfeit goods, perhaps? Chopra knew this kind of man. He was bad news.

'The boy was killed in Marol,' said Chopra evenly.

'Then you are a little out of your territory, aren't you?' The big man turned to Motilal. 'I have some business with you,' he said. 'And that is surely none of your business, Inspector.'

The two men disappeared into the rear office.

Chopra waited, considering his options. He could continue to bluff it out, and tackle the brute and Motilal head-on. But the thug did not look as if he was fazed by Chopra's credentials as a police officer, and he could not afford to have his bluff called. Alternatively, he could wait for the brute to leave and try to tackle Motilal again on his own. He sensed that while the thug was around he was not going to get anything useful out of the shop owner, assuming there was anything useful to be had. He had come here on a hunch; it was only in the movies that hunches paid off each and every time. Most of the time they led precisely nowhere.

The peon hovered around Chopra, unsure of how to treat him. Clearly he was a police officer, and therefore to be handled with care. But at the same time he was also someone who was causing his master some anxiety. In the end Chopra solved his problem by leaving the shop.

He walked across the parade to the tree where he had tethered Ganesha. The children playing cricket had finished their game and disappeared back into the slum. As he approached, the elephant lumbered to his feet. For the first time Ganesha seemed to show some recognition of him, extending his trunk and touching Chopra's hand. It was an encouraging sign. 'We're not going just yet, boy,' he said.

They waited. Around them the life of Dharavi continued. People drifted down the parade, some on private errands, others flirting with the various leather shops before deciding to enter a particular one. A handcart-wallah selling lime water rattled by. Chopra purchased ten glasses, one for himself and nine for Ganesha, who slurped up the cool liquid with his trunk and shot it into his mouth. Even the little elephant seemed to be feeling the extraordinary heat.

Finally, just when he was about to give up, the big man emerged from the shop.

Chopra moved behind the tree and watched him as he clambered astride a motorbike parked outside the shop and stamped on the starter pedal. Nothing happened. The man swore and tried again. Still nothing. He got off the bike and bent down to examine it. He lifted the engine cap and fiddled inside. Then he tried to start it again. The machine remained coolly unresponsive. Enraged, the thug kicked the bike forcefully, toppling it onto its side. He continued to kick at it on the ground, all the while abusing it loudly.

Eventually, he stood back and looked up at the sky. He wiped the sweat from his pitted skull with the back of his hairy arm. Then he reached behind him and pulled something from the pocket of his jeans. It was a hat, like a combat beret, but bright red, made of a shimmering velvety fabric. Red velvet.

Chopra stood frozen behind his tree. He remembered the motorbike tracks that he had seen at the site of the boy's murder; how they had suggested to him that two men had been on the bike, perhaps Santosh and a second heavier man. A big man. Homi Contractor had surmised that the fibres found under Santosh's fingernails came from a red velvet *shirt*. But that had just been a guess. The fibres did not have to come from a shirt at all.

The man put the hat on, reached inside the waistband of his jeans and took out a package wrapped in brown paper. He examined it, then tucked it back inside his denims. Then he set off down the road. Chopra unchained Ganesha and began to follow him.

THE ATLAS MEGA MALL

Chopra was glad that the man had chosen to walk, rather than take a taxi. As it turned out they did not have far to go.

They tramped along Station Road and onto the Sion-Bandra Link Road, which served as a bridge over the Mahim creek. Almost as soon as they crossed over to the far side, the man turned off the road and walked down into the newly redeveloped business district that ran along the bank of the creek. He carried on walking right up to the Bandra Kurla Complex, which was now home to such global giants as Google. Here the reclaimed land had been cleared and flattened and a whole new shopping development had been created, with wide lanes, huge car parks and gigantic superstores.

At the centre of the new shopping zone was its star attraction, the Atlas Mega Mall, said to be the largest shopping mall in the whole of Asia. Over a million square feet in retail space, with one thousand-plus outlets under one roof providing a 'one-stop destination for every shopping, leisure, entertainment, lifestyle and eating requirement of every customer'.

Even from a distance the mall looked imposing, thought Chopra, who had never been inside. In fact, he had never been inside any of the new malls that had recently sprung up around Mumbai.

He found something intrinsically vulgar and alien about them, from the sheer arrogance of their size, to the conveyor-belt so-called hospitality of their service. He had made a point of continuing to patronise the smaller shops that he had always frequented, even though they were rapidly being forced out of business by the new behemoths.

His tailor, Ramesh, had bemoaned his dwindling customer base. 'Who wants my shirts any more, Inspector Sahib?' he had griped. 'Now they can go to the mall and buy shirts by Mr Van Hussain, and Mr Loose Phillips.'

Chopra did not need Van Heusen and Louis Philippe shirts. He had no use for Apple accessories and Ray-Ban sunglasses. Sometimes it seemed to him that the whole country was being rebranded. He imagined lines of Indians moving past booths manned by representatives of foreign multinationals; as each Indian went past he was stripped of his traditional clothes, his traditional values, and given new things to wear, new things to think. Branded and rewired, this new model of Indian went back to his home thinking that he was now truly a modern Indian, and what a fine thing that was. But all Chopra saw was the gradual death of the culture that had always made him proud of his incredible country.

Poppy, of course, did not share his views.

Poppy had been an early victim of the mall mania. She had been instantly beguiled by the bright lights, glitzy displays and insouciant sales-boys with their slicked-back hair and garishly coloured uniforms. She loved to have them buzzing around her, telling her how she looked like such-and-such movie heroine in this outfit or that.

The mall was fronted by a grand plaza in which fountains in the shape of drooling lions sprayed water majestically in all directions. Coloured pennants fluttered at the top of forty-metre-high flagpoles. The mall's façade was covered in a skin of stainless-steel panels, which reflected the sun blindingly into the eyes of the dazed customers moving lemming-like towards the grand parade of glass entrance doors set above a flight of marbled steps.

Chopra was finding it increasingly difficult to track his target, but, thankfully, the man's height and the brightly coloured beret made his task simpler. He watched now as the man disappeared into the mall.

Chopra surged forward, pulling Ganesha up the flight of shallow steps. At the entrance doors a liveried guard halted him. 'Sir, you cannot enter the premises!'

'Why ever not?' said Chopra, bristling.

The man's eyes drifted behind him, as if the answer to this question was self-evident.

Ganesha! In the excitement of the chase, Chopra had almost forgotten that he was currently accompanied by a two-hundred-kilo elephant.

He looked around. The crowds poured around them, a few stopping from their headlong rush into the theatre of dreams to shoot a quizzical look at the strange man and his elephant. Ganesha had drawn close to him; he could feel the little elephant's nervousness. Chopra knew he could not leave him out here, amidst this sea of strangers. Dr Lala had said that elephants were highly emotional creatures. He imagined how a young human child would feel being left alone amidst a crowd. No, he could not do that.

'Step aside,' Chopra said to the doorman. 'This is official police business.'

'But sir!'

Chopra barged past the man, pulling Ganesha behind him. Luckily the doors were very wide, and the elephant had no trouble passing through. Behind them, he could hear the doorman complaining to a colleague, and the crackle of a walkie-talkie summoning reinforcements.

Inside, the lobby was a bedlam of noise and movement. Rock music blared from hidden speakers. There were glass elevators moving up and down, and a giant tropical fish tank. A curtain of water fell from above into a rock pool. People moved in all directions, like shoals of fish – groups of teenagers, couples, whole families with babies and grandparents in tow. There were jugglers and face-painters and even a fire-breather in bright red leather tights. It was more like a carnival than a place for shopping, thought Chopra in horror.

Or a lunatic asylum where the inmates had taken over.

Suddenly, he felt a tug on his arm. He looked down. A small child in a bright yellow Nike T-shirt and sports shoes that lit up with red runway lights looked up at him with a belligerent expression. 'I want to ride your elephant,' he said.

'This elephant is not for riding,' said Chopra.

A fat man in a similarly bright red Nike T-shirt and glistening, permed hair in which were parked designer sunglasses, stood in front of him. 'Come now, fellow, my son wants to ride on your elephant. How much is it?'

'This elephant is not for riding,' he repeated, a little more gruffly.

'Nonsense,' barked the fat man. 'What do you want? Fifty rupees? One hundred? Whatever my son wants, my son gets. Come now, how much? Don't haggle with me, I'm no tourist, you know.'

'Get out of my way,' growled Chopra, brushing past the fat man.

In the middle of the lobby a series of grand escalators took centre stage. He could see the man in the red hat on one of them, gliding up to the next floor of the mall.

He moved to the foot of the central escalator and stepped on board. Suddenly, he found himself tugged back. Behind him, Ganesha had planted his feet and was making it clear that he had no intention of boarding the moving staircase.

'Come on, boy,' grunted Chopra, pulling on the chain and furiously backpedalling as he sought to maintain his balance on the ascending steps. Ganesha dug in his heels, and with a quick jerk of his neck, yanked Chopra from the escalator. The inspector landed in a heap. Ganesha snorted and moved further backwards.

Around him, Chopra heard people laughing.

'Come on, do another one!' someone guffawed as he rose to his feet and dusted himself off.

'Yes,' said a portly woman in a bright orange sari, 'do the one where the elephant rolls over.'

'We are not part of the entertainment,' muttered Chopra grimly. He bent down to Ganesha and looked the little elephant squarely in the eye. 'Listen to me, my friend,' he said. 'I need your help. Don't be afraid. I won't let any harm come to you. You must trust me.'

He patted Ganesha on the head, then turned, walked forward . . . and was swiftly brought back down to earth again.

He swore under his breath.

The man in the red hat had vanished onto the level above. He knew he couldn't just leave Ganesha in the lobby. There was nothing for it. He would have to give up the chase.

'Here, try this.'

Chopra turned. An elderly gentleman held out a bar of Cadbury's Dairy Milk chocolate.

'I do not require chocolate,' he said, stiffly.

'It is not for you,' said the man with a kindly smile. 'When I was young, my father worked in the Grand Kohinoor Circus. It was his job to train the elephants.'

Chopra took the bar of chocolate and examined it suspiciously. The old man nodded encouragingly. Unconvinced, he broke off a piece from the slab and offered it to Ganesha. The elephant sniffed at it with his trunk, then took it and put it into his mouth. He blinked. His tail twitched. His ears flapped. Then, with a shake of his head, he reached out his trunk for the rest of the bar. Chopra pulled it away, then backed off to the escalator. 'Come and get it, boy.'

In this way, he managed to coax Ganesha onto the escalator, which, like everything else in the mall, was made to a gargantuan scale, easily wide enough to accommodate a nervous baby elephant. As they travelled up to the next floor, a buzz of laughter erupted around them.

On the first floor, Chopra followed the gallery of shops and designer boutiques around the curve of the mall. Benetton, Nike, Burberry, Marks & Spencer, GAP, The Body Shop. Suddenly, he came to a large store with mannequins in the window modelling stylish leather coats. He peered inside and saw the man in the red hat standing at the counter, chatting idly to one of the pretty young attendants. As he watched, a man in a well-tailored suit emerged from the rear of the store. The man in the red hat pulled him aside, removed the package from inside his jeans, and handed it over.

Chopra had a sudden idea of what was in the package. Cash. A very thick bundle of cash. To him the whole transaction smelled of one thing: payoff. But for what?

The two men finished their business and, with a last flirtatious leer at the salesgirl, the man in the red hat left.

Chopra turned and pretended to be looking into the store behind him, which was a specialist cake boutique. Immediately, a sales attendant ran outside and enquired: 'Sir, is there some special occasion for which you require a cake? We can make any kind of cake you like. Any shape, also. Even in shape of elephant!'

'No thank you,' growled Chopra.

THE MAN WHO WAS SUPPOSED TO BE DEAD

Inspector Chopra and Ganesha followed the man in the red hat as he left the mall. Instead of leaving through the front lobby, he exited from the rear doors, which led onto a grand concourse packed with parked cars.

The man in the red hat wandered up to the taxi rank, where he spoke briefly to a driver. He was about to step into the cab when his phone rang. He signalled to the driver to wait, and lit a cigarette while he chatted. Chopra looked around. He didn't have much time. There was no way he could continue to follow this man, unless . . .

Not far away an emaciated man in a grey uniform and shorts was standing idly beside a small truck with a drop-down tailgate. On the side of the truck was written ATLAS MEGA MALL DELIVERIES.

Chopra approached him and said, 'Official police business. I am commandeering your truck.'

The driver, who had not been born yesterday, was instantly suspicious. 'If you are a policeman,' he said, 'why do you have an elephant?'

'It is a police elephant,' said Chopra.

'Pull the other one, sahib,' said the man. 'The police don't use elephants.'

'You have heard of police dogs?' said Chopra, sternly. 'Well, this is a police elephant.'

The man looked at Ganesha with renewed interest. Chopra looked around. The man in the red hat had finished his call, and was leisurely finishing his cigarette as he eyed the young girls passing by, occasionally making lecherous remarks.

'Listen to me,' said Chopra. 'I am going to commandeer this vehicle. If you don't help me, I am going to have you arrested. Do you understand?'

The man blanched. 'OK, OK, no need to get upset, Inspector,' he said. 'I will have to answer to my boss, that's all. If there is even one scratch on it, I will lose my job. Wherever you want to go, I will drive you.'

'Let's get the elephant into the back.' The driver dropped the tailgate and, using the remaining chocolate, Chopra coaxed Ganesha into the rear of the truck. They were just in time.

They followed the taxi as it made its way towards the suburbs, passing through Ambedkar Chowk and onto the Western Express Highway. The taxi raced through Bandra,

Santa Cruz and Vile Parle until they were back in Sahar. Once off the expressway and onto Sahar Road, the taxi turned into the old industrial sector that lay behind the abandoned Gold Spot factory.

This massive sprawl of derelict buildings was scheduled for gentrification and a planned 'elevated road' that would directly connect the nearby international airport to the highway, but the grand project had become mired in red tape and the unscrupulous machinations of politicians.

The taxi snaked into the interior of the derelict zone until finally it parked outside what looked like a gutted warehouse. Facing the warehouse was another, equally derelict-looking building.

The man in the red hat got out, paid the taxi driver and entered the warehouse.

Chopra ordered the truck driver to park out of sight around a corner and wait. Leaving the driver and Ganesha in the truck, he positioned himself at the corner of the alley so that he could keep an eye on the front of the warehouse.

Just when he felt it was safe to move in, the sound of an approaching vehicle stopped him in his tracks. As he watched, a large white Mercedes with blackened windows came bouncing along the rutted road.

It parked in front of the warehouse, and waited, engine idling.

After a while, the man in the red hat came out of the warehouse with two other equally rough-looking men in tow. A driver in a spotless white uniform jumped out from the Mercedes and held the rear door open. A man emerged, wearing a crisp white suit and sunglasses. He was tall, with short dark hair, and wheatish skin. His face was made distinctive by its long chin, partially covered with a stubbly beard. The man stepped forward. Chopra noticed that he used a cane; his right leg seemed to be troubled by a limp. Then the man removed his sunglasses and looked up at the sky. Chopra stood frozen in shock.

That face! *He knew that face!* It was a face that was supposed to be no more: the face of his old nemesis, the underworld crime lord known as Kala Nayak.

A man Chopra had killed nine years ago.

Poppy had been baking. As she herself would have been the first to admit, she was not the most skilled of bakers, but it was her favourite activity nonetheless, because it helped her to think, particularly when she was feeling anxious.

And right now, Poppy was more anxious than she had ever been in her life.

The idea that had come to her when she had sat with Kiran at her fancy home in Bandra had now had time to grow. As she considered it once again her arm became a blur, whisking away at the flour mix, whisking and whisking, and whisking some more.

A child! A child of her very own! That was what Poppy wished for, more than anything else in the whole world. And now fate had dropped the opportunity into her lap.

Oh, but how could she possibly! How could she hope to get away with it?

When she had first outlined the plan to Kiran, and then to Kiran's daughter Prarthana, she had done so with a breathless feeling of incredulity. Surely they would not agree, she had thought.

But it made sense, certainly on the basis of the facts that she had been given.

Kiran's daughter was pregnant with an illegitimate child. She did not wish to abort the child, nor raise it. The child would be given up for adoption. Poppy had no children, and could not have any . . . Why then, should *Poppy* not become the mother of Kiran's daughter's child?

Wasn't that preferable to sending the child to be raised by strangers in some impoverished orphanage?

After all, wasn't Poppy the child's great-aunt, anyway? Certainly, Kiran had leaped at the possibility of salvaging her family honour. She had already helped to convince her daughter who, though not without qualms, had reluctantly accepted the eminent practicality of the solution.

The problem, of course, was Chopra.

Her husband had made it clear that he would not entertain adoption. She did not understand why, but she knew him well enough to know that once he had made up his mind about something like that he was not going to change it. And if she tried to talk to him about adopting Kiran's grandchild, then that would ruin any chance she had of putting her plan into effect. Because Poppy's plan was this: she would pretend to be pregnant.

For the next nine months, she would carry out the charade of pregnancy. And then, when the baby was born, she would present it as her own.

It seemed, at first glance, absurd; every time she thought about it her heart galloped inside her. But when she considered it rationally, she realised it was not as far-fetched as all that.

Chopra was a detective, but in matters such as this men were renowned for their ignorance. As long as she put on a little weight, and feigned morning sickness and the occasional foul mood, he would believe that she was pregnant. This was not the West, after all, where men seemed to be involved with every aspect of what should be a woman's private experience, and even attended the birth, something that struck Poppy as an affront to common decency.

Her mother might be harder to fool, but Poppy could manage Poornima. If necessary, her mother would become a grumbling co-conspirator; after all, hadn't she complained for years about her daughter's childlessness?

As for the birth itself, Poppy would insist on a good old-fashioned midwife, not a hospital birth. She would insist on moving in with her good friend and cousin Kiran for the final few weeks; Kiran who herself would have moved by then to a little cottage in Silvassa, just outside of Mumbai, to help her ailing daughter recover from her 'illness'. The baby would be born a good three weeks before everyone had been told it was due; a premature birth. And then, finally, Poppy would be a mother.

Poppy believed that becoming a mother might also help dispel the feeling that was growing inside her that something was wrong in her relationship with her husband. She loved him dearly, but since his heart attack he had seemed increasingly distracted, even distant, at times. Perhaps that was understandable, given the upheaval in his life . . . But there were other changes in his behaviour that she found strange.

Take, for instance, the mysterious phone calls he had been receiving over the past months. Whenever the calls arrived Chopra would excuse himself, even if he was halfway through dinner, and retire to his study. And when Poppy asked, he would simply say, 'Police business.' But there had never been police business before that necessitated so many calls at home, and such secrecy.

Poppy was worried. And the answer to her worries, she now felt, had been delivered to her by Prarthana's baby.

She paused and looked at the wall, where the framed and garlanded photographs of both her father and Chopra's father were placed side by side. 'Am I doing the right thing?' she asked the two venerable and long-deceased gentlemen.

After a while she went back to her whisking.

Narendra 'Kala' Nayak had been just one of a number of gangland criminals who had ruled Mumbai's underworld in the early nineties. Back then they had been arrogantly open about their activities, seemingly unafraid of the authorities. It was not uncommon for celebrities to be gunned down in the street after refusing to pay extortion money; or for local politicians to be similarly despatched when a crooked deal went awry.

By the standards of the Mumbai underworld Kala Nayak had been an entrepreneur. He had been the first to graduate from hashish to large-scale importing of cocaine, and, later, designer drugs such as ecstasy, acid and butterfly, feeding the growing market of hip young things in the newly fashionable suburbs. He had quickly built up a network of distributors, using the city's beggars, eunuchs, and men recruited from the poorest segments of society. He had become incredibly wealthy, seemingly overnight.

But that much money attracts attention and it wasn't long before Nayak was fighting battles on every front – with the police, with rival gangs, with dirty politicians unhappy with their monthly payoffs, and even with ambitious lieutenants from his own organisation.

Nayak had upset the old order: the dons who had ruled over their local neighbourhoods with iron fists, creaming profits from the old staples: extortion, gambling, prostitution and smuggling. Nayak had boldly moved into new enterprises: real estate, film production and waterfront commerce, all twisted in some way to add to his ever-fuller coffers. Because of his brashness, and because of his refusal to negotiate territorial arrangements with other gang lords, Nayak had trodden on the toes of almost everyone who mattered in Mumbai. He had made so many enemies that soon even his enemies' enemies were his enemies.

Heedless, Nayak had continued to expand his organisation, throwing his ill-gotten money around; and where money didn't get him his way, he resorted to violence. By the mid-nineties he was top of the Most Wanted lists, and had been declared a bona fide menace to the city of Mumbai in particular and the country in general.

A special citywide taskforce had been put together to tackle Kala Nayak. Because his stronghold had remained in the Sahar and Marol districts, Chopra had been seconded to the taskforce. They had put together a case, and a warrant had been issued for his arrest. But the panicked gangster had gone underground. The word was that Nayak was still in the city; the search was on.

One evening, when Chopra had been working late at the station, the eunuch Anarkali had come to see him. She had information about Nayak.

Over the years, Chopra had learned that little happened in the locality without Anarkali knowing about it. A six-foot-tall, muscular transgender individual in a purple sari, she was, he had discovered, an intelligent and thoughtful person who made the best of her circumstances. Like most eunuchs she was enmeshed in the world of petty crime, but Chopra had been willing to look the other way in return for the occasional titbit of useful information.

It was one of his few concessions. Chopra, as a rule, did not believe in compromising in such matters.

Above this, however, was another belief, one that he had held almost since the day he had first arrived in this fantastical city: that Anarkali, like millions of others on the lowest rungs of Mumbai society, was merely a product of the crushing poverty into which she had been born. Many years ago he had discovered her under the Airport Flyover where she lived, beaten and close to death after a gang of drunken men had violated her. He had taken her to the hospital, argued with the horrified doctor, and paid the medical fees himself.

Following Anarkali's tip-off, that evening Chopra and a team of officers from the Sahar station had staked out an old garment warehouse in the heart of the area known as MIDC-SEEPZ, the Maharashtra Industrial Development Corporation and Santacruz Electronic Export Processing Zone. The area was a hive of small industrial units, and, over the years, because of the preponderance of cash-intensive jewellery operations, had become a hotbed of criminal activity. Chopra and his men were no strangers to the bustling cantonment.

An hour into the stakeout, a face had appeared at one of the warehouse windows. Kala Nayak!

Chopra had wasted no time, leading his team in an all-out assault on the building. Immediately, they had found themselves in a pitched battle with Nayak's men. The shootout had raged through the four floors of the warehouse; then, out of nowhere, a fire had sprung up. The policemen had retreated and watched while the building burned down.

When they sifted through the ashes, they found a number of charred remains, including one body wearing the distinctive jewellery that Nayak had been famed for.

The case had been closed, and Inspector Chopra had subsequently received the Kirti Chakra.

In time, others had moved in to take Nayak's place, but for Chopra there had been a deep personal satisfaction in seeing the back of Kala Nayak. Not only had Nayak been responsible for bringing a wave of crime to the area that he had made his home, but the gang lord had also been responsible for the death of a close colleague and friend from the station, Sub-Inspector Pereira, who had been shot dead by Nayak's men some two years previously. Pereira and Chopra had passed out through training school together; Pereira had left behind a wife and three teenage children.

Chopra watched now as the man he believed to be Kala Nayak entered the warehouse. His every instinct was urging him to hurl himself after his quarry, but he somehow held himself in check.

The minutes ticked away. Sweat beaded on his forehead, and rolled down his back. He heard Ganesha noisily pacing inside the rear of the truck. He heard the truck driver wander up behind him and strike a match, and smelled the pungent whiff of beedi smoke.

He looked at his watch. Fifteen minutes!

Just as he had all but decided he could wait no longer, Nayak re-emerged, trailed by the man in the red hat.

Briefly they exchanged words, and then Nayak got into the Mercedes. The vehicle left in a cloud of dust. The man in the red hat followed on a motorbike that he had rolled out from inside the warehouse.

Chopra turned back to the truck. 'Come on, let's go!' he said to the driver, who was now crouching by the front right tyre.

'I'm sorry, sahib, but we cannot go anywhere,' said the driver ruefully. 'Puncture.'

Chopra looked down and saw the flattened tyre. He swore under his breath, and trotted back to the corner. But the Mercedes had vanished.

Dammit! He hadn't even noted the vehicle's registration plate! It was the sort of oversight for which he would have roundly berated a junior officer. But he had been so disoriented by the fact of Nayak's reappearance that he had not been thinking straight. There was nothing further he could do, not now. At least he had the location of this warehouse, whatever Nayak was using it for.

Now he needed time to think.

THE RAIN FINALLY ARRIVES

Inspector Chopra dreamed. He dreamed that he was inside a mall, a mall so vast that it took up the whole world. The mall was brightly lit; everything – walls, floors, ceilings – shone with a pearly white light.

As he wandered around the mall, people jumped out at him, offering him incredible bargains. *Would sir like to purchase a brand new soul, special offer this week only, ten per cent off with your loyalty card?*

He arrived at a long counter. At the far end of the counter, he could see the tiny outline of a man. He walked towards the man; it seemed to take for ever.

Finally, he reached the man, who had his back turned to him, as he stood facing a row of shelves that stretched upwards to infinity and were crowded with shiny, indistinguishable packages of all shapes, sizes and colours. The man was dressed in white, but had very dark hair. 'Excuse me,' said Chopra, 'can you tell me where I am?'

The man turned around and Chopra saw that it was Kala Nayak. Nayak grinned, and as he did so flames erupted around the outline of his body. But he did not burn. Grinning in the centre of the fire, like a maharishi, he said: 'Didn't you know? They made me a god. God of the new India. You can't kill me. Nothing can kill me.'

Chopra woke up, his heart hammering inside his chest. For a second he thought he was having another heart attack . . . and then he realised that the hammering was not his heart – it was the rain hammering against the windows of his bedroom, hammering loud enough to drown out even the noise of the air-conditioning unit.

Rain! At last, the long-awaited monsoon had broken! Chopra felt an overwhelming sense of relief. He had grown up on a village farm, and although he was now a city boy through and through, something inside him, some creature of the fields, still yearned for the annual deluge. It was inside every Indian, he supposed, this primeval connection to the ancient rhythms, the cycle of planting, inundation, harvest; the cycle of life on the subcontinent.

He got up and went into the living room. Here the rain hammered even more fiercely on the windows. It wasn't really rain, thought Chopra. This was a vertical flood!

Sheets of water raced down the windowpanes, torrents of wonderful, life-giving water, blasting away the heat and humidity of the prolonged summer.

The water made him thirsty, and he fetched a glass of orange juice from the fridge.

His thoughts turned now to the extraordinary day he had had. He realised that his leg muscles ached; all that walking! He hadn't walked so much in years. And the revelations, one after the other, that had surprised and shocked him throughout the day, culminating in the final, incredible possibility that Kala Nayak was still alive.

Now, in the dead of night, Chopra considered the evidence of his own eyes. He had never doubted himself before, but now . . . could it really have been Nayak? Surely he would have heard something before today, through his network of street informants, if Nayak had somehow survived the police raid? And how had he done that, anyway? Whose was the body they had found wearing Nayak's rings and gold chains? A body too burnt for identification.

Conveniently too burnt? wondered Chopra, now.

And if it *was* Nayak, what did he have to do with the death of a poor boy from Marol? Or did one thing have nothing to do with the other? After all, what *really* tied them together? A visiting card? A red beret? Had he put together a chain of evidence that in fact was as full of holes as the average Bollywood potboiler?

He shook his head and moved to the windows. One of them had been left open to allow a breeze into the flat. He peered out. He could hardly see anything, such was the ferocity of the rain. He looked down: Strange . . . the ground, fifteen floors below, appeared to be moving. He peered closer. Not moving, *swirling*.

The water was rising, flooding the rear of the courtyard, that odd declension that sloped down to the guard hut, creating a sort of shallow pool. Poor old Bahadur, thought Chopra. He would have had to abandon his guard hut and was probably even now shivering on the ground-floor landing wondering when he would get his hut ba—

Chopra froze. Oh no. Surely, Bahadur would have—?

He raced across the room, slapped down the glass of juice – spilling some onto the antique sideboard – and flung open the front door. Still in his shorts and vest, he raced to the elevator.

Which was not working.

Cursing, he turned to the stairwell. *Fifteen flights!* He had never really considered it much of a challenge, not for a man who had always prided himself on his fitness, but now it seemed to take for ever.

He reached the ground floor, huffing and panting. His heart really was pounding now, dangerously so.

He found Bahadur leaning against the wall at the top of the ground-floor stairwell, staring, as if hypnotised, at the fast-rising tide. The water, inky black, had already crested the fourth step. 'Bahadur!' gasped Chopra, massaging his chest. 'Where is Ganesha?'

Bahadur looked at him in incomprehension. He had his answer. 'You fool!' he raged. He looked down. The water was now at the fifth step, and rising fast. That meant about two feet. Add another two feet for the declension at the rear of the courtyard. Four feet. How tall was Ganesha? Three and a half feet? Maybe three ten?

Chopra knew he didn't have much time.

'Give me the key to his chain.'

Bahadur shivered to life, and rummaged in the pocket of his trousers. His face blanched. 'Sahib, I have left it in the hut.'

Chopra swore. He turned, and, without hesitating, waded down into the water.

By the time he got out from the entrance it was up to his crotch. The water swirled around him, making it difficult for him to keep his footing. He could barely see a few feet in front of him.

How long could elephants breathe underwater?

He worked his way around to the rear of the courtyard. Suddenly, he slipped as the declension fell away below his feet, and tumbled forward into the water. Gasping, he leaped up again, splashing wildly around him with his arms. Now the water was up around his chest. Chopra felt panic take hold of him, paralysing his muscles. The realisation that he had been forcing himself not to acknowledge now came home to him: he did not know how to swim.

Was it possible to drown in your own courtyard?

He took a deep breath and plunged ahead. Above him, the blue lantern that Bheem Singh and Bahadur had strung over the rear courtyard shone down, illuminating the heaving water with a ghostly light. Suddenly, he was confronted by a strange sight: it looked for all the world like a snake balancing on the water by its tail! The snake was moving from side to side, as if searching for something, or performing a dance.

That is no snake, thought Chopra. That is my Ganesha. And if his trunk is above water then the little elephant is still alive.

The thought spurred Chopra out of his paralysis. Hot on the heels of this thought came another one, courtesy of Dr Harpal Singh: 'Contrary to common perception, elephants are thoroughly accomplished swimmers. Their large bodies provide excellent flotation, and they are able to use their muscular legs to swim long distances with ease.' He held onto this thought now as he surged forward, hopping against the current, using his powerful arms to muscle his way through the water, now up to his armpits.

Chopra reached the guard hut and pushed his way inside. He knew Bahadur kept the key to Ganesha's chain on a nail on the wall just inside the door. Quickly Chopra looked for it. It was not there. *Damn!* But Bahadur did not have it either . . . There was only one other possibility. Taking a deep breath, Chopra dove under the water. He crouched down and moved his hand along the base of the wall. Nothing. He turned and moved it along the base of the wall in the other direction. His hand hit something, something cold and metallic. *He had it!*

Gasping, Chopra broke the water's surface. He waded back out of the hut and over to the metal pole to which Ganesha was chained. The elephant's trunk reached out and touched his face. It tried to wrap itself around his neck, but he forced it firmly away. Taking another deep breath he dove into the water again. His hands found the chain. It was stretched taut; Ganesha had been trying to get away, but did not have the strength to break the chain. Chopra fumbled for the padlock. Precious seconds were lost as he tried to insert the key into the lock, performing the action blind . . . and then it was done. The lock fell away, and Ganesha surged ahead.

Chopra pushed himself out of the water, which was now up to his neck. On tiptoe, he splashed and slid his way to the front of the courtyard.

Gasping and shivering, he struggled out of the water and up onto the ground-floor landing, dragging Ganesha behind him using the chain around the elephant's neck.

For a while he just lay there, flat on his back, listening to the erratic beating of his heart and the hammering of the rain on the water. He was conscious of Bahadur's concerned face hovering above his own, but he could not hear anything the man was saying. He was surrounded by an amniotic silence, as if someone had stuffed cotton wool in his ears. He turned his head. Beside him, slumped against the wall on all fours, was Ganesha. The elephant had closed his eyes, and his trunk was wrapped in a tight curl under his face. His body trembled – from terror or cold, Chopra could not be sure.

Eventually, he staggered to his feet. 'Come on, boy,' he said. 'Let's get you warm.' Bahadur looked as if he was going to protest, but then thought better of it.

Chopra led Ganesha to the lifts. They were working again, he was glad to see. He was also glad that the building had such expansive elevators.

They got off on the fifteenth floor. Chopra opened the door to his apartment and led Ganesha inside. The elephant became wedged in the doorframe. Sensing an opportunity to make up for his earlier negligence, Bahadur put his shoulder against the little elephant's backside and pushed. Ganesha surged forward, and into the flat, taking a section of the right doorjamb with him.

'Over here, boy,' said Chopra. Ganesha collapsed in the middle of the living room, in front of the sofa, on Poppy's faux Persian rug.

Chopra fell onto the sofa. He felt completely drained. A shroud of darkness rushed at him.

Moments later both man and elephant were fast asleep.

NO PLACE FOR AN ELEPHANT

The next morning Poppy awoke to find an elephant had taken up residence in her home.

'But this is too ridiculous!' she admonished her husband. It was all very well fighting to keep the elephant in the complex, but to see a wild animal parked in the centre of her living room on her best rug, like some sort of living sculpture, was quite another matter.

'Madness,' muttered her mother, who had been rudely surprised that morning when she had wandered into the living room and tripped over the creature. 'Cracked, cracked in the head.' This last was directed at her son-in-law, against whom she had always held a grudge for not being Jagirdar Mohan Vishwanath Deshmukh, landowner and erstwhile suitor of her daughter.

The source of all this consternation lay folded up on the floor, wrapped in Poppy's warmest winter quilts, looking none the worse for wear after the excitement of the previous night. Occasionally, the little elephant would shudder and, with a preparatory sniff of his trunk, unleash a sneeze into the room. A drift of Dairy Milk chocolate-bar wrappers lay strewn around him, as if a children's party had just taken place.

Chopra frowned at his wife and mother-in-law. 'This elephant is my responsibility, just as you both are. If his welfare requires that he stay in my home for a day or two then so be it. I do not wish to hear another word on the matter,' he added crossly as he headed towards the door of his office.

Earlier that morning, Chopra had sent Bahadur to the hole-in-the-wall grocery shop across the road to buy the chocolate. Bahadur had returned not only with the chocolate but also a breathless report of what was happening in the city.

The intense rain had flooded many parts of Mumbai. Such had been the delinquent monsoon's ferocity that flash floods had claimed more than one hundred lives. Bloated bodies lay in the streets, like the fallen dead from some forgotten war. Vehicles had been abandoned at junctions and in the middle of the roads. In some cars, dead bodies sat in the seats, staring glassily out into the afterlife; so fast had the water risen that their occupants had not had time even to undo their seatbelts before they were engulfed. There was an air of shock around the city; a strange silence hung over the malls and call centres, the glassy offices and fancy restaurants, the slums and the high-rise towers. For the first time in living memory, Mumbai had been brought to a standstill.

The authorities were slow in responding, and would later be accused of gross incompetence, charges that they would dismiss as uncharitable. After all, it was not every day that Mumbai was struck by such severe flooding.

In the courtyard below, the high sun had already dried the concrete. Bahadur had hauled his charpoy out into the centre of the courtyard to allow it to dry. It gave off great curls of steam, a potent symbol of the tempest of the night before.

Chopra had received a number of calls from friends eager to talk about the rain. He did not find the subject as fascinating as many of his friends appeared to. His mind was preoccupied once again by the events of the previous day: Kala Nayak, and the man in the red hat.

His first instinct was to contact his old colleagues on the force, in particular Amit Ghosh of the Detection Crime Branch. The DCB unit was specifically responsible for tackling organised crime in the city. The media loved to call it the 'Mumbai Encounter Squad' because of its reputation for prematurely retiring known gangsters in shooting incidents. He could ask Ghosh if any rumours of Kala Nayak resurfacing had been doing the rounds. But then he would have to explain why he was asking these questions. He was very reluctant to offer himself up for ridicule to his old colleagues. He imagined how the conversation might go.

'So you say you saw Kala Nayak?'

'Yes.'

'You are aware his body was identified and cremated nine years ago?'

'Yes.'

'Were there any other witnesses who could identify Nayak?'

'No.'

'Did you obtain any physical evidence? A photograph, for example?'

'No.'

'Did you note down the registration number of his vehicle?'

'No.'

He could imagine the looks that would be exchanged by his old colleagues. He could imagine what they would be thinking. Chopra was a good officer, sincere and committed to his duty. Now he has retired, and like many who retire before their time, he is struggling to manage his new circumstances. He is seeking attention, perhaps, some means of staying *involved* . . .

No, Chopra could not face the prospect of his colleagues thinking of him in this way. Everything he had achieved in his life would be undone. They would remember him not as the fine officer he had been, but as that sad specimen who had started seeing the ghost of Kala Nayak.

Just before lunch there was a loud knocking on the front door. Chopra opened it to find Mrs Subramanium blocking his view, Bahadur peering nervously over her shoulder.

'Mr Chopra,' said Mrs Subramanium primly, 'I have heard a very disturbing thing. I have heard that the elephant that you have forcibly lodged in the courtyard, against the regulations of this building, I might add, has now been brought into the actual living premises. In fact, I have heard that this creature is even now inside this very apartment.' Her voice seemed to indicate her utter incredulity.

'You have heard correctly,' said Chopra calmly. Not for the first time he thought that Mrs Subramanium, with her short hair and her severe manner, reminded him of Indira Gandhi.

As a young man Chopra had greatly admired Mrs Gandhi, but then had come the Emergency Years when Gandhi, following her conviction for electoral malpractice in the 1971 elections, had refused to step aside and instead imposed President's rule and ordered the arrest of her opponents. Those had been black years when the police, mandated to defend the central government's position, had been given extraordinary powers to detain ordinary citizens and to ensure that the curfew was upheld. Chopra knew of many officers who had enjoyed the new powers immensely, and committed terrible acts of injustice simply because they knew they could get away with it. He himself, as a young officer, had often been put in a position where he felt that he had compromised his own high ideals. He had never forgotten that time, and had never forgiven Mrs Gandhi.

To his amazement, Mrs Subramanium did not respond with a tirade, as he had half expected her to do; instead, she merely pursed her lips. 'Please step aside, sir.'

Chopra found himself automatically moving aside.

Mrs Subramanium marched into the apartment. She stopped short as she caught sight of Ganesha. Only the elephant's head was visible from inside the igloo of quilts that were piled up around his body. Mrs Subramanium stepped in front of the little calf and looked down at him. Ganesha tilted his head upwards as if determined to meet the old woman's disapproving gaze head-on.

'This is completely unacceptable, Mr Chopra,' said Mrs Subramanium, finally. 'Completely unacceptable. I cannot even begin to tell you how many building regulations are being flouted here.'

'Please explain to him!' came the voice of Poornima Devi, who had suddenly appeared at Mrs Subramanium's shoulder. 'He will not listen to us. The beast almost trampled me to death this morning!'

'The elephant nearly drowned yesterday, Mrs Subramanium,' said Chopra, ignoring his mother-in-law. 'I could not leave him in the flooded courtyard, so I brought him up here.'

'It is an animal,' said Mrs Subramanium sharply. 'A dumb animal. If its fate was to die in the rain, then that is that. Its place is not inside *my* building.'

'No, Mrs Subramanium, that is not that! This is *this!*' Poppy had materialised from the bedroom. She stood now with narrowed eyes and folded arms, glaring at her nemesis. 'This elephant is a living, breathing creature. He is an avatar of our Lord Ganesh. The poor baby nearly died last night. Now he is very, very ill. He is welcome to stay in *my* home as long as he wishes.'

'But he is not welcomed by *me*, Mrs Chopra,' growled Mrs Subramanium. 'He is a danger to children; he is a menace to hygiene; he is a threat to the security of our infrastructure; he is a—'

AAATCHOOOO!

The sneeze reverberated around the room. Mrs Subramanium froze. Gradually, the echoes of the monumental sneeze faded. Mrs Subramanium looked down at her sari. She did not like what she saw. 'Filthy, filthy creature,' she growled. Without a further word she turned on her heel and marched from the room, stopping only to mutter: 'You have not heard the last of this, Mr Chopra. This is really too much.'

After Mrs Subramanium left, Poppy served lunch. Chopra watched her carefully. 'Did you really mean what you said?' he asked, eventually. 'About Ganesha staying as long as he needs to?'

'Well, if Mrs Subramanium thinks she can tell me what to do in my own home, then she has another thing coming.' She set down the plate of steaming brinjal curry with a bang, and went back to the kitchen. Chopra watched her go, thinking that she had never been more magnificent.

After lunch Chopra retired to his study. From the display cabinet he removed the medal that he had been awarded nine years ago, following the raid that had ended in the death of Kala Nayak. *Presumed* death. The Kirti Chakra was a significant honour for any policeman, particularly one as relatively young as he had been at the time. But the award was a reflection of how serious a problem Nayak had become to the city, the state and even the country. Although he had tried to play down the award, as was his nature,

Chopra had been quietly proud of the accolade. He had been proud of the fact that he had helped to finish off Nayak and his gang, helped to make the city that he loved a safer place. Now, he felt like a fraud.

He sent his mind back to that night, a very hot, humid night in the month of October, just after the rainy season had ended. He remembered waiting outside the building that Anarkali the eunuch had tipped them off about, waiting for Nayak and his gang to show their hand. He remembered seeing Nayak's face at the window. But now, looking back, he thought . . . why? Why, if Nayak was in hiding, had he come to the window and spent a good minute there, smoking a cigarette? With the benefit of hindsight, it seemed to be an overtly deliberate gesture. It was as if Nayak had been making sure that he was clearly identifiable to anyone watching from below.

Had he known that they were there? Had he planted the information on the street knowing that it would eventually find its way to the authorities? And inside, in the chaos of the shootout, who had actually *seen* Nayak's death? Reviewing the debriefing sessions that he had conducted with his men, it seemed that a number of his officers had claimed to have seen Nayak engaged in the shooting. But Chopra himself had been in the middle of that chaos, and he would have been hard put to say exactly what he had seen among all those flying bullets and the smoke from the fire.

And the fire . . . they had never really figured out who had started it. Certainly, the building seemed to have gone up in flames very quickly – suspiciously quickly, he now thought. Was it possible that all of it, the whole thing, from start to finish, had been orchestrated by Nayak himself? That the point of the operation had been for Nayak to vanish, leaving behind a burnt and smoking body, an impostor decked out in Nayak's own jewellery?

Chopra picked up the framed photograph of his father that stood on his desk. It showed Masterji with his two sons, standing beneath the ancient lychee tree in the dusty courtyard of their village compound. The tree had been a fixture of Chopra's childhood. The picture had been taken on the occasion of his elder brother Jayesh's marriage. Jayesh was dressed in his groom's outfit; Chopra himself was resplendent in his own glittering costume. Their father was wearing his usual attire, a staid kurta and dhoti, a schoolmaster's waistcoat. His hands were placed on the shoulders of his sons. His pride was evident, filling the picture.

Chopra stood up and paced the room. He knew that he was agitated, and he knew that this was not a good mental state to be in if one hoped to conduct an investigation of any kind. To calm himself he sat down again and took out the diary that he had taken from Santosh Achrekar's home. He considered it now to be a sort of talisman, a guide that kept him locked on to his true objective – finding the murderer of a poor boy from Marol.

He went through the diary again, looking for anything he might have missed. But the entries were still either bland or enigmatic: 'SNBO – how to expose them?'

As he riffled through the pages, he noticed a sliver of white peeking out from the inside leather jacket of the diary. He teased out the paper, and unfolded it. On the paper were names and numbers:

Dilip Phule	Rs. 800,000
Ritesh Shinde	Rs. 750,000
Sanjay Kulkarni	Rs. 900,000
Ajit Kamat	Rs. 750,000
Suresh Karve	Rs. 700,000
Shabbir Junjunwalla	Rs. 800,000
Chandu Pandit	Rs. 800,000
Anthony Gonsalves	Rs. 700,000

Chopra was astounded. He had an immediate idea of what this list represented; he had seen something like it before, many years ago, taken from the pocket of a member of the underworld . . . He was certain that this was a bribe list.

And the individuals named on this list must be reasonably high-ranking officials to deserve payments in excess of seven lakh rupees!

He recalled now the bundle of cash that he had seen the man in the red beret give to the leather shop-owner in the Atlas Mega Mall. It seemed he had been right to guess that this cash had been a payoff. Was the shop-owner one of the names on this list? Why did he need paying off? The more important question was: what was this list doing in Santosh Achrekar's diary? What did these names have to do with his death?

The answers to all these questions, Chopra suspected, lay with the man he believed to be Nayak. The names on this list could only be men that Nayak had bribed.

But who were they? Their names were not familiar to Chopra; certainly they were not senior policemen of his acquaintance. But then, he did not know every policeman in Mumbai. And why should they be policemen? Perhaps they were customs officials, or tax men. Why not high court judges, or government ministers? There were so many men that someone like Nayak would need to bribe in order to smooth the terrain for whatever illegal activities he was engaged in.

And somehow, Chopra was certain, these activities had led to the death of Santosh Achrekar.

One other thing was also certain: Chopra now had in his hands compelling evidence that there was more to Santosh's death than simply a crime of passion or a fight between friends that had gone too far. Which left him with the question of . . . what next? Well, he did have one clear lead.

Inspector Chopra (Retd) made his decision. 'I am just going out,' he called to Poppy, as he made his way to the front door.

After Chopra had gone, Poppy found herself alone in the apartment with Ganesha. Her mother, exasperated by the morning's events, had wandered down to the eleventh floor to share her woes with her friend Lata Oja. Poppy found that she was suddenly overcome by a strange feeling of nervousness. Mrs Subramanium's unwarranted intrusion had forced an automatic reaction from her, but now, faced with the somewhat dreamlike reality of an elephant in her living room, she found herself at a loss. What did Chopra expect her to do? After all, what did she know about elephants, anyway? What did *he* know about elephants, for that matter? Really, her husband could be such a duffer at times!

And then something curious happened. As the little calf continued to snuffle and sneeze, hunched down inside its quilts, the very picture of misery, Poppy felt her long-suppressed mothering instincts rising to the fore. Perhaps it was the influence of her recent thoughts about Kiran's daughter's baby, but suddenly she was overcome by a desire to nurse the baby elephant that her husband had seen fit to deposit inside her home.

'OK, young man,' she said determinedly, 'first things first: let's get you cleaned up.'

She took a large tin tub from the pantry and filled it with steaming hot water from the bathroom. Into this she added some lemon-scented soap and half a bottle of her favourite bath scent. She dragged the tub out into the living room and set it down in front of Ganesha, who eyed it with a look of sudden trepidation. Poppy then removed all the quilts from around the little elephant and set down some plastic sheets around the rug, which she had already mentally consigned to the wastebin. She fetched her largest scrubbing brush from the bathroom, and set to work.

First she washed Ganesha's back and flanks. 'Stop wriggling,' she told the elephant sternly as he writhed beneath her ministrations. She cleaned his legs and his bottom. She scrubbed his feet and his large, square toes which were caked in mud. Finally she cleaned his face, even scrubbing his trunk. 'Don't moan,' she said as Ganesha mooed in complaint, trying to draw his trunk as far away from her as possible. 'It's for your own good.'

Just as she finished, Ganesha dipped his trunk into the tin tub, sucked up the remaining quantity of soapy water and then shot it all over her.

She stood there gasping, and then wiped the water from her face. She glared at the little elephant, who returned her glare with a defiant look of his own. 'Young man, if you think *that* will get you out of it, you don't know Poppy very well!'

She stalked off into the bedroom and returned with a large cotton towel with which she violently patted Ganesha down. Then she fetched a bottle of mustard oil and rubbed it onto Ganesha's head. 'My mother swears by this,' she said. 'She is sixty years old and still has skin like a baby.'

Finally, she fetched a small plastic tub of Vicks VapoRub. 'This will frighten away your cold in a jiffy,' she said. Ganesha sniffed the bottle with his trunk; his eyes fluttered in alarm. He tried to lumber to his feet, but Poppy prevented his escape by telling him sternly in a no-nonsense voice to 'SIT!'

Ganesha huddled in miserable silence while she coated his trunk in the smelly ointment.

Finally, her work done, Poppy cleaned herself up, changed her clothes, and then made herself a pot of tea. She sat back on the sofa. Ganesha eyed her warily. 'Now,' she said, 'what shall we watch?'

BASANTI RIDES AGAIN

Meanwhile, Inspector Chopra had made his way to his friend Kapil Gupta's garage. The streets of Mumbai were gradually filling up again. Like crabs emerging from the sand after the tide, Mumbaikers were reclaiming their city. The rain had instantly vaporised much of the road surface and Mumbai's infamous potholes were back, adding to the traffic woes. There was a curious smell in the air: a sweet smell of jacaranda blossom and re-breathed dust, as if the earth itself had exhaled. Or perhaps it was the smell of death.

One hundred dead, thought Chopra. And yet, in a city of twenty million, what did that mean? Almost nothing.

No, he said to himself. Even a single death means something. To those who care, and even to those who don't. Even a single death makes a demand on us all.

Kapil's garage was busy. The rain had damaged many vehicles. Chopra found his old friend knee-deep in irate customers. 'This is extortion!' blubbered one; 'Highway robbery!' roared another; 'Blatant profiteering!' growled a third. 'If this was wartime you would be shot.'

'Lucky we are not at war with anyone, then,' said Kapil sweetly.

Spotting Chopra, he pulled away from the angry mob.

'What's all the fuss about?' asked Chopra.

'I have decided to temporarily raise my rates.'

'But with all the rain damage you must be flooded with customers.'

'Exactly,' said Kapil, a broad grin breaking over his moustachioed face. 'One must make hay while the sun is shining, yes? Or I should say when the sun is not shining.'

Chopra smiled, then said: 'I've come to take Basanti.'

'Shiva have mercy!' exclaimed Kapil. 'I thought the day would never come.'

He led Chopra to the rear of the garage, where a blue tarpaulin covered a hidden object. With no further ceremony, he removed the tarpaulin. 'Here you are, old friend. Tuned up and ready to go.'

Chopra drew in his breath. He felt that old excitement welling in his breast. Basanti! After all these years!

The Royal Enfield Bullet gleamed. With its 500cc of unbridled horsepower, the motorbike stood there like a lion ready to pounce, the very embodiment of mechanical puissance. Its bulbous black petrol tank shone like the carapace of some giant beetle; its enormous tyres looked as if they could tackle the Himalayas.

He remembered when he had first bought her, back when Poppy would still ride pillion, and they would tear around the city: across to Juhu Beach for kokum ice shavings, or down to Nariman Point to eat bhel puri at Chowpatty and walk around the curved, palm-tree-lined promenade of Marine Drive, known as the Queen's Necklace, watching the sun go down on the Arabian Sea. Back then, Poppy had been as thrilled as he was by the bike's power, the feeling that one was riding a wild stallion. And then, in a mad instant, everything had changed. Damn that donkey-cart-wallah!

Afterwards, when Chopra had returned from the hospital with his leg in a plaster cast, Poppy had refused to sit on the infernal machine ever again, and nagged him endlessly to get rid of it. In the end she had made him promise to give up the bike.

But now, thought Chopra, it was time for his self-imposed penance to end. It was time for Basanti to tear up the Mumbai roads again.

Chopra parked the Enfield in the courtyard. Bahadur rushed over to examine it, his eyes shining.

'If Poppy Madam asks,' said Chopra, 'this is not *my* bike.'

'Yes, sir!' said Bahadur. 'Chopra Sir's bike is not his bike.'

Upstairs, Chopra discovered Poppy and Ganesha transfixed by the goings-on in a soap opera about a newly married woman's travails with her mother-in-law and her new family. This seemed to be the latest craze in Mumbai – family soap operas. Poppy and her mother were addicted to them. And now it looked as if the latest addition to their home was also being weaned onto the over-the-top melodramas.

Chopra shook his head sadly and retired to his study. He had to complete his preparations.

From the bottom of his cabinet he removed a locked steel box. Inside the box was a pistol wrapped in oilcloth. It was Chopra's spare service revolver, which he was supposed to have handed back to the police armoury, but had not got around to doing. He had not fired the weapon for years, had not needed to. His work had become increasingly desk-bound. In some ways this had been a relief, as it had given him time to concentrate on the strategic aspects of local policing; and yet he had often found himself wishing, wistfully, for the old days when he could get out into the streets and get his hands dirty with the guts of an investigation.

With great care Chopra cleaned the gun. First he disassembled it and degreased the frame, scrubbing it out with a nylon wire brush. He cleaned each part, then lubricated them with oil, paying particular attention to the contact surfaces of the hammer and the trigger pin. Then he reassembled the revolver and loaded it with .32 calibre bullets. He knew that the gun was old-fashioned, a long-barrelled Anmol revolver that carried only six rounds. Nevertheless, he had always preferred it to the newer German automatics that his colleagues now favoured. There was something reassuringly *traditional* about the Anmol.

Next, he removed a cloth bag from his cabinet. From inside the bag he took out a pair of high-powered binoculars and a digital camera that Poppy had given him for his birthday two years ago and which he had never used.

He cleaned the binoculars, checked that they were still focusing properly, and then sat down and read the operating manual for the camera. Finally, he charged the camera's battery and practised taking photographs. When he was satisfied that his preparations were complete, he put the gun, the binoculars and the camera, together with its stand, into a rucksack. He stood for a while, thinking. Then he added a folding metal stool, his notebook and his calabash pipe.

Chopra looked at his watch. There were still many hours to go before he could put his plan into action.

He returned to the living room, where Poppy and Ganesha had moved on to watching a Bollywood potboiler starring Poppy's idol Shah Rukh Khan. Shah Rukh was engaged in giving the suitably pantomime villain a good thrashing, but would occasionally pause for spots of comedic jackanapery. Poppy had placed a large bowl of fried banana chips on the floor. Occasionally, without taking their eyes from the screen, both his wife and the little elephant would lift chips from the bowl and insert them into their mouths. Not wishing to disturb them, Chopra took the newspaper from the sideboard and returned to his study.

CHOPRA GOES ON A STAKEOUT

The next morning Inspector Chopra (Retd) woke up just before dawn. Having dressed quickly, he stood for a moment looking down at his sleeping wife. He thought: it is not too late to tell her where I am going. But he knew Poppy would make a fuss.

In the end, he simply left, closing the bedroom door gently behind him.

In the living room, Ganesha was also awake. Poppy had left a shallow tin tub filled with water next to him, which was now empty. A second tin tub waited in readiness should Ganesha feel the need to exercise his bowels.

Chopra patted the little elephant on the head. 'Good boy,' he murmured. Ganesha reached up with his trunk and caressed Chopra's face, like a blind man running his fingers over the features of a friend. 'Got to go,' said Chopra. He went to his study and retrieved his rucksack.

Downstairs, he discovered that Bahadur, who was

supposed to be at his guardpost, was fast asleep on his cot, still in the centre of the courtyard.

Chopra climbed onto the Enfield and kicked it into life, causing the somnolent guard to immediately awaken, jerking up in a shiver of fright.

As he roared out of the compound in a cloud of exhaust fumes, dawn was breaking. From the nearby Al Noor mosque the sound of Imam Haider's call to prayer came floating over the city.

When Chopra reached the warehouse, he stopped at the same corner from which he had previously spied upon the man he believed to be Kala Nayak. He waited for twenty minutes, but there was no sign of life. Then he quickly rode his bike to the back of the derelict building directly opposite the warehouse. At its rear he found an old worm-ridden door.

Chopra kicked the door in and rolled the Enfield inside.

Leaving the bike by the door he made his way through the abandoned building, which appeared to be an old printing works. On the scarred, paint-peeled walls Chopra discovered framed, yellowing front pages of the *Maharashtrian Weekly Samachar*, a newspaper that he recalled briefly flourishing some ten years ago, and just as quickly going bankrupt.

On the third floor, a vast open space where, Chopra imagined, a cramped team of reporters and editors had once sweated and boiled, he set up his folding stool before the enormous, cracked windows overlooking the warehouse opposite. He removed the camera and screwed it on to its stand. He debated whether to clean the windows, which were grimy with decades of dust, but decided against it. He did not wish to alert those below to his presence. He sat down on his stool, took out his notebook, checked the time on his watch and made a note. Then he sat back to wait.

It had been a very long time since Chopra had been on a stakeout. It was not a tactic often utilised by the Mumbai police, simply because the sheer mass of people on the streets at any time of the day or night made a successful one rather a hit-and-miss affair. But he had realised that with no other leads to pursue, his best option now was simply to hope for some luck. He knew that he had seen Nayak and the man in the red hat enter this warehouse. He was betting that one or both of them would be back. At the very least he might get an idea of *why* they had come here. Even that might provide a clue, something with which to continue his investigation into the death of Santosh Achrekar. In spite of Nayak's reappearance, Chopra had not lost sight of the fact that he had made a promise to the parents of the murdered boy. Whoever had killed Santosh must be brought to justice.

An hour passed and the sun continued to climb, heating up the room. At 7.04 a.m., Chopra noted the first signs of life.

A short, thin, rat-faced man wearing a blue Indian cricket team shirt with the number eight on the back emerged from the warehouse, stretched himself in a yawn, then stood against the building urinating. A stray dog came limping down the alley. The rat-faced man called the dog over, then, when it came close, kicked it hard on the side of the head, laughing raucously. The dog slunk away, yelping piteously. The man went back inside.

A short while later he returned, this time accompanied by a tall, thickset man with a heavy paunch wearing a garish orange shirt. Both men sat down on old packing crates and took out cigarettes which the thickset man lit using a gold-plated lighter in the shape of a curvaceous woman. They chatted for a while, their voices drifting up to Chopra, who watched them with his binoculars through a gaping hole in the corner of one of the windows. But their talk was inconsequential, of movies, friends, their favourite whores . . .

After a while, they went back inside the warehouse.

By midday, the abandoned printing works, whose roof was made of tin sheeting, had heated up considerably and Chopra found himself sweating profusely and increasingly uncomfortable. It was as if the rain had happened a long time ago. Mumbai was sweltering again.

Suddenly he noticed a movement from the corner of his eye. Startled, he nearly fell from his seat. But it was only a gecko, come to investigate the intruder. An hour later, the gecko was joined by another, and then another, until a whole family of them had clambered out from their hiding places to arrange themselves on the wall around the windows. Chopra stilled the panic that threatened to overcome him. The sight of the silent lizards made him shiver, but he knew that he had to hold his ground.

To calm his nerves he took out his calabash pipe and stuck it into his mouth.

By the middle of the afternoon he realised that he had made an elementary mistake. In spite of his meticulous preparations, he had overlooked two crucial things: food and water. By four o'clock his stomach was rumbling loud enough to wake the dead, and his mouth was parched. But there was nothing for it. He couldn't abandon his post; he would simply have to put up with it. He heard another sound and turned. It was the limping dog from the street below. The dog approached him warily, expecting another kick, perhaps. Once it realised that Chopra was not about to beat it, it sniffed around his rucksack.

But there was nothing for it to eat.

It sat down on its haunches next to him, silently keeping him company in his vigil.

Nothing else happened for the remainder of the day. The two goons occasionally appeared outside the warehouse, to urinate, smoke or stretch their legs, but other than that the day was uneventful. There was a minor scare when Poppy tried to call him on his mobile. Chopra had forgotten to set the phone to vibrate mode, and the rousing tones of 'Vande Mataram', the national song, rang out around the deserted space, which seemed to amplify the sound. Chopra was certain the goons must have heard. But no one emerged from the warehouse to investigate.

He shut off the phone, and threw it into his rucksack.

At 11 p.m. he finally decided to pack up his operation, making his last notebook entry.

He arrived home famished, and immediately sat down at the dinner table, drinking a litre of water while Poppy and Ganesha watched him in astonishment. 'Where have you been all day?' asked Poppy eventually. Her tone made no secret of her displeasure.

'Oh, just doing some things,' mumbled Chopra vaguely.

'What things?'

'This and that,' he muttered, not meeting her eyes. Poppy watched with a troubled expression as her husband finished his meal and then, with barely a mumbled thank you, retreated into his office.

This and that! thought Poppy. What was the meaning of 'this and that'!

Her husband had been acting very strangely of late. Of course, she understood that ever since the shock announcement of his heart problem, and the terrible news that he would have to retire early, he had been forced to adjust to major and unexpected changes in his life – but still! He had always been a creature of habit, predictable. He was not a keeper of secrets. Even when he was working on important cases and could not share the details with her, he had still been an open book for Poppy to read: his anxieties, his moments of triumph. But lately he had become an enigma.

Take all the strange phone calls that he had been getting over the past few months, calls that her husband took great pains to conceal from her . . . And today! Vanishing without a word before she had even awoken. He was a retired man now, so what was he doing skulking around, keeping his activities hidden from her as if they were some sort of state secret! And ignoring her calls when she had telephoned him – not once, but eight times!

If Poppy had not been so preoccupied with her own concerns and the whole business with Kiran's daughter, she would never have let the matter lie. She would have dragged it out of her husband, and discovered what it was he was up to.

The next day the situation worsened. Chopra again disappeared before Poppy had woken, and only reappeared late at night. He remained tight-lipped and mysterious, even though she complained to him directly that he was acting strangely. He told that her he was 'tying up some loose ends; can't talk about it right now'. And then he had brushed past her and locked himself in that infernal study of his.

Her mother had been of no help. Instead of comforting her, she had poured fuel on the fire. 'Make sure it's not another woman,' she had said, articulating the very concern that was eating away at Poppy herself.

'Of course it's not another woman,' she snapped at her mother, who merely gave her one of her pointed looks.

And yet, in spite of her scorn, Poppy was worried. More than worried – she was terrified. Certainly, another woman might explain the secret phone calls, the skulking around. And although Chopra had been steadfastly loyal all these years, now that he was undergoing this incredible upheaval in his life, perhaps he had finally decided that it was time to move on. He was a retired man now. He had time on his hands. Now that he had no work to occupy him, he had time to reflect deeply on his life. He had time to think about the disappointments of his marriage; the fact that the woman he had chosen had borne him no children.

A man needed a son; Poppy knew that. Particularly a man like Chopra. But she hadn't even been able to give him a daughter. And while before, his dedication to his work might have papered over this missing part of his life, what was there now to invest his days with purpose and meaning?

Her husband had clearly decided that he had had enough.

There was another woman out there, Poppy felt certain; another younger, prettier woman, who had sunk her claws into him, who was making him promises of a son, many sons, a whole cricket team's worth of sons!

What kind of woman was she? A scheming witch, no doubt. Maybe someone like Mrs Gopaldas from the tenth floor, who was always telling Poppy how lucky she was to have such a handsome husband, so virile in his police uniform, completely unlike her own husband who was such a . . . such a . . . such an accountant!

Poppy sat on the sofa and wept. Suddenly she felt a touch on her shoulder. She looked up and found the face of the little elephant looking at her with grave concern. Ganesha brushed the tip of his trunk over Poppy's face, lightly wiping away her tears. 'You don't understand, do you, Ganesha?' said Poppy miserably. 'How could you? It is a woman's lot to endure pain and suffering in this world; always the woman's lot.'

Poppy thought once again of her plan to become the mother of Prarthana's baby. Suddenly, the plan, the wisdom of which she had been debating endlessly with herself, almost to the point of abandoning it, seemed now to represent the only way to save her marriage . . . if it wasn't already too late.

Kiran and Prarthana had now both agreed. Indeed, Kiran was pestering her to get on with it. All that remained was for Poppy to deliver the news of her 'pregnancy' to Chopra. Each time she thought of it she felt an unwillingness rising up inside her. How could she possibly lie to her husband, particularly such a lie as this?

But now she realised that she would have to act. She had

to tell him, convince him that all was not lost if he chose to stay with her.

Yes. She would tell him. Soon. As soon as she could. Very soon.

QUEEN OF THE NIGHT

On the third day of his stakeout, Chopra finally got his breakthrough.

It was late in the evening, and dusk had fallen. It had been another tiring day, but this one had been relatively eventful.

Some time in the afternoon, Chopra had watched the two goons leave the premises and wander off down the alley and out of sight. His heartbeat had quickened immediately. Before he had time to change his mind, he hurried down from his hideout and made his way across the alley. His senses were on red alert. Hefting his service revolver, he advanced into the shadowed entrance of the warehouse. To his surprise, the door was unlocked. Proceeding with caution, he opened the door and entered.

He found himself in a largish space, within which he could see a number of barred iron cages; they reminded him of the cages he had seen at the Byculla Zoo. In one corner of the room, a sort of photographic studio had been set up, with an expensive, professional-looking camera perched on a tripod, a complicated lighting rig, and a backdrop screen.

For a moment he felt completely disoriented. He had expected to find contraband: narcotics or illicit weapons. What were these empty animal cages doing here? And then it hit him! Something he had recently read in one of his policing journals . . . This set-up looked for all the world like the sort of thing that those involved in the poaching and animal trafficking trade might use.

Was this what Nayak was up to? Chopra knew that the poaching trade had, almost unnoticed, become big business for organised criminals in India. As certain species became rarer and rarer, there were fortunes to be made by those unscrupulous enough to treat animals as commodities to be slaughtered for their material value. Newly minted billionaires in the superheated economies of the East were willing to pay huge sums for a tiger's claw or penis, or rhino horn, or, worst of all, elephant ivory. (Chopra had read that a single rhino horn could fetch four hundred thousand US dollars.) Often, these rare animals would die simply to provide the essential ingredient for some primitive recipe; a shaman's charm to promote virility, or a cure for illnesses ranging from gout and snakebite to demonic possession.

Chopra stood in the silent room for a moment, gathering as many impressions as he could. Then he remembered that he had his camera with him. He quickly snapped off a number of photographs of the silent cages before moving on.

The rest of his expedition proved fruitless. The other rooms on the ground floor of the warehouse were empty, except for one that had clearly been set up as sleeping quarters for the two goons. A quick trip to the next floor up showed that it was unused: cobwebby and deserted.

Chopra realised that the two caretakers of the warehouse might be back at any second. He turned on his heel and raced back down to the ground floor, out of the warehouse, and back up to his hideout. He fell onto his stool just in time. Laughing and clapping each other on the back the two goons came sauntering down the alley, bottles of beer in their hands.

The only other noteworthy incident of the day was a phone call Chopra had made to the vet Dr Lala. He had realised that in his single-minded pursuit of Santosh Achrekar's killer, he had allowed himself to become remiss in his duty to Ganesha. A follow-up with Lala was overdue.

Chopra dialled the vet's number. He found Lala preoccupied with a schizophrenic Pomeranian, the pampered pet of a noted Bollywood heroine. The Pomeranian accompanied his mistress on all shoots, and had lately begun to attack her male co-stars in what the actress claimed to be fits of rabid jealousy. She explained, with perfect sincerity, that the Pomeranian was the reincarnation of her first husband, who had died in a tragic accident some years previously. Lala had been tasked with curing the pooch's violent tendencies. Four major Bollywood films were on hold until he could do so, as the actress refused to film without her beloved pet by her side.

Lala apologised for not having called Chopra himself. There was good news. The medical analysis of Ganesha had not turned up anything untoward. Aside from his subdued demeanour, and a certain undernourished aspect to his physique, the baby elephant appeared to be in pretty good health.

Lala had more good news. He had spoken to his friend in Visakapatnam. As luck would have it, a place was available for a baby elephant in the sanctuary run by his friend. Lala had been busy. In three days' time a truck would arrive to take Ganesha to his new home.

Chopra was struck by mixed emotions. He felt glad that the problem had been so swiftly resolved. But at the same time, he could not suppress the twinge of guilt that assailed him. 'Are you sure that this sanctuary is a safe place for a baby elephant?' he asked Lala.

'I have been there myself,' the vet confirmed. 'It is ideal. You have my word.'

By the time night descended Chopra was finding it hard to keep his eyes open. The previous three days had taken their toll. He was tired and his body ached; muscles that he did not even know existed had been crying out their protest. He was also acutely aware of the frosty reception that awaited him at home. But he could not share what he was up to with Poppy. She would not understand.

She had been after him to retire since the day they had

discovered that he had an ailing heart. If he told her that he was camped in a derelict building, opposite a cabal of hardened gangsters, waiting for the notorious crime lord he was supposed to have killed nearly a decade ago, she would have a fit. Once Poppy got a bee in her bonnet about something, it was hard to make her see reason. She would never understand that this was something he simply had to do, no matter where it led him, no matter even if it consumed him.

And all the time that Chopra was thinking about Kala Nayak, he could not stop thinking about the murdered boy and his mother, who, even now, was waiting for justice, waiting for him to fulfil his promise. In a way, that boy had become Chopra's own son; he *had* to know why Santosh Achrekar had died; he had to find those responsible, even if that trail led him into dangerous waters.

And then, just as he had all but decided to go home, the roar of a motorbike cut into the alley. The man in the red beret had reappeared.

As Chopra watched, the man parked his bike and dismounted in front of the entrance to the warehouse. It was a new bike, a Hero Honda, bright red, with painted black chevrons and gleaming chrome spokes. The man in the red hat lit a cigarette, then called out.

A few minutes later the two men stationed in the warehouse emerged. The bigger one scratched his hairy belly; the shorter one rubbed sleep from his eyes. The man in the red hat loomed over the shorter one, then slapped him in the face, knocking him to the ground. He kicked him in the stomach a couple of times until the man curled into a ball. He flicked his cigarette at him, then turned his attention to the other thug, whose own drowsiness had evaporated in a hurry. As Chopra watched, the man in the red hat forced him to his knees, reached into the waistband of his jeans and took out an automatic pistol. He forced the barrel of the pistol into the paunchy man's mouth, then growled something into his ear which Chopra could not catch.

Clearly, the man in the red hat was displeased. But what about?

The man straightened, then loudly counted out one, two, three . . . and pulled the trigger.

Nothing happened.

With a snarling laugh, he pushed the terrified goon onto his back. 'The next time it won't be empty,' he shouted. 'You idiots better shape up or I'll bury you right here in this warehouse.'

The man in the red hat straddled his bike, then lit another cigarette.

Chopra swept his things into his rucksack, then raced downstairs to his own bike. He leaped onto the Enfield, and stepped on the clutch. It refused to start. 'Come on, Basanti!' he pleaded. 'Don't let me down now!'

The clutch caught and the engine roared to life.

Chopra picked up his target's trail at the next traffic junction. He followed the Hero Honda along the Western Express Highway, heading north, until they got off at the next underpass and drove into Andheri West. He continued to follow him as they passed through Jogeshwari and into Lokhandwala.

In Lokhandwala, the man in the red hat pulled his bike to the side of the road. He got off the bike and walked into a building with darkened windows and a red neon sign that said 'Queen of the Night'. A ladies bar.

Chopra dismounted and followed his quarry inside.

Immediately, he was confronted by a thick smog of cigarette fumes. Men were crowded around tables, drinking and smoking in the dim red lighting. Scantily clad women wandered around the room, serving drinks and stopping to whisper into the ears of the patrons. Every few minutes an agreement was reached and a man would rise from his table and follow the woman to the rear of the room where a staircase led upwards.

Chopra's eyes pierced the smoky miasma, searching for the man in the red hat. *There!* He was sitting with his back to Chopra, laughing heartily with two friends. As he watched, a woman in a short skirt, high heels and halter-neck top shimmied up to their table with a tray of drinks. The man in the red hat immediately pulled her onto his lap and said something at which the others burst out laughing.

'Sahib, can I take you to a table?'

Chopra turned around. A small man in a purple uniform was looking at him expectantly. He hesitated. He did not know the etiquette of this sort of place. Ladies bars were a Mumbai phenomenon that had long disconcerted him. Part-bar, part-brothel, part-gentlemen's club, they had mushroomed around the city during the past decade. Some were seedy dives while others were so upmarket as to be almost indistinguishable from the trendy international bars one found in south Mumbai. He knew that some of his police colleagues frequented such places, even boasted openly about how much fun they had, going into some detail about their nightly conquests. But Chopra had never been that type of officer, and had made it clear, when he had taken over the Sahar station, that his attitude in such matters was uncompromising. If any of his own officers indulged themselves in this way, then they had been smart enough to keep it from his ears.

'Yes,' he muttered, 'a table.'

He was given a small table on the far side of the room from the man in the red hat.

'Sahib, what will you have?'

'What?' Chopra realised the waiter fellow was still hovering around him.

'What will you have, sahib?'

Chopra looked at him uncomprehendingly.

'To drink,' said the man, encouragingly.

'A Coke,' he said, automatically.

'Coke?' repeated the man. He seemed nonplussed. Chopra realised his mistake. The clientele who frequented this sort of place did not order a Coke.

'Yes,' he said gruffly. 'Coke with a whisky. What's the matter, can't you hear properly?'

The man's face broke into a smile of relief. This was more like it.

He returned quickly with the order. As a rule, Chopra did not drink. He had seen what happened to officers who did.

It would begin as a small peg, just to be sociable. Then a couple of tots to help clarify things on a particularly tricky investigation. Soon it would be three or four glasses to relieve the tensions of the day. Before you knew it a perfectly fine officer had ruined his career, earmarked by his colleagues as 'that drunk'.

No, it was a slippery slope, and he had never set foot on it.

He poured the Coke into the tumbler of whisky and pretended to sip at it while he watched the man in the red hat, who, by this time, had been pawing and petting the girl in his lap for a good ten minutes. For the first time he could get a good look at the man's skull. He knew what he was searching for, but his eyes, which were still 20-20 over distance, couldn't find the scratch marks that he had almost convinced himself must be there. Had he made a mistake? Was he chasing the wrong lead? What if this man had nothing to do with Santosh Achrekar at all? Surely that was Chopra's priority, not his sudden conviction that Kala Nayak had returned from the dead?

Suddenly, the girl stood. She lifted the man's red beret from the table, placed it on her own head, and, to the raucous laughter of his friends, sashayed towards the staircase. The man slapped hands with one of his friends and followed her. Chopra felt his stomach tighten. His every fibre urged him not to lose sight of his quarry, but he couldn't very well follow him up into one of the private rooms. *Dammit!* There was nothing to do but wait.

He realised that someone was hovering at his elbow. 'I don't need another whisk—' he began, and then saw that he was talking into the buxom chest of a woman. The woman appeared to be Asian, maybe one of those girls from Assam or Nagaland, who came to Mumbai to seek their fortune and so often ended up in places like this.

She smiled at him through a mask of make-up. She was attractive, Chopra couldn't help but acknowledge, with shapely legs and an incredible bust, barely contained inside her halter-neck top. Her silky black hair was piled into a pineapple coif above her head.

'Hello, sir,' she said, in a husky voice, which made Chopra wince. 'I haven't seen you here before.'

'No,' he mumbled, 'it's my first time.'

'Your first time?' smiled the woman. 'You look very experienced, sir. I can't believe that for handsome man like you, this can be first time.' She giggled lewdly.

He felt himself blush. 'I didn't mean that it was my first time with a – I mean . . . what I mean is it is my first time in this particular establishment.'

She continued to smile at him, moving closer so that her bosom was only inches from his face. Chopra realised that he had broken into a sweat. She looked down at him with her blue-lined eyes and whispered, huskily, 'Would you like to come upstairs with me?'

'Not now,' he muttered. 'Maybe later.'

'Oh,' said the woman, looking crestfallen, 'so you do not think I am beautiful? You think I am ugly?'

'Not at all,' said Chopra desperately. 'You are, ah, very attractive.'

The girl brightened. He knew that it was an act; he knew that he was being manipulated, and yet he felt like a rabbit caught in the headlights of an onrushing express train.

'Then what is the problem?'

'No problem,' he muttered. 'I'm just here to drink, that's all.'

'Just here to drink?' The woman had raised her voice. 'What do you mean?'

A very large man in a black safari suit materialised behind her. 'What's the problem here?' he asked gruffly.

'Mister says he is only here to drink. He does not like me.'

The large man looked down at Chopra. He had dark skin and a very thick moustache. 'What's your game, Mister?' he growled. 'No one insults my girls.'

'I didn't insult anyone,' said Chopra through gritted teeth.

'You turned her down, yes?'

'Yes, but—'

'He says he is only here to drink.'

'Only here to drink?' The moustache bounced up and down above the man's mouth in utter incredulity. He glared at Chopra. 'What the hell do you think this is? A five-star hotel?'

Chopra could see that the situation was spinning out of control. Men at the surrounding tables had turned to listen. Any more of this and his cover would be blown.

'If you don't want *her*, pick another girl. We have a good selection, something for all tastes.'

Chopra now had two choices. He could leave and wait outside for the man in the red hat to emerge. But if he did that he would not be able to see what happened inside the bar. What if Kala Nayak was in here somewhere, maybe even in one of the private rooms above, and the man in the red hat had arranged to meet him? No, he had to stay inside.

'Look,' he said desperately, 'she is fine.'

'Good,' said the man, and wandered off.

The woman grinned at him. She bent down and whispered, 'Come, let's go upstairs.'

Chopra realised that he had no choice.

He followed the woman as she made her way through the maze of tables and up the stairs. His face was flushed with embarrassment. He was sure that every eye in the place was turned towards them, that every man was staring at him. But when he sneaked a quick look he saw that no one was watching them. No one cared. This was all part of the business of this place. He was just another customer, on his way to get his slice of heaven.

The woman led him into a dimly lit room with whitewashed walls and a single bed. She turned and said, all business now, 'The rate is five hundred rupees.'

Chopra began to protest, but then simply took out his wallet and counted out five one-hundred-rupee notes. The woman took them and put them into a drawer beside the bed, which she locked with a key hanging from a chain around her neck. She had taken something from the drawer and handed it to him. It was a contraceptive. 'Put that on,' she ordered. Without further ado, she removed her halter-neck top and shimmied out of her skirt and shoes, then lay down on the bed.

Chopra stared at her naked body. He was struck dumb, by her beauty, and by his own feelings. He was a good man; he knew that. He should not be standing here, looking at this young woman, who was waiting for him to – to . . . waiting as she did for God only knew how many customers each night. He knew the wave of lust coursing through him was wrong. He looked away from the woman. 'Listen to me,' he said, 'I need your help.'

ON THE BOAT

When he came back downstairs, some fifteen minutes later, he saw that the man in the red hat had also returned. Chopra went to his own table, where his Coke and whisky still waited.

'Were you satisfied?'

He turned and saw the big man in the black safari suit looking down at him.

'Yes,' he said. 'Very satisfied.' The man nodded and left.

Chopra continued to watch the man in the red hat. A few minutes later, the Asian girl came downstairs. She made her way to Chopra's table and pretended to flirt with him again, sitting down on his lap and putting her arms around his neck as she whispered into his ear. 'I spoke to my friend. She says the man did not meet anyone in her room. As far as she knows he does not meet anyone here except the friends he is sitting with. Do you want to know what he did with my friend?'

'No,' said Chopra. 'I can guess.'

'Chopra! My God, it is you!'

Chopra turned his head to find a man in a police inspector's uniform bearing down on him on somewhat unsteady legs. 'Wah! Wah! I never thought I would see the sun rise in the west!' The man brandished a bottle of Kingfisher beer. He was tall and thin, with a brisk moustache and heavily oiled hair slicked back over a perfectly round skull.

Chopra was mortified. He knew the man. Inspector Amandeep Singh from the Chakala station. Singh was a passing acquaintance, rather than a friend. Over the years he had heard rumours that Singh played fast and loose with the rules, and led a cavalier lifestyle both in and out of his office. He cursed his luck that their paths had crossed tonight.

'I admit, Chopra, you had us all fooled, yaar! We used to joke behind your back that Chopra's so straight he'd arrest his own mother for spitting betel-nut in the street. Hwaw! Hwaw! Hwaw!'

Chopra winced. He remembered now the last time he'd heard Singh's laugh, at a meeting of the local station heads a year ago. It sounded to his ears like a donkey being castrated.

'By the way, I heard you retired.' Singh raised his bottle in a toast. 'Here's to living the good life! Hwaw! Hwaw! Hwaw!'

Chopra felt himself blushing all over. Damn this clown! Surely his cover was blown now! His eyes flicked over to the man in the red hat, but he was on his mobile phone, his back turned to Singh's circus act.

'Look, Singh, let's keep this to ourselves, yes?'

Singh tapped the side of his nose. His eyes revolved in their sockets. 'Ah, yes! The wife! What was her name? Chippy?' He winked lewdly at the girl on Chopra's lap. 'Much better here, I say. Different wife every night and no nagging afterwards! Hwaw! Hwaw! Hwaw!'

As Singh staggered away, Chopra felt a terrible sense of impending doom. He knew that by the next day, his reputation would be dust. Everyone would be talking about Chopra, the secret ladies bar aficionado.

He imagined the boys at the Sahar station shaking their heads in disbelief, refusing to accept the story at first, then becoming angry when they recalled how he had always pretended to be such a stickler. 'You never know what lies beneath,' they'd say, and their faith in human nature would ebb just a little bit lower.

The man in the red hat left the bar three hours later. By that time it was deep into the night. He walked, somewhat unsteadily, to his bike. Chopra followed him out. He was not feeling terribly steady himself. It had been impossible to maintain his seat in the bar for three hours without drinking. His head was beginning to throb, and he could feel a burning sensation in his throat. It took him three attempts to gain his footing on the Enfield's clutch.

He followed the man in the red beret through Lokhandwala and into Versova. The roads were empty now, and the rushing wind helped clear Chopra's head a little. He thought of the last thing the young woman in the Queen of the Night had told him. 'You asked me to find out this man's name. His name is Shetty.'

Shetty. On the day that he had died Santosh had written in his diary: 'Meet S. at Moti's, 9 p.m.' Was Shetty 'S.'? Chopra could not be sure, but he had to believe that he was on the right track. Had Santosh kept his meeting with this Shetty at Motilal's that evening? If so, a few hours after that meeting he had been killed.

They followed Yari Road as it curved around to its terminus in the Koli fishing village behind Versova Beach. Chopra found it difficult to track the man in the red beret – Shetty – through the narrow winding alleyways of the village, but every time he thought he had lost him, he would catch a glimpse of red.

The village was quiet, bedded down for the night; a few lungi-clad fishermen smoked beedis on their verandas and watched them pass with slitted eyes, but otherwise there was little activity.

There were many such villages dotted around the coast of Mumbai. Chopra knew that they were insular communities descended from the city's original fisherfolk, when Mumbai had been little more than a series of marshy islands. Most were intensely distrustful of the police, and for good reason. Fishing was a hard life and many communities supplemented their income by aiding and abetting organised smuggling operations.

Finally they emerged onto Versova Beach.

Chopra had been here once before, many years ago, in the company of an enthusiastic friend who had got him out here at an ungodly hour so that they could buy fish directly from the boats as they came in. Pomfret and Bombay duck; tiger prawns and baby shark; squid and ladyfish; mackerel and surmai; hilsa and rohu. Now, the fishing boats lay beached, colourful hulls exposed to the night. Above the beach a crescent moon shone down, glazing the water with a silvery sheen.

On the water, a large trawler bobbed by the wooden jetty which stuck out from a concrete apron overlooking the beach. The trawler was tethered to a mooring post at the end of the jetty.

Shetty parked his bike and walked over the gangplank and onto the trawler. He disappeared inside.

Chopra parked his own bike on the concrete apron behind a row of oil drums lined up next to an old abandoned shack. The air stank of drying fish.

He took out his binoculars. Peering out from above the oil drums, he settled down to watch the boat.

After an hour, during which nothing happened, he heard the rumble of a powerful engine behind him. He ducked down as bright lights swept the beach. A Mercedes slid to a halt on the far edge of the concrete apron. Two men got out, one of them in a white suit and holding a cane. Chopra watched through the binoculars as the men walked along the jetty and went onto the trawler. Just before he ducked into the boat the man with the cane turned around; his eyes swept the beach. For a brief second moonlight caught his face. Chopra felt his breath catch in his throat. Nayak.

He waited for thirty minutes. After that, he could wait no longer. He had to know.

Chopra took out his revolver and checked the chamber one more time. He walked along the concrete apron and onto the wooden jetty. Just before he stepped onto the trawler he was overcome by a sudden wave of self-doubt. What was he doing?!

All his life, he had been a by-the-book officer. What he was now proposing to do was reckless; foolhardy in the extreme. As a policeman, it showed a blatant disregard for procedure. But that was the point – he was no longer a policeman. Chopra knew that if he called for backup, as a former officer he would probably be sent a team from the local police station.

But what if he was wrong? There would be hell to pay! And the terror arose within him again – not the terror of what he might face on the boat, but the far greater fear of ruining the reputation that he had taken a lifetime to build.

No, he thought, he could not take that risk.

Chopra took his notebook from his pocket and wrote down the registration number of Nayak's car. The number was a start, but if Nayak had managed to stay hidden for so many years he would not be foolish enough to leave such an easy trail. He needed definitive proof.

And there was something else . . . Chopra needed to confront Nayak. It was his fault that Nayak had slipped through the net. Nayak had made a fool of him and, by extension, of the force. It was Chopra's responsibility to bring the man in. It was the policeman's code.

He would board the boat and locate Nayak. Once he had identified his nemesis, he would make a citizen's arrest. Anyone who got in his way would be dealt with. Then he would take Nayak to his superiors.

Chopra considered the plan and acknowledged to himself that it was naïve in the extreme.

After all, he had no idea how many people were on board the trawler. It was practically a certainty that most, if not all, would be armed. There was also the possibility that Shetty had spotted Chopra tailing him. The Bullet was a hard thing to miss, particularly in the dead of night. Could Shetty have been luring him here? Was he now waiting on the boat hoping that Chopra would be foolish enough to step aboard, alone and armed with only his old Anmol revolver?

Sweat pooled on his upper lip as he wrestled with the dilemma. He knew that he should turn around and leave. And yet, his feet would not move.

Finally, after agonising with himself for what seemed an eternity, Chopra decided that for once in his life he had to leave rationality aside. His instincts were urging him forward, urging him to strike while Nayak was still on the boat. He could not let this chance pass. He could not walk away.

He gripped his revolver and moved silently forward, all the while thinking that it had been a long time since he had last fired a weapon in anger.

The trawler bobbed gently beneath his feet. He walked along the narrow corridor of decking between the boat's hull and the superstructure. He reached a doorway. Holding his revolver before him, he swung the door open and entered.

He was in a short passageway, closed doors on either side of it. He picked the door on the right. He walked into a darkened room, lit only by a single lantern that swung gently with the rocking of the boat. There was a charpoy leaning up against one wall. A wooden pillar rose from the centre of the room to meet a crossbeam. A bucket rested in one corner, next to a tangle of fishing nets. In the other corner was a small table flanked by two stools. On the table was a bottle of whisky, two glasses, a metal ashtray with a lit cigarette resting on its lip, and tattered playing cards laid out in two hands.

'Where are they?' murmured Chopra. He was not given the opportunity to complete his thought. The blow caught him on the back of his head, whirling him into blackness.

When he awoke it was to the sound of dripping water. His head ached. He shook it to clear his thoughts. He realised that he was sitting down, trussed to a chair. He could not move. A cotton rag was tied around his mouth.

He turned his head. He was still in the small room where he had been ambushed. The chair to which he was tied was in turn roped to the wooden pillar in the centre of the room. On the small table he had noticed earlier was Chopra's gun

– but it might as well have been a million miles away. The sound of water that he could hear was the gentle plink-plonk of rainwater falling into the bucket in the room's corner from a leak in the ceiling. The boat bobbed gently below him. He knew, from the moonlight streaming in from the room's solitary window, that it was still the dead of night outside. He could hear the rain drumming on the boat's wooden timbers.

Inspector Chopra (Retd) tried to calm his mind. *Think!* There was no point cursing his stupidity; it was too late for that. He had allowed his desire to track the man he suspected to be Kala Nayak to get the better of him. And now he was well and truly in hot water. As a rule the Mumbai underworld did not kill policemen; it caused too much disruption for their own organisations, too many of their own men subsequently shot dead in police 'encounters'. But Chopra was no longer a policeman, and that made all the difference.

He wondered what his obituary would say?

'Inspector Ashwin Chopra (Retd). Expired in Versova, Mumbai, at hands of criminal elements in the line of what-was-no-longer his duty. A model police officer and good citizen of Mumbai for over thirty years. Recipient of the Kirti Chakra for gallant action above and beyond the call. Lover of cricket and vada pao. Owner of one elephant. He is survived by his wife Archana Chopra.' Perhaps to this should be added: 'Silly fool who is dead because he ignored the most basic precautions of police work.'

What would Poppy say, he wondered? No doubt she would be furious with him for dying on her just when he had retired. She would certainly be furious that he had ignored the doctors' edicts not to excite himself. Chopra felt a sudden lifting of his mood. At least she was still young and attractive enough to remarry. And if he knew his wife she was certainly not the type to spend the rest of her life as a widow, mooning about all dressed in white. He wished the best for her, always had done.

He thought briefly of the new property on Guru Rabindranath Tagore Road, still unfinished and now likely to remain so. Poppy would find out about that sooner or later. What would she make of it? She would be angry, no doubt; angry at his plans, at the fact that he had kept this secret from her. But in the end what did it really matter? What did anything matter once a man was gone from this world? Karma. That's all a man could do. Husband his karma, so that in the next life he had a fighting chance.

Chopra tested his bonds, but they were too tight; tied by an expert, he thought. If this were a Bollywood movie and he were a Bollywood action hero, he would, no doubt, be able to call upon the deity of his choice, find the superhuman strength to tear apart these ropes, and then, muscles bulging, leap into action to summarily dispatch a dozen or so villains, before a final showdown with Kala Nayak.

He wondered when the fishermen would wake up and go out in their boats. Surely that would be his opportunity, perhaps the only one he would get, when the beach would be crawling with fisherfolk, fish buyers, litter pickers, ice-sellers. The trouble was, he couldn't even shout for help . . .

Suddenly he became aware of another sound, a low keening sound just below the edge of hearing. He strained his ears. The sound seemed to be coming from somewhere below his feet. He wondered what it could be. It was difficult to isolate from the sound of the rain, and he began to suspect it was simply his imagination. But before he had a chance to analyse the sound further, the door to the room swung open and two men entered. One was a thin dark-skinned man wearing a Hawaiian print T-shirt; the other was the man in the red beret. Shetty.

'He's awake,' said the Hawaiian T-shirt.

'Welcome, Inspector,' grinned Shetty with an expansive wave of his arm. 'How do you like our boat?'

Chopra glared at him.

'He doesn't have much to say, does he? Normally, these policemen can't stop yakking. Isn't that right, Inspector?'

The two men grinned at each other as if they had just told a fabulous joke. Chopra watched them with wary eyes. He could sense the threat of violence that lay behind their words.

Shetty picked up Chopra's gun and pretended to examine it. 'This is why the police are so useless,' he said. 'You have such old guns. Me, I have a German automatic.' He reached into the waistband of his jeans and took out his pistol. He weighed both guns in his hand, then said: 'What do you think, Chotu? Revolver or automatic?'

'Only one way to find out, boss,' grinned Chotu.

Shetty placed his automatic onto the table. Then, with mock ceremony, he pretended to examine the revolver, before emptying five of the six bullets from its chamber. He twirled the chamber around, snapped it back into place, then put the gun to Chopra's forehead. 'You know, it's not very polite to follow people around, is it, Inspector?' He grinned, displaying a mouthful of flat, broad teeth. 'You have to be very lucky not to be spotted. Let's see how lucky you are, today.'

'*Stop!*'

All three of them looked to the doorway. Another man came into the small room, trailed by a second goon. Chopra froze, his eyes narrowing.

'Ram, ram, Chopra,' said Kala Nayak. 'It is so nice to see you again, after all these years.'

NO ORDINARY ELEPHANT

Poppy awoke. For a moment she splashed around in confusion, swimming out of the depths of her dream. She had imagined herself to be lost in the jungle, unable to find her way out while strange creatures with nine legs and seven eyes chased her through the trees, trees which themselves sprang to life and joined in the chase, reaching out with viney limbs to clutch at her throat and choke the life from—

She sat up.

A sound had woken her. She could hear it now. It rose above the sound of the rain hammering on the windows, above even the sound of her air-conditioning unit. Poppy turned to her side to nudge her husband awake . . . and discovered, to her horror, that he was not there. And then she realised that he had probably risen to go to the bathroom or drink a glass of water, as was his habit.

This realisation was overtaken by the memory of the previous evening, when she had gone to bed alone, seething because he had neither returned nor called to inform her of his whereabouts. She had been determined to stay up in bed, waiting to give him the shock of his life as soon as he walked in the door; she would show *him*, Mister This-and-That! But the stress of the past few days had worn her out and she had fallen asleep almost as soon as her head had hit the pillow. That was another thing: Chopra had always been a much lighter sleeper than her, which had bothered her at first until he had reassured her that she did not snore in her sleep. It would be just terrible if a woman snored, Poppy thought.

She sat upright, listening. The strange sound, a sort of dull scraping, was clearer now. What could it be? Surely her husband was not making it.

Filled with an incipient sense of trepidation, Poppy slipped out of bed and crept into the living room. A glance at the kitchen area and through the open doors of the bathroom and the study confirmed her worst fears: Chopra was not in the flat.

For a moment she was stunned, rooted to the spot by shock. In twenty-four years of marriage this was the first time her husband had been away for the night without informing her first. Surely, this was the last piece of evidence that Poppy needed; surely, now, it could only be another woman!

Poppy tried to picture her husband in the arms of some floozy, some two-bit hussy dripping sweet poison into his ears. She was overcome by a terrible rage that made her whole body flush. Coupled with the rage was shame; shame that she had not been able to hold on to her husband; shame at what the neighbours would say, what her family would say. How would she ever face anyone again? Poppy, who had always been the fearless one, the confident one. Now she would not even be able to meet the eyes of her friends. A woman abandoned by her husband had no value in India. She would become invisible, a ghost that no one wished to associate with. She might even be forced to return to her native village, back to her parents' house, to live out her days like a leper in the company of her idiotic brother and her exasperating mother, who would, no doubt, never let her hear the end of it. A deathly panic trembled through her, and tears began to seep from the corners of her eyes.

It was at this point that she realised that the strange scraping sound she had heard was coming from the front door. She turned and saw Ganesha rubbing his head against it.

She wiped the tears from her eyes and moved towards him. 'What is it, boy?' she said. Ganesha ignored her and butted the door gently with the top of his knobbly skull. It was obvious that he wished to leave the apartment.

Poppy opened the door and followed him out into the lobby.

Ganesha circled the lobby anxiously until he came to the marble staircase. He dangled one leg over the top step, but then moved back, confused.

'This way, boy,' said Poppy and summoned the lift. Together they rode down to the ground floor.

As Ganesha trotted out into the courtyard, Bahadur, who had just that moment got up to visit the lavatory, let out a yell. The sight of the elephant suddenly materialising out of the darkened lobby had frightened him to the point where he no longer needed to use the toilet.

Together, he and Poppy watched Ganesha as he butted the gates to the compound. Bahadur looked at Poppy, who nodded. He went to the gates and unlocked them. They watched as Ganesha lumbered away towards the main road.

Now that Chopra could get a good look at his face, he realised that Nayak had not changed as much as he had at first thought. If you took away the stubbled beard, the altered hair and the pale eyes – clearly the work of coloured contact lenses – he felt confident he would have recognised this man anywhere.

Nayak stood before him, a gaunt, imposing man in a white linen suit, leaning on his cane. The cane was made of ivory, with a silver base and finely wrought handle.

'You like this?' said Nayak, noticing Chopra's gaze. 'Pure elephant ivory, carved from a single tusk taken from a giant bull. A gift from you, Inspector, in a way. That night in MIDC you nearly upset my plans. A bullet caught me in the hip. It was only a grazing blow – at least that's what I thought at the time. But the wound became infected; a bone fragment went the wrong way. The doctors had to operate. They didn't do a good job, as you can see. Take off that gag.'

Chopra felt rough hands pulling away the gag. He sucked in a deep lungful of air as it fell away.

'You must have so many questions,' said Nayak.

'Why?' said Chopra finally.

'I had to disappear. Things were going badly for me. We were in a gang war, the old dons fighting to hold onto power. They got together, pooled their strength; sooner or later they would have finished me off. Then we had you and the special taskforce, closing in. I could feel the noose tightening around my neck. I suppose I could have tried to shoot my way out of trouble. But I preferred to use this.' Nayak tapped the side of his skull. 'The whole thing at MIDC was a set-up. Only one of my men knew what I was up to, a loyal lieutenant who knew that I had planted the police information, knew that a raid was coming, knew that we would start the fire ourselves, knew that I would be replacing my 'corpse' with another. It was a high-risk strategy; many things could have gone wrong. But it had to look real, or else it would never have fooled you.'

'Whose body did we find?'

'The loyal lieutenant's. I could not leave any loose ends. You understand that, don't you, Inspector?'

'How did you get out of the building?'

'I changed into a police uniform and limped out with the rest of your men. In all the smoke and chaos of the fire, no one noticed. By the next day I was out of the city. A day after that I was in Dubai.' Nayak shifted his weight on the cane. 'Have you ever been to Dubai? I highly recommend it. For a person like me it is a Mecca. I had been putting money there for a long time. Within a month I was up and running again. But this time I stayed in the shadows. You taught me a valuable lesson, Chopra – there is nothing to be gained by being a hero. In this business the ones who live to a ripe old age are the ones who play the cautious game, who manage the risks and stay out of the limelight. In the past nine years I have built up my organisation again; now it is stronger than it has ever been. Drugs, guns, construction . . . anything you can think of, I am making money from. But almost no one even knows that I exist. That is the real secret!

'And I will tell you one other thing: I am older, I am wiser. I know what to spend my money on now. Not the flashy ornaments of a young man, but the one thing that can guarantee a long life and prosperity. Do you know what that is? Power. With the money I make, I buy *power*.' Nayak smiled. 'Do you know, there is even a word for people like me now: *entrepreneur*.'

'And yet,' said Chopra, 'for all your fine talk, your fine clothes, you are still nothing but a petty crook. A *goonda*.'

For a moment Nayak said nothing. Then he smiled ruefully. 'It is a shame that our paths have crossed again, Chopra. The world is a more interesting place with men like you in it.'

He turned and left.

Shetty now spoke to the two goons. 'Take him onto the beach. Put him in the sea. It must look like a drowning. No knives, no bullets, no punches – do you idiots understand? You already left a bruise on his skull. If you mess up again you'll be joining him in the water.' Shetty looked down at Chopra and grinned. 'What do you think of Boss's idea, Inspector? "Recently retired policeman commits suicide." "Depressed inspector drowns himself." Too good, yes?'

'Did you kill him?' asked Chopra.

'Kill who?'

'The boy. Santosh Achrekar.'

Shetty frowned. 'Santosh? Poor kid. He killed himself. This suicide business, it's becoming a craze.' He guffawed loudly.

'Why?' asked Chopra. 'Why did he have to die?'

Shetty stopped laughing. 'You know your problem, Inspector? You ask too many questions. The kid is history. Who cares why?'

'I care.'

'And that's why you're sitting here now,' growled Shetty, tiring of the game. 'Come on, why are you two idiots looking at my face? Take him.' Shetty waved his automatic at the two thugs. 'When you finish, I want the pair of you to get out of town for a few weeks. Go to the Pune office.'

'But boss, what about the . . . cargo?'

'You don't have to worry about that. Mangesh and Namdeo will be along any minute. I'll be back in a couple of hours myself. I don't want to see your ugly faces here when I return.'

The gag was tied back around Chopra's mouth. He felt his bonds being loosened, then removed. Rough hands pulled him up. He tried to struggle but his captors were too powerful.

Flanked by a goon on either side, he was dragged along the deck, onto the jetty and from there down onto the deserted beach. The rain had momentarily relented; it fell now in a light spray. The sound of the surf was a gentle susurration that filled Chopra with a sense of sudden calm. The wet sand sucked at the soles of his shoes.

The goons held him upright as they turned and watched the white Mercedes leaving. Shetty followed the Mercedes on his motorbike.

'Come on!' One of the goons pushed Chopra in the back, toppling him onto his knees in the surf. He rested there a moment, like a Muslim about to commence his prayer. Then he was pulled roughly to his feet again, and dragged forward until they were knee-deep in swirling black water. An old discarded tin can rode up on the surf and ricocheted off his leg. With a swiftness of movement that belied his size one of the thugs pincered Chopra's arms behind his back. The other pulled off his gag, but before Chopra had a chance to yell out, a rough hand grabbed his hair and he was pushed down into the water, his face submerged with a shocking suddenness.

He thrashed around, but the grip on his head was implacable; a knee was planted in his back. He held his breath, wriggling for all he was worth; suddenly, the knee slipped. With a monumental effort he shook off the hand from his skull and lifted himself up, drawing in a huge, gasping breath as he broke the surface of the water. The two thugs, one of whom had fallen into the surf, grappled with him.

From the corner of his eye, Chopra saw a grey shape bundling over the sand. The next thing he knew Ganesha had materialised out of the rain and steamed into one of the thugs, striking the man forcefully at his hip. Chopra heard the crack of bone; the thug screamed and tumbled backwards into the surf. The other thug, eyes wide in astonishment, reached into his jeans for his pistol, but the weapon fell from his water-slippery hands and was lost in the swirling sea. He fell onto his hands and knees, groping under the water for his automatic.

As Chopra watched, rooted to the spot in astonishment, Ganesha butted the man from behind, splaying him face-first into the water. Then, rushing forward, the elephant had stepped onto the man's back, then his head.

Chopra came to his senses. He had no idea how or why what had just happened had happened. But it had happened all the same.

He tried to imagine how Ganesha could possibly have found him.

On foot Versova Beach was at least an hour from his home. He knew that few people would have commented on an elephant on the roads of Mumbai. What he didn't understand was how the elephant had known where he was.

Chopra had read that many animals possessed senses that were still a mystery to human beings, particularly in the realms of tracking and navigation. He knew from Dr Harpal Singh's book that the trunk gave the elephant an extraordinarily acute sense of smell, capable of detecting scents over a distance of several miles. He knew that in times of drought elephants had been shown to detect where water was to be found even when that water was over ten miles away . . . In the end, the only thing that really mattered was that he was alive.

'Come on, boy,' he said, patting Ganesha on the flank.

Chopra ran back up the wet sand, climbed the stone steps onto the concrete apron, and ran into the fishing village, Ganesha close at his heels.

When Chopra arrived back at his compound, he first settled Ganesha downstairs by the guard hut. It was time for the elephant to move out of the apartment.

He crouched and patted him on the head as Bahadur looked on with round eyes. 'You saved my life, boy,' Chopra murmured.

Ganesha yawned and collapsed onto all fours. He blinked, then closed his eyes. The night's exertions had exhausted him. They had walked back from the village, Chopra forcing a steady pace through the still-quiet streets. He had sensed the elephant's fatigue but he knew that time was of the essence now. A plan was already forming in his mind . . .

Within moments Ganesha was fast asleep.

In the apartment Chopra found Poppy curled up on the sofa. He knew that she must have waited up for him, fretting herself finally into a troubled sleep. Chopra considered waking her, but then decided against it. He was still shaken and not yet ready to talk to anyone about what had transpired that night.

He walked into his office, sat down in his wicker chair and closed his eyes.

He still could not believe that he was alive. How close had he come? He had tasted it, all but accepted it, gone halfway there and back. But now, miraculously, he had returned to the land of the living. Chopra lifted his hands to his face. He realised that he was weeping.

Afterwards, he crept back into the living room, and stood there looking down at his wife's sleeping face. He imagined her once again as a widow. If he knew Poppy, she would make a cause of herself. Plenty of theatrics and melodrama . . . but in the end his wife was irrepressible, a force of nature; she would survive.

Chopra walked to the window and looked out over the sleeping city. His city. Yes, that was how he had always thought of it. *His* city. His because he felt a duty towards it. People said he had inherited this sense of duty from his father, but Chopra did not believe this. You could not inherit such a sense, the way you could the colour of your eyes, or your hair. Such a sense had to be born within each man, had to be nurtured by the decisions he made, particularly the decisions he made at the most critical times in his life. Times like this moment.

Chopra did not wake Poppy. She would not understand what he was about to do. Instead, he took a notepad from the telephone stand and wrote her a message. 'Dear Poppy, do not worry. I am safe. I have gone out. I will be back soon. I will explain then. Ashwin.'

He left the note on the table, took one last look at his wife, then went back downstairs.

He found Ganesha hunkered down in his furrow next to the metal pole. Bahadur had reattached the chain around the little elephant's neck. Chopra looked down on Ganesha's guileless, sleeping face. Had it really happened? Or had it been some incredible dream? How had the elephant found him? How had he known? None of it made any sense.

Chopra realised that he might never know the answers to

these questions. The only thing he could be sure of was what his Uncle Bansi had said: 'This is no ordinary elephant.'

Chopra recalled something from Harriet Fortinbrass's memoirs: 'Indian mythology elevates the elephant to the position of *navratna*, one of the nine jewels that rose to the surface when gods and demons searched the oceans for the elixir of life. Indians are convinced that elephants possess mystical powers and an innate sympathy for the trials of humankind. They are our friends; they are our keepers.'

Chopra had to move fast.

He took a rickshaw back to Versova, to the fishing village. It was almost dawn. Soon the villagers would be bustling about their business.

Chopra found his Enfield where he had left it, hidden behind the oil drums on the concrete apron above the beach. He looked down at the beach to the trawler in which he had so recently been imprisoned. At the end of the jetty, parked by the mooring post, he could see Shetty's Hero Honda. Shetty had returned as he had promised.

Chopra peered at the surf. There was no sign of the bodies of the two goons. The sea, that ultimate collector of human waste, had done its work.

Chopra settled down to wait, knowing that what he was doing now far exceeded in foolishness everything he had so far done. But he was beyond caring about consequences; he felt like a man who had already died, and was living now on borrowed time. The only thing that mattered was completing his self-appointed mission.

Thirty minutes later, just as dawn was breaking, Shetty emerged. Chopra watched him as he straddled his bike, stamped on the clutch and roared away.

Chopra followed him as he made his way back along Yari Road, back through Andheri West and back to Sahar.

On the east side of Sahar he drove into the affluent new Mount Kailash development. This was one of many new developments in the suburbs, designed to cater to the burgeoning wealth in the city and the exodus from the crowded southern zone. Large, well-constructed bungalows lined the road, each with a fancy gate and security guards stationed outside. Shetty stopped at the gate of one particularly lavish mansion. For a while he chatted to the guards, who clearly knew him. Then the gate opened and he roared off inside.

Chopra counted to one hundred then revved his bike towards the gate. He signalled to one of the guards.

'Hey, you, I'm looking for the bungalow of Prakash Jain, do you know where it is?'

The guard exchanged looks with his colleague. 'No, sir.'

'What about this one,' said Chopra. 'Are you sure this isn't his bungalow?'

'No, sir,' grinned the guard. 'This is Jaitley Sahib's bungalow.'

'Jaitley? Yes, I have heard of him. Mr Jain told me about him. Tall man, wears a white suit, walks with an ivory cane, yes?'

'Yes, yes,' nodded the guard enthusiastically. Chopra roared away.

So this was where Kala Nayak now lived. Right out in the open! How many years had he been here, right under Chopra's very nose? How was it even possible? How could it be that he had heard nothing, that all his informants on the streets had heard nothing?

In the end it didn't really matter. Nayak was back in Chopra's city, and now he knew where he was. And what was more, there was no longer any doubt: Nayak was behind the killing of Santosh Achrekar. Santosh had worked for businessman Arun Jaitley, the alter ego of Nayak. Chopra did not yet know why Santosh had been killed, but he vowed to himself that he would find out.

He had to plan his next move carefully. Who could he call on? Not ACP Suresh Rao, who had always been at loggerheads with him. Perhaps his old friend ACP Ajit Shinde might believe him, might even call his former superiors in Mumbai and convince them on his behalf. But Shinde was halfway across the country in the jungles of Gadchiroli, fighting Naxals. Would he really act with alacrity on a call from his old friend? Or would he put it onto his to-do list, and then, when he finally got around to it, call and check on Chopra first, probably with Inspector Suryavansh.

Chopra imagined the conversation: 'Old Chopra's come up with this incredible story, is there any truth to it?'; 'Nayak still alive? Preposterous! Back in the city, under our very noses? Ridiculous!'; 'Chopra seemed very sure of his information. Claimed he'd seen the man with his own eyes.'; 'Well, retirement does funny things to a man. And he's been quite ill. Dicky heart, and all. Very stressful, I'd imagine.'; 'Shame, he was such a reliable fellow.'

No, thought Chopra, he would not call ACP Ajit Shinde. But there was one other person who could help. One other person who had the welfare of the city at heart, particularly the welfare of Sahar, and who had the power to do something about it.

A MEETING WITH AN MLA

The offices of the Member of the Legislative Assembly for the Andheri East constituency, Ashok Kalyan, were located in a dour sandstone building on Sahar Road, the premises announced by a large billboard halfway up the front elevation sporting a colourful, hand-painted picture of Ashok standing shoulder to shoulder with the grinning party leader while a horseshoe of fawning acolytes from the party ranks looked on in awe. In the background was the logo of the party, and the party slogan: 'From behind, we are moving the common man in front'.

Chopra knew that if Ashok had wished it he could have relocated to much fancier premises. But Ashok was a canny operator. 'How can I be a man of the people if I don't live like the people?' he had explained with a big grin on his genial face.

That had been nearly five years ago, at the time of the last elections, when Ashok had first gained a seat in the state Legislative Assembly. Chopra had visited him on occasion since then, but those occasions had become rarer and rarer as each had become busier and busier, particularly Ashok. Yet they continued to talk on the telephone, felicitating each other at Diwali, asking after each other's families, and generally keeping up with each other's careers. As a former police officer and now MLA, Ashok continued to take a strong interest in local policing. He worked closely with the soon-to-retire state Home Minister, whose remit included law and order for Maharashtra. There were rumours that Ashok would be championed by his party as an able replacement for the outgoing minister.

A security guard sat outside Ashok's office. It seemed the man of the people now needed protection from his people.

During the elections many politicians had been attacked around the country. The divide between rich and poor had been growing dramatically; and the common man was beginning to get fed up. While the incumbent government talked about 'India Shining', the opposition asked, 'Shining for *who*?' It didn't help that many politicians openly lined their own pockets while pretending to be sanctimonious servants of the masses. Unfortunately, even the good ones were tarred with the same brush.

Through the glass screen of Ashok's office Chopra could see his old friend sitting at his desk, a young clerk leaning over him holding a clipboard.

Chopra rapped on the glass door, ignoring the protests of the khaki-clad security guard. Ashok looked up. For a moment his expression was irritated at the interruption, and then he recognised Chopra and broke into a smile. He stood up, swept past the clerk and opened the door himself. 'Ashwin! What are you doing here!'

The two men embraced. Ashok ushered Chopra into the office and pushed him onto a wooden chair. The clerk hovered around them like a nervous bat.

'What can I get you? Tea? Soft drink?'

'Nothing for me,' said Chopra.

'Nonsense,' said Ashok. 'First time we've got together in ages and I can't even get my old friend something to drink? It's a shame you're a teetotaller; I have a bottle of Johnnie Walker in the Ambassador. Raju, go downstairs and get a Limca for the inspector sahib.'

'But sir, the papers—'

'Yes, yes, I'll look at them in a minute. Go on, go now.'

The clerk bustled off with an aggrieved look.

'The trouble with these young modern types,' sighed Ashok, 'is that they think everything can be done in a day. They have no concept of how things actually work. They come into my office without the faintest idea of how much effort and manoeuvring it takes to effect the slightest change in this great nation of ours. Anyway, how is retirement treating you?'

'Not well,' said Chopra. 'Ashok, I need your help.'

Ashok regarded him with an amused smile. 'You said that with such a serious face one would almost think you had the weight of the world on your shoulders. Correct me if I'm wrong, but isn't retirement supposed to be the time when you relax and let someone else deal with all the problems?'

'There are some problems a man has to deal with himself.'

Ashok shook his head and chuckled. 'Same old Ashwin. What's bothering you, old friend?'

'Kala Nayak is back.' Quickly Chopra explained what he had discovered, then: 'I know that what I am saying is hard to believe, but I have seen him, I have spoken to him. It is him.'

Ashok Kalyan regarded Chopra carefully. The MLA was a handsome man, with a cap of curly black hair and a well-groomed moustache, dressed in a dazzling white kurta-pajama, a contrast against his coffee-coloured skin. The eyes radiated warmth and Ashok's smile, Chopra had always thought, was like a personal assurance of friendship and trust. On Ashok's desk sat his Nehru cap, which he had adopted as his personal trademark a couple of years back.

Two decades ago Ashok had made the move from policing into politics with consummate skill. Unlike Chopra he had always been an excellent public speaker, an open and approachable fellow with a flexible bent of mind. Tall and well built, he also displayed a physical dynamism that made him popular with the masses, like a Bollywood hero of their very own. Chopra had often asked him why he had chosen to move into the murky world of governance; Ashok had always laughed away his concerns. 'We have so many crooks in our government,' he would joke, 'it's about time we had a policeman or two as well.'

Ashok had quickly made a name for himself with his forthright manner and his undoubted charisma. And as his rallies became increasingly well attended, the leaders of his party had begun to sit up and take notice. He had progressed from ward councillor to MLA with relative ease, a rising star in whom others saw both possibility and opportunity. Now, with a state Home Ministership beckoning, there was even hope that should his party be successful in the current general elections – as many pundits were predicting they would be – he might well end up with a seat on the Cabinet in the not too distant future. 'Imagine that!' he had said to Chopra, the last time they had spoken on the phone. 'A boy from our own village holding the ear of the Prime Minister of India! What do you think I should ask for?'

Ashok stood up from behind his desk and walked slowly to the window. 'Come here,' he said. Chopra stood up and joined him. 'Look down there. Tell me what you see.'

Chopra looked down onto the road, and the passing traffic. This was a poor neighbourhood and there were few expensive cars. The Toyotas and Skodas that were now a common sight in the inner suburbs were nowhere to be seen. Here auto-rickshaws ruled the road, battling fiercely for lane space with battered Marutis, psychotic motorcyclists and obstinate handcart-wallahs. Women carrying vast baskets of fruit and dried fish swayed up the street, doggedly pursued by begging street urchins.

Across the street a building was rising. A white billboard declared it to be the 'DOCTOR AMBEDEKAR GENERAL HOSPITAL'. Bamboo scaffolding climbed around the three half-finished floors. A narrow lane passed by one side of the building. In the lane Chopra could see a number of men squatting and defecating into the open sewer that ran alongside the new hospital. The men chatted amongst themselves, their pajamas hitched down around their ankles, cigarettes in their mouths.

'Every day, I come to this window and look out there,' said Ashok. 'In four years that hospital has barely risen two floors. And it is not for want of trying. But just as I know that if I can get that place completed it will do great credit to my reputation and the reputation of my party, there are others who know that every day they can delay me will do me harm. And then I look into that little lane, and see grown men sitting down in broad daylight and shitting against the hospital wall, as if this were the most natural thing in the whole world, and I begin to laugh. Sometimes I laugh so hard tears fall from my eyes. Tell me, old friend, where else in the world can a man go and see such things?'

Ashok turned to face Chopra. 'Men like Nayak are an ugly fact of our nation, one we would rather pretend did not exist. Like those men down there, shitting against the wall of the very hospital that might one day save their lives. If you say that he is alive and prospering then I believe you. If you say we must do something then something must be done. I will help in any way that I can. But I will be honest; it is not going to be easy to convince the Commissioner to investigate this. His resources, as well as his concerns, are presently engaged with the election. Rallies and riots, my friend, are what is troubling the police chiefs of this city. As far as they are concerned, Kala Nayak is old news, dead and buried with most of the underworld. The days of gangsters holding the city to ransom are a thing of the past. They are a dying breed, running like rats from our brave men in khaki.'

Ashok put his hand on Chopra's shoulder. 'For both our sakes, I hope that you are not mistaken. I will use up valuable collateral requesting an investigation into this matter, and in my line of work collateral is everything. But you know what they say: if one lives in the dung heap, one cannot smell of roses.'

The clerk returned. With great ceremony he handed Chopra a bottle of cold Limca. He also gave Ashok a small fragrant parcel wrapped in newspaper. 'For you, sir,' said the clerk. Chopra noticed that he was even younger than he had first thought. A slim, good-looking young boy with slicked-back hair and the beginnings of a faint moustache.

Ashok broke into a grin. 'Do you see this, Ashwin? This is why India is great! The young! There are one billion of us now, and most of that one billion are young, ambitious and fiercely competent like my Raju here. Each day, at this time, he fetches me my favourite snack, whether I remind him or not. He knows that this will bring a smile to my face. And when I am smiling Raju knows that I will sign his papers and listen to him as he tells me what I must next do. Isn't this right, Raju?'

The young man murmured something that Chopra could not hear, and looked uncomfortable as Ashok continued to beam at him. 'Don't be shy, now. Tell the inspector what you achieved in your HSC examinations.'

'I was state topper, sir,' mumbled the boy apologetically.

'State topper! Do you hear that, old friend? State topper! And where did you grow up, Raju?'

A flush of embarrassment clouded the boy's face.

'Well?'

'In an orphanage, sir.'

'An orphanage!' echoed Ashok. 'Do you know what it takes to climb out of a place like that? It takes determination. And something else too: a helping hand. The sad fact of our country is that there are many young people like Raju who have the potential but not the contacts to get ahead. Even in the biggest multinationals, the old codes of nepotism still hold sway. It is up to people like me to give the Rajus of this world an opportunity to prove themselves. That is why I make it a rule not to surround myself with fawning flunkies and pretty young girls with short skirts and vacant smiles. Instead I find young men like Raju here, who roll their eyes at me when they think I am not looking, and tut-tut me under their breath when I am lax in my duty.'

'But, sir—!'

'Oh, don't deny it,' said Ashok good-humouredly. He opened the parcel and the smell of freshly fried samosas filled the room. 'Ahhh,' he breathed theatrically. 'Doesn't that remind you of old Hari Uncle back in the village?'

A loud rapping sounded on the door and the security guard burst in. 'Sir!' he blurted. 'There is a petitioner from Sakinaka in the lobby! He is threatening to set fire to himself!'

Ashok rolled his eyes. 'Again?' He grinned at Chopra. 'Don't worry. This drama happens nearly every week. All the poor chap wants is some attention. Really I should have him locked up, but I don't have the heart to do it. Wait here, old friend. I'll be right back.'

'But sir, what about the Shivaji Ground rally?' protested Raju desperately.

'The rally will wait for me,' declared Ashok imperiously as he swept out of the room, the samosa still in his hand. 'After all, I am the star attraction, yes?'

Raju followed him out, casting a last despairing look at Chopra, as if to say, 'Do you see what I must deal with?'

Chopra returned to his seat to wait. Ashok's words had filled him with a renewed sense of purpose, and a determination to see this matter through. Whatever it took, he would bring the killers of Santosh Achrekar to justice.

He looked at the clock on the wall behind Ashok's desk. It was already late in the morning. Assuming Ashok could convince the Commissioner, a raid could be organised by that very evening. *Three* raids, in fact. One on the derelict warehouse in Vile Parle, one on the boat at Versova, and one on the mansion of one Arun Jaitley, the alter ego of Kala Nayak. Chopra would insist on being there for that final raid. They would protest, but he would be there nonetheless. He wanted to see Nayak's face when they led him out in handcuffs; he wanted to look into his eyes.

The wall behind the desk was lined with framed photographs, pictures of Ashok with famous personalities. Chopra noted that there was also a picture of Ashok back in the village, being garlanded by the village council. He smiled. Ashok never missed a trick to remind his voters of his humble origins. Alongside this photo was a picture of Gandhi sitting cross-legged before his charka, spinning cotton. Chopra knew that Ashok, in his own cynical way, had always been a big fan of Gandhiji. 'Now *there* was a born "spin" doctor,' he would say, laughing at his own joke.

'He understood how to market his image before we even had media relations officers!'

There were other pictures of Ashok with various senior politicians, some of whom were so old and mummified in the pictures that they had probably passed into the next life by now. There was a picture with a prominent Bollywood film star, a man who had risen from the local community. There were many pictures of Ashok with his public: Ashok at rallies, shouting into a mike; Ashok grandstanding in front of a packed audience of black-suited lawyers; Ashok being garlanded and felicitated by various charities and welfare organisatio—

Chopra froze.

Seconds ticked away, and then he rose from the chair and walked behind the desk to take a closer look at the picture that had caught his eye.

The photograph showed Ashok placing a garland around a slim young man in a white shirt and navy trousers. A number of other similarly dressed young men were gathered around the boy, watching the award ceremony. In the background was a large banner that said: Shanti Nagar Boys' Orphanage Annual Sports Day. Above these words was the legend S.N.B.O.

Chopra felt something catch deep inside his throat. S.N.B.O. . . . SNBO. Could it possibly be? He moved back to the window and looked down into the street. SNBO. Shanti Nagar Boys' Orphanage.

Chopra stared at the half-built hospital across the road. His mind was whirling with possibilities. Was he clutching at straws, or had he, through sheer chance, stumbled across the vital clue that might finally unlock the mystery of Santosh Achrekar's death?

Chopra knew that there was only one way to resolve these conundrums – he had to find out for himself.

Chopra took an auto-rickshaw to Shanti Nagar, a poor, bustling suburban community with narrow overcrowded streets, overhanging balconies and a preponderance of roadside rubbish tips.

By stopping and asking directions he quickly found his way to the Shanti Nagar Boys' Orphanage.

The building looked like a convent, with black wrought-iron gates, shuttered windows and tall whitewashed walls. Chopra explained to the security guard that he was here to visit the orphanage's administrator. The guard swung aside the gate then went back to reading the newspaper he had been perusing.

The orphanage's main building was fronted by a withered lawn and a cement statue of the freedom-fighter and politician Dr T. S. S. Rajan.

Chopra walked through the front doors and into a low-ceilinged rotunda, which housed numerous display cases holding trophies and award plaques. Decorating the walls was a series of blown-up photographs showing destitute young boys taken in by the orphanage and inducted into a programme of wholesome activities and educational pursuits.

One photograph, garlanded with flowers, showed Ashok Kalyan standing in line with a number of other serious-looking gentlemen. The caption in the photograph read 'SHANTI NAGAR BOYS' ORPHANAGE BOARD OF GOVERNORS'. At the bottom of the photograph were the names of the governors. Against some names, in brackets, were the words: 'Not present in photograph'. One of the names against which this was written was 'Shree Arun Jaitley'.

'Excuse me, sir, may I help you with something?'

Chopra turned to find an elderly woman in a navy blue sari looking at him with hawkish eyes. For a moment he did not speak. His thoughts were still churning around inside his head. Then he said, 'My name is Inspector Chopra. I have some questions about the orphanage.'

'What is this about, Inspector?' said the woman.

'A missing boy,' said Chopra. He turned back to the Board of Governors photograph. 'How long has MLA Ashok Kalyan been on the Board of Governors here?'

'Kalyan Sir? Why, he was one of the founding members. Without his help this sanctuary would never have been established, or any of the other four orphanages that we now run. We will be celebrating our fourth anniversary in one month's time. But what is this you say of a missing boy?'

Chopra removed the picture of Santosh Achrekar from his pocket and handed it to the woman. 'Do you know who this boy is?'

The woman hesitated, a fraction too long, then said, 'No. I have not seen him before.'

'Are you sure?' persisted Chopra.

The woman could not meet his eyes. 'I have said no, sir. I have not seen this boy. Now, we are really busy, you must excuse me.'

He knew that the woman was not telling him the truth. 'Madam, this boy is dead. Murdered. If you do not cooperate with me then a full investigation will be conducted. We will turn this place upside down. Do you understand me?'

'Murdered! My goodness!' The woman appeared genuinely alarmed. Then she calmed down and said: 'Inspector, you must do what you think is right. But I tell you I have not seen this boy before.'

She narrowed her eyes and met his gaze with a look of stubborn defiance.

Finally, Chopra nodded and turned to leave. The woman watched him go then scuttled off down the tiled corridor.

He stopped as he reached the gate. He looked back and saw the turbaned, bespectacled stone figure of Dr T. S. S. Rajan staring down at him with an expectant gaze.

He turned and went back into the building.

His shoes squeaked as he walked along the newly scrubbed corridors. From the rotunda he followed the sign that said 'Boys' Wing'. He walked past a classroom where young boys of perhaps six or seven years of age were sitting at wooden desks reciting in unison behind their English teacher. A few doors down he found a small gymnasium lined with blue matting. Further along he saw an open door and looked inside. It was an empty dormitory, two rows of single beds facing each other. Each bed had been made meticulously.

A little further down the corridor he came across a small room in which a temple had been set up. A portly, middle-aged woman in a navy blue sari, the uniform of the staff at the orphanage, was lighting incense before a statue of Lord Krishna. Chopra waited for her to finish her prayers. The woman touched her joined palms to her forehead, then turned.

'My goodness!' she gasped, raising a hand to her throat.

'Do not be alarmed,' said Chopra. 'My name is Inspector Chopra, and I must ask you a question.' He took out the photograph of Santosh and held it below the woman's nose.

The woman looked at the picture . . . and then her face crumpled into tears. She buried her face in her hands, sobbing. 'I told him to leave it alone,' she sobbed. 'I told him he was putting himself in danger. But he didn't listen to me.'

'*I* am listening to you,' said Chopra gently. 'Please tell me what happened.'

'I cannot,' said the woman, still weeping into her hands. 'They will kill me.'

'No one will harm you,' said Chopra. 'You have my word. Now tell me, from the beginning . . .'

When Chopra arrived back at his apartment, it was to discover that everyone was out. He had wanted to talk to Poppy, to tell her what he had been doing, to confess everything: not just about the private investigation he had undertaken into the death of Santosh Achrekar, but also about the *other thing* and what that meant for their future together.

He knew that he should not have kept Poppy in the dark for so long. He knew that he should have spoken to her that morning when he had narrowly escaped death. He had made a mistake. If there was one person deserving of his trust and confidence it was his wife. And right now he had a desperate need to share his thoughts with her.

The disturbing information that he had uncovered at the orphanage had devastated him. He needed to talk to Poppy, if only to unburden his mind.

She would be shocked and furious, furious at the revelations but also furious at him. Poppy had made a crusade of his heart attack. He knew that she would be mortified at the things he had been doing, and even at the future plans he had put in place with Shalini Sharma, plans which would not lead to the stress-free life that Poppy had envisaged for them both following his retirement. Which was precisely why he had not told her about them.

None of that could be helped.

He had almost died; and there was a good chance that he was going back into danger. He had to make his peace with her before that.

Chopra trudged back downstairs. 'Bahadur, where is Poppy Madam?'

But Bahadur did not know where Poppy was. Chopra felt a tug on his arm. He looked around and saw that Ganesha had twined his trunk around his wrist. The elephant had stood up and was padding back and forth, one step forward, one step back. He was clearly agitated. 'What's the matter, boy? What is it?'

Chopra patted the little elephant on the head. He looked down into Ganesha's eyes. 'You know what I'm going to do, don't you?' he murmured. 'I don't know how you know, but you know.'

Suddenly there came the sound of an auto-rickshaw pulling into the compound. Chopra turned and saw Poppy bearing down on him. She looked deeply unhappy.

'So,' she said, 'you have finally decided to come home.'

'I must talk to you,' said Chopra.

'Yes, and I must talk to you too,' said Poppy stiffly. 'I do not know what you think, Mister big-shot C.I.D. man, but I am not some born-yesterday girl that you can treat in this way.'

He blinked in confusion. 'What? What are you talking about?'

'You know exactly what I am talking about!' said Poppy, her voice rising to an exclamation point. 'Just tell me, who is she?'

Chopra felt himself beginning to sweat. Beside him Bahadur was listening agog. He looked up. A couple of heads were poking out of windows, staring down on the scene with growing interest. 'Look, whatever is troubling you, let's go upstairs and talk about it. This isn't the place.'

He walked into the lobby. Poppy had no choice but to follow him.

In the lift she refused to look at him. Instead she said: 'Just tell me, who is she?'

'Who is who?' said Chopra exasperatedly. 'You're not making any sense, Poppy.'

'Oh, so now I am senseless, am I? You didn't think I was senseless the day you sent your father to beg for my hand!

You didn't think I was senseless these past twenty-four years! My mother was right to warn me about you.'

Chopra felt himself floundering in an unfamiliar sea. 'Look, clearly you are labouring under some sort of misunderstanding.'

But she was no longer listening. 'You thought you could pull the wool over Poppy's eyes. Well, I'll show you, mister.'

They entered the apartment, where Poppy threw down her bag dramatically onto the sofa.

'Whatever is troubling you—' began Chopra, but she did not give him a chance to finish.

'I am telling you now,' said Poppy, her hands on her hips, 'it is me or her!'

'Or *who*?'

'You know who.'

'*I* know who?' said Chopra, now thoroughly bewildered.

'You see,' cried Poppy, looking theatrically up at the ceiling, 'he confesses!'

Chopra stood there, momentarily unsure of what he should say or do next. He had come here to talk to Poppy, to clear the air, but she appeared to be suffering from some sort of delusion. He knew his wife. There would be no way to have a sensible conversation with her until she had calmed down. In that sense, she had always been like a child; quick to anger, and as moody as a storm.

Poppy walked to the sofa and rummaged in her bags. 'I want to tell you something else, Inspector,' she said, holding aloft a white packet. 'I know why you want this floozy of yours. But let me tell you one thing: anything she can give you I can too. Do you see this?' She waved the packet under his nose. On it, in black letters, were the words DR REDDY'S HOME PREGNANCY TEST KIT. 'Yes,' declared Poppy, 'I am pregnant!'

Chopra looked into his wife's eyes. She had been crying, that much was evident. Clearly, she had come to some erroneous conclusions about him. And now, in desperation, *this*. 'That is not possible,' he said gently.

'Miracles can happen,' said Poppy, angrily. 'They happen every day.'

Chopra did not know what else to say. He was completely out of his depth. 'Look, there is something I must do now,' he said finally. 'After that, we will talk.'

'Where are you going?' shouted Poppy. 'Back to that hussy?'

'You have no idea what you are saying,' said Chopra softly. Then he turned and left the apartment.

Sub-Inspector Rangwalla had had a bad week. The departure of Inspector Chopra and the arrival of his new commanding officer had placed a great strain upon both his time and his patience. And the fact that his new CO was proving to be an odd bird, the very antithesis of Chopra, a man Rangwalla had both admired and learned from, was all the more galling.

Rangwalla was a man who prided himself on his ability to thrive in any environment. He had worked too long in Mumbai to be fazed by a man like Inspector Suryavansh; and yet there were limits even to his tolerance. The inspector's drinking had not bothered him; he knew other officers who drank themselves into a stupor each evening but were nevertheless very capable policemen. Neither did the inspector's intimidating manner bother him – he knew many men who liked to throw their weight around; he could deal with that type of personality. No, the straw that had broken the camel's back as far as Rangwalla was concerned had occurred that very morning, when, on only his third day at the station, the good inspector had ordered Rangwalla to close the file on the Kotak case.

The Kotak case was close to Sub-Inspector Rangwalla's heart.

Sunil Kotak's business card stated that he was a property developer. In Rangwalla's opinion it should have stated that the man was a born crook.

Over the past year Kotak had managed to gain control, through underhand means, of an apartment complex in Sahar populated almost exclusively by Muslim families. As soon as Kotak felt confident of his position he had issued an eviction notice against the tenants. It seemed that he had made a deal to sell the land to a foreign developer who intended to create a boutique department store on the site. Kotak stood to make millions. The families, poor ones, had little recourse. They had no money to fight a legal case or to relocate to similar accommodation elsewhere . . . and so they had come to Rangwalla.

Rangwalla knew a number of the families there on a personal basis. In fact, his first cousin Jamil lived there with his wife, five young children and his elderly parents, Rangwalla's aunt and uncle.

For eight months Rangwalla had conducted an investigation into Kotak, with Chopra's blessing. Slowly but surely he had made progress, gathering evidence that could have put the unscrupulous developer behind bars, thus bringing the whole deal to a grinding halt.

And then, that morning, Kotak had come in and spent two hours with Suryavansh. He had left with Suryavansh's arm around his shoulders, the pair of them laughing and joking as if they had been best friends their whole lives.

An hour later Suryavansh had summoned Rangwalla to his office. Without ceremony he had ordered him to close the Kotak file, and stop bothering the man. Rangwalla's protests had fallen on deaf ears.

When the phone rang Rangwalla was still in a foul mood. 'Who is it?' he barked. But his mood instantly brightened as he heard Chopra's familiar voice.

'Rangwalla, I need your help,' said Chopra. 'But it is something you will have to keep from Inspector Suryavansh. Will you help me?'

It did not take Rangwalla long to make up his mind.

A RAID ON THE WATERFRONT

When Rangwalla arrived in the blue police truck, Chopra was waiting for him in the courtyard of Poomalai Apartments, Ganesha by his side.

'Lower the tailgate,' ordered Chopra.

Rangwalla looked from his old boss to the little elephant and said, 'Is this why you wanted me to bring the truck, sir?'

Chopra nodded. 'You will have to trust me on this, Rangwalla.'

Rangwalla shrugged. He had respected Chopra's judgment for twenty years. He was not about to start questioning it now.

He dropped the truck's tailgate. Chopra led Ganesha into the back of the truck. Suddenly, a dark shape rose up from the rear seating, startling both man and elephant.

Chopra regarded the sweating figure of Constable Surat.

'What are you doing here?' he asked in astonishment.

'Sir, I overheard Rangwalla Sir talking to you, and asked to come along.'

'I told you to come alone,' frowned Chopra, turning to Rangwalla.

'I know, sir. Sorry, sir. I couldn't stop him.'

'Please, sir,' begged Constable Surat, 'let me come with you! I won't let you down.'

'I have no doubt of that, Surat. But this could be very dangerous. I do not want you to get hurt.'

'I am not afraid, sir.'

Chopra considered the plump young man, then shook his head. 'My instincts tell me to send you back to the station. But I don't suppose that you would listen to me anyway.' He turned and climbed out of the truck, then got into the driver's cab with Rangwalla.

'Where are we going, sir?'

'To Versova,' said Chopra.

By the time they reached the fishing village the sun had set. Darkness shrouded the maze of narrow lanes. The residents of the village watched from their porches with interest as the police truck nosed its way towards the beach. Rangwalla parked the truck on the concrete apron overlooking the beach. Chopra got out and looked along the wooden jetty.

The trawler was still moored in the same spot. Chopra guessed that either they did not yet know that he had survived the attentions of the two departed goons, or they were so arrogant that they simply did not believe that he would be foolish enough to raise the alarm. After all, they had all but killed him once; the next time they would be more thorough.

He could see no one on the boat's deck. 'Did you bring the gun?' he asked Rangwalla.

Rangwalla handed him the service revolver. Chopra checked the chamber, then ordered Rangwalla and Surat to follow him. Ganesha, who had been let out of the truck, trotted a few steps along the wooden jetty and then stopped. His trunk crinkled as the odour of drying fish swept over him.

The three men clambered aboard the trawler. Chopra heard the sound of water lapping gently against the boat's hull. The door to the wheelhouse swung open and a man sauntered out onto the deck. He stretched his arms into a yawn, then scratched at his groin. From behind him the sound of a Bollywood dance number drifted out into the warm night air. The man turned, and came face to face with Chopra.

'Wh—?' he began, but Chopra cut him off by hitting him on the head with the butt of his revolver. The man fell back against the side of the boat, then flopped forward onto his stomach. A trickle of blood dribbled from his skull and onto the deck. Chopra bent down and put a finger to the man's neck. The pulse was strong.

He stood and went through the door.

The passage was as he remembered it, with doors leading off it on both right and left. The left door led to the wheelhouse. He signalled to Rangwalla and Surat. *Right door.* Then, counting to three under his breath, he kicked in the door and charged into the room, Rangwalla and Surat close behind him.

There were two men in the room, sitting at the small table that Chopra had seen before. A bottle of unlabelled whisky sat on the table, surrounded by playing cards and two neat piles of cigarettes. From the cot in the corner a portable CD player bellowed out music. Everything else seemed exactly as he remembered: the bucket and fishing nets in the corner; the pillar in the room's centre to which he had been trussed.

'Stand up,' said Chopra, pointing his gun at the two goons who were staring at him in open-mouthed astonishment. The men exchanged looks, then slowly got to their feet. 'Surat, take their weapons.'

Constable Surat lowered his rifle and slung it over his shoulder. He quickly frisked the two men, uncovering two pistols.

'Now,' said Chopra, 'I want you to take me to them.'

One of the goons, a bearded man with a nose that appeared to have been crushed at some time in the past, narrowed his eyes. 'Take you to *who*?' he said, his voice a growl.

Chopra walked forward and put the muzzle of his revolver next to the man's temple. 'If I have to tell you again, it will be too late, do you understand?'

The man stared into Chopra's eyes. Sweat beaded on his forehead. Then he blinked. 'OK, OK.'

He led them out of the room, and through another door at the end of the connecting passage. That door opened onto a spiral staircase leading down into the belly of the trawler. The policemen followed the two thugs down into the darkness.

On the lower floor they found themselves in a narrow passageway, lit only by a single lantern. The smell of mould wafted from the walls. They clattered along the corridor and stopped outside a door. Chopra could hear the low keening sound coming from inside that he had heard when he had last been on the boat. The room behind the door was directly below the one in which he had been imprisoned.

'Open the door,' he ordered. The goon lifted a set of keys from a hook by the side of the door. Suddenly, the keys fell from his hand. The goon bent down to retrieve them; his hands fumbled at his ankle . . . and then he erupted from his crouched position with a snarl, the blade of a knife flashing in his fist. Before Chopra had time to react he had buried the knife into the upper part of Constable Surat's chest.

There was a loud bang.

The goon fell back against the wall. He clutched his belly and slid down onto the floor.

Chopra turned.

Smoke curled from the tip of Rangwalla's revolver. The sub-inspector's eyes were shrouded in darkness. His arm swung around to cover the second goon, whose eyes were wide with shock.

Chopra turned to Surat, who was doing his best to stay upright. His hand was gripped around the hilt of the knife. Chopra could see blood leaking out from between the constable's fingers. 'Let me have a look,' he said.

'Don't worry about me, sir,' said Surat weakly. 'I'm all right.'

Chopra gently prised the constable's fingers from the knife. It had entered the fleshy area between the front of the shoulder and the upper pectoral muscle.

'You're a very lucky young man,' said Chopra, relief washing over him. 'It could have been much worse.'

Surat gave him a sickly grin.

'Rangwalla, get the medical kit from the van.'

'Really, sir, it is no bother for me,' trembled Surat, blinking the sweat from his eyes. He was swaying on his feet.

Chopra helped Surat to sit, taking care to cover the second thug with his revolver as he did so.

They waited while Rangwalla fetched the kit.

Minutes passed as the sub-inspector doused the wound with antiseptic, then applied a patch. 'It's not critical,' he said. 'You'll live, Surat.' He tapped the constable on the shoulder, a reassuring gesture.

Chopra bent down to the thug who had been shot. The man's eyes had closed and his hands lay lifelessly in his lap. His head lolled forward onto his chest. Blood had pooled between his thighs. He looked like a drunk taking a rest in an alleyway. Chopra placed two fingers at the man's neck, waited. Then he stood up, and turned to the other goon.

'Now, open the door.'

The goon bent down, picked up the keys and, with shaking hands, opened the door.

Chopra went in.

It was a good-sized space, lit by an oil lantern that threw shadows over everything. In the room, sitting on the floor with their backs against the walls, were eight adolescent boys. They were shackled together. Manacles ran from their ankles to iron loops embedded in the floor. The low keening sound was coming from the boys; a chorus of despair expressed without words. As Chopra stepped forward into the room, some of them lifted their heads and looked up at him. He could see the confusion, the deep misery, etched on their faces. And something else, too. Hopelessness. Resignation. They did not expect anyone to come for them. They did not believe in miracles.

'What *is* this?' said Rangwalla, looking around the room with narrowed eyes.

'This?' said Chopra. 'This is evidence of the evil men are capable of.'

He looked at the goon. 'Where are the keys to their chains?'

The man held up the ring of keys with which he had opened the door.

'Unchain them.'

One by one the boys were released from their manacles. They rubbed their ankles and wrists, but did not rise from the floor. Chopra turned to Rangwalla. 'I want you to call Inspector Chedda at the Versova station. Explain what you have discovered. Tell him to send a team here. He will know what to do.'

'Sir,' said Rangwalla, 'what if Chedda is . . . ?'

'I know,' said Chopra. 'But it is a chance we have to take. If Nayak has bought himself protection, then it will be more difficult. But this is not something that can be hidden. Not any more.'

He turned back to the goon. 'Now . . . where is Nayak?'

CHOPRA CONFRONTS KALA NAYAK

The truck rumbled through the night-time city, past the trendy bars and the dhabas; past the sleeping beggars and the urchins; past the handcart-wallahs supine on their carts; past the ladies bars disgorging their woozy and satisfied clientele; past the call centres operating on foreign time; past the cows lying down by the side of the road; past the glitter-eyed pye-dogs prowling the empty streets, masters once again, if only for a few short hours, of their ancient dominion.

Occasionally Chopra would glance in the rear-view mirror. In the back of the truck, Ganesha stood quietly, wreathed in shadow. Now and again, a passing streetlamp would throw a burst of light over the little elephant's eyes and he would blink and his trunk would twitch.

Thirty minutes later Chopra arrived at the bungalow of Arun Jaitley, aka Kala Nayak. The rain had begun to fall. It clattered on the metal lid of the boot, and splattered the windscreen with big, heavy droplets. Rain swirled in the beams from the headlights.

For a full two minutes he sat in the truck, just watching the rain and the swishing wipers. A dog raced down the road, stopped in the headlights, shook out its sodden fur, then ran on. In the open gutters rats squealed, borne along by the sudden torrent.

Chopra thought about everything that had happened. He realised that when he had retired, something essential to his survival had been taken from him. It was something more than his identity as a policeman. It was the exhilaration of piecing together a puzzle; it was the quiet feeling of satisfaction from knowing that justice had been served and that he had been a small instrument in the serving of that justice. He knew now that whether he wore a uniform or not he would always be driven to pursue justice, a notion that he cherished like a precious flame within him.

He got out of the truck. He walked to the rear and lowered the tailgate. Ganesha trotted down the ramp and into the rain. The little elephant's ears flapped as raindrops bounced off his hide.

Chopra walked to the gate of Nayak's mansion. He peered through the curlicued ironwork and saw that beneath the awning of the guard hut the security guard was sitting with a white-liveried chauffeur in a peaked cap. Both men were smoking cigarettes and peering out at the rain. A glass of tea steamed in the chauffeur's hand.

'Open the gate,' ordered Chopra.

Rain drummed off the awning, rat-a-tat-tat, rat-a-tat-tat. The guard rose from his stool and squinted at Chopra through the bars of the gate. He did not seem to recognise him from the previous day. 'What do you want, sahib?'

'Official police business,' said Chopra gruffly. 'I have come for Nayak.'

Instantly, the guard's face took on a frightened, owlish aspect. He gave a quick telltale look to the driver, who had lowered his glass of tea. 'Sahib, there is no Nayak here. This is the bungalow of Arun Jaitley Sahib.'

'Open the gate,' said Chopra.

The driver looked along the road to where the police truck waited, its beams like two spikes in the darkness.

'I am sorry, sahib. But you have the wrong place.'

Chopra regarded the man's face. He could read the fear. The guard was caught between incurring the wrath of his brutal master and the possibly even more brutal wrath of the police.

Chopra turned and walked away into the darkness. The guard watched him melt into the rain, then returned to his seat under the awning. He picked up his cigarette with shaky fingers. He turned to the driver, to ask his opinion . . .

And then, out of the swirling rain, came a dark, lumbering shape. With a brief trumpet Ganesha steamed into the gates, knocking them from their hinges. The left half of the gate clanged onto the gravel of the driveway, while the right section spun away and struck the guard, who fell to the ground in a dazed heap.

The chauffeur had sprung up from his seat. For a moment he stood there, his mouth flapping open, the glass of tea still in his hand. Then he threw the glass at Ganesha. Turning tail, he ran into the rain, towards the side of the bungalow, the little elephant in hot pursuit.

Chopra walked along the driveway, his feet crunching on gravel. His clothes were soaked; he blinked as water dripped from his hair onto his eyelashes.

The house was set back some way from the gate, behind an ornate cement fountain. The rain had swelled the water in the fountain's basin and it gurgled loudly as it threatened to overflow. Behind the fountain, a number of expensive cars were parked, including the white Mercedes.

Chopra looked up at the house. The façade of the mansion was lined with expensive granite tiles. The large sash windows were rectangles of yellow in the darkened exterior. But he could see nothing moving behind them.

He ascended the marbled steps that led onto the bungalow's front porch. Above him the rain drummed loudly on the porch roof. The front door was open. A servant was framed in the doorway, standing there watching the rain. Chopra raised his weapon. 'Go. Now.' The serving woman stared at him goggle-eyed, then hitched up her sari and splashed off down the drive.

He entered the house.

He found himself inside a vast marbled lobby. A double

spiral staircase with ornamented balustrades and finials in the shape of lions' heads wound up to the first floor. The lobby was tastefully decorated with large Chinese urns and a set of teakwood trestle tables positioned either side of a pond. Exotic fish swam in circles around a profusion of lily pads and floating lotus flowers.

Chopra's heart thundered inside his chest. He clutched his revolver, knuckles whitening on the handle.

He moved through the deserted lobby into an adjoining passage, lined with large rectangular carvings fashioned from Burma teakwood. They depicted scenes from the *Ramayana*, Lord Rama battling Ravana for his beloved Sita. There was something mythological in his own situation, thought Chopra. The hero facing the villain in a final confrontation. In Mumbai, even he could not escape the narrative of the Bollywood potboiler.

He entered a room as sumptuously decorated as the lobby, with a gleaming Italian marble floor, a vast chandelier, and a grand dining table. A giant print hung on one wall, a rural scene of three village maidens carrying pots beside a gurgling river. An arched doorway led onwards. Voices drifted in through the opening. Chopra raised his revolver and moved through the doorway and into another room.

There were three men in the room, two of them sitting on plush red leather sofas that faced each other, the third standing by the floor-to-ceiling French windows that looked out into darkness. The man by the doors was the man in the red beret, the man Chopra knew as Shetty. The two men seated on the sofas were Kala Nayak and Ashok Kalyan.

As Chopra entered the room, the three men turned as one. There was a moment of stunned silence, then Nayak spoke. 'I had hoped that your experience on the boat would have taught you to keep your nose out of my business, Inspector. It seems that I was wrong.'

Shetty moved away from the doors and towards the sofas. 'I told you to let me find him,' he growled. He glared at Chopra. 'I would have cut your throat and watched your blood run into the gutter along with your self-righteousness.'

'You would have made a mess,' said Nayak sharply. 'And I do not need a mess right now.'

Ashok Kalyan stood up. 'You have become an impatient man, Ashwin. I told you to wait.'

'Why?' said Chopra. 'So you could tell me more lies?'

Chopra's face seethed with fury as he glared at Ashok. The revelation of Ashok's involvement had shaken him to the very core. That his childhood friend, a man he had respected as well as loved, was a criminal was bad enough. That he was a man who exploited children for his own gain was almost more than he could bear.

His hands had clenched into fists and it was all he could do to prevent himself from launching an assault on Kalyan there and then.

'Lies?' Ashok shook his head. 'No. So that I can tell you some home truths, old friend.'

'What truths would those be? About the human trafficking ring that Nayak has established in our city? About the boys that you help him find through your orphanages? About Santosh Achrekar, who found out everything and threatened to expose you? Is that why he was killed?'

'Santosh had a bright future ahead of him,' said Nayak. 'I offered him a way out of the filth and poverty into which he had been born. He threw it back in my face. He decided that my business was not to his liking. He forgot the first rule of our country: do not bite the hand that feeds you. He started to snoop around, to ask questions that should never be asked. I think he had the idea that he was going to become a hero. But he made the mistake of trusting the wrong person.'

Shetty moved closer. 'Santosh thought that I would help him expose the operation. We bumped into each other at Motilal's when he came for the monthly accounts. We became friends, for a while. To tell you the truth I quite liked him. I suppose he thought he could trust me, because one day he told me he had found some documents back at head office. He was convinced the organisation was up to shady activities. Hah! What a fool!'

'He found something that led him to the orphanage, didn't he?' said Chopra.

'He saw the account books. It was only a matter of time before he began to ask why what he had come to believe was a crooked organisation was pumping money into those orphanages. He told me he was waiting to find definitive proof before he went to the police. I pretended to be sympathetic; I pretended that I knew all about it, but that I had always been too frightened to go to the police myself. Just another innocent victim. I tell you, I should get a Filmfare award for acting!'

'Why did he trust you?'

'Because I told him that he had finally convinced me, and that we could bring this trafficking operation down together. I told him I knew where we could get the proof he needed.'

'Is that why he went to Moti's on the night he was killed?'

Shetty smiled. 'That evening I asked him to meet me there. I had already told him about how dirty cash was being laundered through the leather shops, moving from one store to another until Nayak Sahib could put it back into 'white' business. We stayed at Moti's all evening; I said I needed to build up my courage for what we had to do. I gave him a Coke, and laced it with drugs. After that, I made him drink whisky with me. I pretended to be in two minds; should I help or should I stay silent? He was eager to keep me talking, so he drank. Typical kid, trying too hard to impress. Pity he wasn't much of a drinker. By this time the pills were kicking in, too. When I could see he was almost gone, I told him I would show him where the boys were kept. On the bike, he was virtually unconscious; I nearly crashed trying to keep him upright. I took him to the place where you found his body. Just before I dragged him to the water, he woke up. Maybe he got some idea of what was going to happen – he suddenly got the strength to fight. He gave me a few scratches, but he had no chance against me. It was a pleasure putting an end to his miserable life.'

Chopra's finger tightened on the trigger of his revolver. He knew that he was teetering on the brink. If this man spoke one more word, he would shoot him down in cold blood. He thought now of the list that he had found in Santosh Achrekar's diary. He had thought that it was a bribe list, but he had been wrong.

It was a list of abducted boys and the prices that they had fetched.

Chopra recalled now his meeting with the woman at the orphanage. About how she had learned, from Santosh Achrekar, that the place in which she worked, a place she'd believed was helping those in need, was actually a vision of hell from which a modern slave trade in children was being orchestrated. The shaken woman had provided many important details to Santosh that had allowed him to further his investigation, not realising then that she was signing his death warrant.

Chopra had promised her that he would avenge Santosh's death and bring a stop to the abuse. At first hesitant, she had finally told him what he wished to know.

He had discovered that the orphanage was besieged by requests from charities and welfare organisations to take in children. In a nation as overcrowded and poor as India this was to be expected. The orphanage, however, had exacting rules. It only took in boys below the age of eight and only those that were healthy. Those with disabilities or family connections were not considered. The boys were schooled and well looked after. But discipline was paramount. Any boy that was disruptive or who did not follow orders without question was dismissed back onto the harsh streets of the city.

Over time the woman noticed that no prospective adoptive parents ever came to the orphanage. Instead, a committee of gentlemen who claimed to represent a charity that helped place orphans into homes would visit the orphanage. Many boys would depart with these gentlemen.

None of the boys would ever return.

The staff at the orphanage were told that the placement organisation had a one hundred per cent success rate. They were told that they had a part to play in assuring that this success continued. They were told that discretion was everything.

Chopra turned to Nayak, keeping his gun aimed at Shetty. 'I saw the warehouse in Vile Parle. Is that where you keep the boys before you take them to Versova to be shipped? Caged like wild animals? Photographed so that you can send pictures of them to the "customers"?'

Nayak said nothing.

'Where do you ship them?'

'What does it matter where they go?' said Nayak eventually. 'They are a commodity, like everything else. They go to the highest bidder. The Middle East. The South. It is all the same. In business, one cannot afford to be sentimental.'

'Listen to him, old friend,' said Ashok gently. 'Listen to what he is saying. It is not too late.'

'Not too late?' Chopra nearly spat the words. 'I should put a bullet in you right now.'

'What will that accomplish?' Ashok clasped his hands in front of his stomach. 'Let me tell you a story. About a policeman, an honest and dedicated policeman who worked his whole life to uphold the principles of justice that someone taught him a long time ago, not realising that the country in which he so diligently applied those principles had changed, its *ideals* had changed. And then one day the policeman retired. What did he have to show for a lifetime of servitude? Was it a mansion as fine as the one in which we are now standing? Was it a Mercedes parked in front of his home? No. Shall I tell you what he had to show for a lifetime's slavery? Nothing. Not a bean.'

'Money isn't everything, Ashok.'

'You are wrong, old friend. It is the *only* thing.'

And Chopra remembered what Nayak had said to him on the trawler: 'I know what to spend my money on now . . . the one thing that can guarantee a long life and prosperity. Do you know what that is? Power. With the money I make, I buy *power*.'

Without warning, Shetty darted between the sofas and charged directly at Chopra. Before he could react, Shetty had grabbed his arm, throwing his weight behind his lunge. Chopra found himself off-balance; the two men tumbled to the floor. The gun went off.

There was a moment of ringing silence.

With a grunt, Chopra heaved the big man aside. Breathing heavily, he struggled to his feet. He looked down at Shetty, who was lying face down on his stomach. Blood oozed out from below his torso. Chopra saw that hidden behind Shetty's right ear were the scabbed-over scars of three short scratches.

A noise behind him made Chopra turn. The French windows were open; a gust of rain blew in from the darkness. Nayak had disappeared.

Ashok, meanwhile, had not moved. 'Don't do this,' he said, calmly. 'There is nothing to be gained. Nayak has spent years putting money in the right pockets. Even if you arrest him, he will never see the inside of a jail cell.'

'I have more faith than you, Ashok. There are still decent men in our country.'

Chopra jogged through the open doorway and into the gardens of the mansion. He was immediately drenched. A solid sheet of water was now falling from the heavens. He could barely see a yard in front of his face. And, unlike Nayak, he did not know the terrain. How could he possibly catch him now?

He ran on.

A shape whirled out of the blackness and Chopra fired on instinct. He squinted closer. It was a concrete statue of a blackbuck antelope raised up on its hind legs.

He ran on, still breathing heavily. He was conscious of his heart thundering inside his ribcage. No time to worry about that now.

He passed another statue. He tripped and fell forward . . . into water.

He splashed around blindly, like a drowning man. He was waist-deep in water, his feet slipping on slime.

He had fallen into a pond.

He lost his footing again and fell, gasping as his face went beneath the slimy water. A shape feathered past his nose, then another. Fish!

Chopra steadied himself, then waded forward, still clutching the revolver. He reached the edge of the pond and, with a sigh of relief, began to clamber out until he was on his hands and knees on the concrete border surrounding the pool. He rested in that position a moment, slimy pond-water dripping from his face, the rain hammering on his back like the fists of an enraged woman . . .

A foot whirled out of the darkness, catching him in the ribs. He tumbled onto his back, momentarily winded. Rain sleeted into his eyes. He tried to rise, and then something struck him in the stomach. It was the point of Nayak's cane. Gasping, he doubled up in agony, tears starting from his eyes, mingling with the rain. The gun had slipped from his grasp. But he could not think of that now; his senses had been overtaken by the sudden, stunning pain, and the thunderous beating of his heart in his ears. Was he having another heart attack . . . ?

And suddenly Chopra was back at the Sahar station, standing inside the interview room, shafts of bright sunlight spearing through the rusted iron grille set high into the whitewashed wall.

He had been interviewing a man that Rangwalla had brought in on a charge of causing public disorder. The man, who claimed to be the reincarnation of the late billionaire guru Sathya Sai Baba, had stood up in the centre of Chakala market and coolly informed his bemused public that one ton of gold from his personal coffers was buried beneath the market.

Enterprising locals had begun digging within the hour, progressively widening their search until the surrounding streets resembled a battlefield of trenches and honking traffic.

Chopra had been grilling the man, attempting to work out if he was a fraudster or simply mad . . . and suddenly a lance of pain had speared through his chest, quickly followed by another, then another. The world slowed down.

Chopra turned his head to look at Rangwalla. The movement seemed to take an age. His hand came up to clutch at his khaki shirt, as if to still the thundering of hooves beneath his ribs . . . and then he was falling, falling, falling . . .

When he had awoken, Poppy's face had been the first thing he had seen. He remembered now the feeling of warmth that had coursed through him as his dear wife had looked down on him with tears in her eyes. 'A heart attack!' she had admonished him. 'Who gave you permission to have a heart attack?'

He opened his eyes and saw Nayak looming over him through the curtain of rain. Nayak bent down onto one knee. He had Chopra's revolver in his hand.

'You have caused me a great deal of trouble, Chopra,' he said, shouting to make himself heard above the rain. 'An honest man in a dishonest city. That is why I have never approached you. I told Ashok, when we first got into business together, when we began to build our power base, that you would never come on board. One crore, ten crores . . . they say every man has his price. But the only price a man like you will ask for is the price of his own funeral.'

Nayak stood. He pointed the gun at Chopra's chest. Chopra felt the sound of his heartbeat slowing in his ears. He thought, suddenly, of Poppy. Poppy who had stuck by his side through thick and thin. Poppy and her never-ending struggles against tyranny and oppression. Poppy and her morbid fear of cockroaches; her habit of biting her lip when she was nervous; her insistence on filling up the apartment with the latest junk that her favourite magazines told her that she simply must have. Her wonderful dosas; the way she would press his shoulders when she knew he was tired, all the while grumbling on about Mrs Subramanium's latest outrage; the way she would whisper in his ear, on the night of every anniversary, even after all these years, that she was so glad that God had brought them together because she simply could not imagine spending her life with any other man. His dear Poppy.

He wouldn't even have the chance to say goodbye. After twenty-four years of being a good husband, fate would deny him even that. Karma, he thought; nothing but karma . . .

Chopra blinked. He saw Nayak standing over him, his face blurred by rain. He blinked again. The muzzle of the gun held his gaze like the eyes of a cobra . . . blink . . . Nayak disappeared . . . blink . . . and now an after-flash . . . Nayak cartwheeling through the air.

With a loud crack the underworld don's head met the concrete edge of the pond. His body slammed into the heaving water. Immediately, it sank below the surface.

Chopra raised himself onto his elbows. A wave of pain lanced around his ribs; the world was spinning like a carousel and he was overcome by nausea. The rain continued to thud onto his skull, plastering his hair to his scalp, ricocheting like a symphony of bullets off the tiles around the pond.

He felt a warm touch on his cheek, and turned. Ganesha snorted, wetly, then continued to pet his face with his trunk, as if assuring himself that Chopra was still in one piece.

He struggled to his knees. With one hand clutching his ribs he peered into the pond.

Nayak floated, face down in the water.

Chopra slipped into the pond and waded over to the floating body. He turned Nayak over. The gangster's eyes were closed. A large gash was visible on his forehead where he had struck the concrete.

Chopra hauled the body to the side of the pond, then dragged it out. He tried to pump Nayak's chest, but it was too late. He was dead.

Chopra got to his feet. He placed a hand on Ganesha's head. He knew that, in spite of Nayak's death, in one sense it was now that the hard work really began. He would have to summon the authorities and pray that there were enough untainted men in the fragile house of Indian justice to permit the visiting of that justice upon all the other corrupt players in this horror.

First among those was his childhood friend, Ashok Kalyan.

'Come on, boy,' he said, 'let's finish what we've started.'

THE BABY GANESH DETECTIVE AGENCY

'Why can't you just tell me where we are going?'

Poppy's face was a picture of worry albeit mingled with curiosity. The past forty-eight hours had been the most trying that she could remember in a very long time.

First there had been the whole business with Kala Nayak and the scandal of the human trafficking ring that her husband had uncovered. She was still furious with him for gallivanting around the city trying to get himself killed when he had a dicky heart and should have been spending his retirement with his feet up, watching cricket and getting fat on her hand-cooked meals. Chopra had attempted to speak to her, presumably to offer some sort of feeble explanation for his foolhardy actions, but she had been so enraged that she had not been willing to listen.

Meanwhile, the newspapers had had a field day. A web of corrupt politicians and policemen had already been implicated in the affair, including local MLA Ashok Kalyan. The

Air Force Colony complex had been besieged with reporters prying into the life of the retired inspector who had cracked the case and in so doing had shaken the very ground beneath the feet of the high and mighty.

Through the phenomenon of the modern Indian media, a howling, insatiable, many-headed beast, the whole country was hooked on the scandal. At the centre of the furore were the rescued orphans who provided a gripping human-interest story. They were presently being put up in the city's most expensive hospital, their plight being used by social agencies as an exemplar of how little Indian society cared for the poorest and most dispossessed. The Chief Minister had been falling over himself to display his concern for the traumatised orphans. The Prime Minister had been forced to make a televised statement, promising an investigation into every orphanage in the country and personally assuring that such a thing would never again be allowed to happen.

Accusations were flying thick and fast of other corrupt practices by politicians in bed with gangsters. Of clandestine arms deals and spurious cattle-feed scams. Vote rigging and paid-for planning permissions. Rivers of black money flowing from the coffers of criminals to the even bigger crooks in elected posts.

To the delight of the masses, politicos of all feathers were running for cover.

And Chopra had achieved all this . . . Poppy had no idea how Ganesha had become involved, but the newspapermen seemed quite intoxicated with the angle of the elephant sidekick. They had made Poppy's life miserable with their constant requests for interviews, just so that they could ask her inane questions about Ganesha: Does he do any tricks? Can he understand everything that you say? Do you think he is God's avatar come to help your husband?

Oh, those silly newspapermen!

The only saving grace had been observing Mrs Subramanium's helpless fury. The old martinet had complained bitterly about the furore but had been powerless in the face of the marauding pressmen who simply thrust microphones in her face every time she tried to chastise them from the premises. Poppy was certain Mrs Subramanium would be sharpening her claws in readiness for the upcoming Managing Committee meeting . . .

And then there had been the whole business with her cousin Kiran. Certain extraordinary developments had put paid to all of Poppy's plans. The boyfriend of Kiran's daughter Prarthana, the wretched scion of the industrialist who had been packed off to a European boarding school, had somehow found his way back to Mumbai. Without informing his parents, he had arrived at Kiran's bungalow and thrown himself at her feet. In the modern way of things he had blubbed on about how much he loved Prarthana and insisted that he was willing to do the right thing by her. He wanted them to be married that very day.

Prarthana had thrown a vase of flowers at him, concussing the wretched boy, and had told him to crawl back to his father.

The boy, once he had recovered from his daze, had threatened to commit suicide there and then if Prarthana did not agree to marry him, proving that he was a true acolyte of the Bollywood school of melodrama. Prarthana had handed him a box of matches and told him to talk less and do more.

Finally, Kiran had got the pair of them to see sense. Without further ado, she had organised the wedding. Her husband, still away in Delhi, had been furious, but for once Kiran had put her foot down. She did not explain the necessities behind the marriage: Anand did not need to know about that, at least not then.

The irate father of the groom had also turned up, the buttons of his shimmering silk bush shirt almost popping from his ample stomach in fury. He had shouted. He had raged. He had shaken his fist, and threatened to call the police. Kiran had swiftly sent him packing.

Poppy reflected that her cousin could be quite the tiger when roused.

And although gossip was rife and would no doubt follow the young couple around for quite some time, at least they would be a *married* couple when the baby was born.

Poppy tried to feel happy for her cousin, but inside, her heart ached. It was cruel of God, she thought, to have given her hope, after all these years, of becoming a mother, and then to snatch that hope away again.

And, of course, there was the whole business of the Other Woman.

Poppy had become more convinced than ever that her husband was about to leave her, about to set up home with his fancy woman, whoever she might be. And now she could not even deliver on her claim that she would finally give her long-suffering husband a child. Her last hope of holding on to the man she had loved her whole life had vanished.

And then, that morning, when she had readied herself for a final confrontation, Chopra had told her to get dressed. He wanted her to accompany him. He did not say where.

In the auto-rickshaw, Chopra had remained determinedly silent, in spite of Poppy's repeated questioning. The bad feeling in her stomach had festered, until she became quite nauseous. She could think of only one place they could be headed. Chopra wanted her to meet his new woman. The question was: how would she react?

I'll scratch her eyes out, thought Poppy defiantly. But she knew that she would not. If Chopra wanted her to meet his future wife, then it was because he wished for a dignified end to their marriage. He had always been a man who prided himself on his dignity. She would give him that, she thought. No matter what it cost her, she would give him that.

The auto-rickshaw stopped.

Poppy looked out. They were on Guru Rabindranath Tagore Road. Traffic buzzed by them on the right, while a steady stream of people moved by on the left. 'Why have we stopped here?'

Chopra did not answer. He got out of the rickshaw and paid the driver. Mystified, Poppy followed him.

They were standing in front of a broad, single-storey building, with a front porch leading into a cavernous room that was decked out with tables and chairs. It looked like a restaurant, a dhaba-style restaurant, she thought. She looked up. Where the restaurant's nameboard should have been there was a white cloth. Perhaps the nameboard was behind the cloth.

Chopra walked up the shallow steps fronting the porch and into the restaurant; Poppy followed.

Above them ceiling fans whirred, churning the hot air. A few flies buzzed lazily around the darkened interior. Poppy was beginning to understand. He did not want to take her to the woman's house. He did not trust her enough to reveal to her exactly where her nemesis lived. Instead he had picked this neutral venue for their meeting.

She looked around, seeking a lone woman seated at one of the tables.

What would she look like? Poppy wondered. Attractive, no doubt. And young – or, at least, younger than her. After all, Chopra was still a handsome man.

Suddenly, she realised that there was no one in the restaurant. It wasn't a popular place, then. That must be why Chopra had picked it; they would have privacy, at least, for her shame. The place seemed to have been newly refurbished. The furniture was unchipped, with bright chequered tablecloths and high-backed comfortable-looking padded chairs. The granite floor tiles had been newly laid, and the paint on the walls was bright and welcoming. She could not see any menus, however, and there seemed to be no staff around. That was strange.

'Well,' said Chopra, 'what do you think?'

Poppy was bewildered. 'What do you mean? What do I think of *what*?'

He smiled. He appeared to be enjoying a joke at her expense. 'When Dr Devidikar told me that I would have to retire, I was terrified. I couldn't tell you just how terrified. What would I do with the rest of my life? I had been a police officer for so long that I could not think of any other sort of existence. But gradually I came to terms with the situation. I started thinking about what else I could do with my time. I didn't want to become that retired old duffer who potters around, reads the newspaper for half the day, spends the other half watching cricket and talking of the good old days. And so gradually I came up with a plan . . . Do you know, in Mumbai now we have every kind of restaurant going. If someone in the world eats it, we're serving it somewhere in this city. But there is one sort of restaurant that I have always wished for that we don't have. Do you know what kind that is?'

Poppy shook her head; her bewilderment was increasing by the minute. What in the world did this have to do with the Other Woman?

'A restaurant run exclusively for policemen!' Chopra said. His face had broken into a rare grin.

'What?'

'Think about it. A policeman is welcome nowhere, not truly. Most restaurants will immediately rush to offer him a free meal, thinking that should they not, they might risk angering him, and no one wants to anger a policeman, even if they have nothing to hide. And as for the other customers – as soon as a policeman sits down they become uncomfortable. There is nowhere a policeman can go in this city and know that he is not only welcome, but positively one of the family. That's when I thought of this place. A restaurant where policemen can gather, knowing that the owner himself was once a policeman, knowing that the clientele are all policemen. A place where they can meet and be themselves, where they can bring their families if they wish, where they can sit with colleagues and discuss the day's work, or simply be at peace for a few moments; a port in a storm; a home away from home.'

Chopra beamed. 'This is our new restaurant.'

'*Our* restaurant? Do you mean you and . . . and the other one?'

'Other one?' It was now his turn to look confused. 'What other one?'

'The other woman,' wailed Poppy desperately. She had promised herself that she would not cry, but she could feel the tears welling at the corners of her eyes. She hoped her mascara would not run. She looked terrible when her mascara ran.

'Oh, Poppy!' said Chopra exasperatedly. 'Come with me.'

He turned on his heel and walked to the front of the restaurant, out into the sunshine. There was a spring in his step that he recognised from his early years on the force.

The past few days had been akin to a rebirth for Chopra. In between his bouts with the media crews, he had spent much of his time fielding a continuous stream of calls from the city's most senior policemen. A few had queried his investigation and the authority by which he had conducted it. But on the whole there had been a genuine feeling that Chopra, a retired officer, had gone beyond the call of duty and in so doing had brought honour to the service. One of their own had cracked a major crime ring and finally concluded the criminal career of Kala Nayak. And Chopra's exposé of Ashok Kalyan's involvement and the collusion of various policemen in the affair had given the Commissioner ammunition with which to launch another root-and-branch inquiry into corruption within the service. With the newspapers behind him the Commissioner was busy fanning the flames, making all sorts of noises about gangsters and corrupt politicians preying on vulnerable, underpaid policemen.

Chopra knew that the Commissioner was a political animal and that he was using the situation to his advantage. But he had also heard that the man was honest – as honest as it was possible for Mumbai's top policeman to be. He felt sure that much good would come of his crusade, even if some of that good was the furtherance of the Commissioner's own career.

One consequence of the furious activity of the past two days was that Chopra had barely had a minute to himself. He had had almost no opportunity to clear the air with Poppy. On the couple of occasions that he had tried she had worked herself into such a rage about his recent behaviour that he had abandoned the attempt. Now that he finally realised exactly what had been going on inside Poppy's head he felt suddenly ashamed. He had caused her much grief and that had never been his intent.

At that moment, a truck pulled up beside them.

Sub-Inspector Rangwalla jumped out of the driver's cab.

'Rangwalla!' said Chopra sternly, returning to the present. 'You're late.'

'Yes, sir. Sorry, sir. There was a problem at the station. A team arrived from the Central Bureau of Investigation to interview Inspector Suryavansh. They took him back to their head office in Colaba. I'm not sure he is going to be back soon.'

'But then who is in charge of the station?'

'ACP Rao put Inspector Modak temporarily in charge, sir. Until Inspector Suryavansh returns.'

'And if he doesn't?'

'We can only pray, sir,' said Rangwalla with a wooden face. 'Of course, this was before ACP Rao himself was requested to attend the CBI offices.'

Chopra's face betrayed no emotion. He remembered how vehemently Rao had opposed his determination to conduct an autopsy on Santosh Achrekar's body . . .

Rangwalla moved to the rear of the truck and let down the tailgate. Ganesha trotted out into the sunlight. Immediately, the little elephant lifted his trunk and petted Chopra's face.

'Just a minute, Poppy,' he said. 'I must deal with our little friend first.'

He led Ganesha down a narrow alley that ran along the side of the restaurant and into a compound at the rear. The compound was securely walled on three sides, with a covered veranda looking out from the rear of the restaurant on its fourth. At the back of the compound was a large mango tree, ripe with fruit. Beneath the tree was a pool of muddy water, surrounded by dry grass. Ganesha trotted to a halt below the mango tree and regarded the muddy pool.

'Welcome to your new home, boy,' said Chopra.

The elephant looked up uncertainly, then dipped the tip of his trunk into the pool as if testing the water. He appeared to be satisfied with what he had divined and stepped forward to plop himself down into the mud. Reaching out his trunk he picked up a fallen mango and popped it into his mouth.

Over the past few days the little elephant appeared to have fully regained his appetite and had abandoned his self-imposed fast. To Chopra's dismay he remained addicted to junk food, in particular bars of Cadbury's Dairy Milk. But at least he had begun to eat a more regular elephant diet as well. Chopra hoped that in a few months Ganesha would begin to fill out.

'Why didn't you tell me you were moving him here?' said Poppy crossly, her other worries momentarily forgotten. 'You know that Mrs Subramanium will think that she has beaten me.'

'Mrs Subramanium was right. An apartment building is no place for an elephant.' And neither, thought Chopra, was an elephant sanctuary a thousand miles away, not for my Ganesha. That very morning he had called Dr Rohit Lala. Thanking the vet for his efforts, he explained that in the end he could not discharge the responsibility his uncle had bequeathed him by sending the young elephant away.

Dr Lala had expressed surprise. 'Are you sure you know what you are doing?' he had asked.

'No,' Chopra had said with feeling. 'I only know that it is the right thing to do.'

Chopra turned to Rangwalla. 'Did you pick up the plaque?'

'Yes, sir,' said Rangwalla. He reached into the sack he had been holding and took out a large metal plaque, about two feet long on each side. The plaque glinted in the sun as he handed it over. Her curiosity piqued, Poppy looked over her husband's shoulder to read the engraved inscription on the burnished piece of metal:

THE BABY GANESH DETECTIVE AGENCY

'What is this?' she asked suspiciously. Poppy had become increasingly confused by her husband's behaviour. She had come prepared for an emotional showdown and some manner of explanation, but instead Chopra was leading her around as if nothing were going on. And now this . . .

'This, my dear, is my second great idea.'

'What do you mean?'

Chopra put down the plaque and turned to her. 'Poppy, I am a detective. I may no longer wear a uniform, but that is what I am. This restaurant will practically run itself. I must have something else to occupy my time, something else that makes me feel that I am still the same Ashwin that you have known all these years. This whole business with the Achrekar case gave me the idea. I have spent thirty years learning how to be a detective. Just because I am retired it does not mean my brain has also retired. I can continue to do what I have always done, only now I can choose the cases that I wish to work on.'

'But what about your heart!'

'I am not a fool. From now on I will take only cases that

don't almost get me killed. You know, missing husbands, lost wills, that sort of thing. But this is something that I have to do. It is as simple as that. I hope you can understand.' Poppy opened her mouth to protest, but then hesitated. As long as she had known him, her husband had been a policeman. She could not imagine what it had meant for him to give that up. It must have been like giving up a part of himself. Could she really deny him this?

A private detective. Surely that would be a safer occupation than an active police officer?

She sighed. 'Where will be the office of this fancy-shmancy detective agency?' she asked finally.

Chopra smiled. 'You are standing in it.'

Her eyes widened, and then she began to giggle. 'And I suppose he is your partner, is he?' she said, pointing at Ganesha, who was happily rolling around in the muddy water.

'Don't forget what Uncle Bansi said: he is no ordinary elephant.'

Rangwalla had wandered over to the mango tree. 'Sir, you don't believe all that mumbo-jumbo, do you?'

Ganesha looked up at Rangwalla. Then he siphoned up a trunkful of water and shot a jet all over the sceptical sub-inspector, soaking him to the skin.

Poppy and Chopra laughed as Rangwalla beat a swift retreat, cursing under his breath.

'Come on,' said Chopra. 'I haven't shown you the best part.' He led Poppy back to the front of the restaurant. 'You didn't ask me what our new restaurant will be called.'

'*Our* restaurant?'

'Yes. Yours and mine.'

'But . . . but . . . what about the . . . other woman?'

'Poppy, for the last time, there is no other woman!'

'So you haven't been planning to leave me?'

'Leave you?' said Chopra. He seemed genuinely astonished. 'Why in the world would I want to do that?'

She looked down miserably. 'You know why.'

Chopra placed an arm around her shoulders. 'God has been very good to me. He has given me you. I don't need anything else.'

Poppy looked into her husband's eyes and knew that he was speaking the truth. She felt tears brimming from the corners of her eyes.

In her heart she had known that the plan to adopt Kiran's baby was an act of desperation. For it to succeed she would have had to lie to the most honest man she had ever known. The thought had festered inside her and thus, in one sense, it had been a relief that the plan had not come to fruition.

Chopra's words were now the perfect balm for her wounded heart.

She was lifted by a sudden feeling of hope.

'But then who is it that has been calling you? I thought it was . . . another woman.'

'Shalini Sharma? She is a restaurant consultant I have been meeting. She has given me much valuable advice.'

Poppy's smile morphed into a frown. 'A restaurant is a very stressful business. If you had told me about this I would never have allowed you to go ahead with it.'

'Which is precisely why I had to keep it a secret from you,' said Chopra. He watched the shadow on his wife's face. 'I will hire good people to help me run it. I will be like one of those big-shot restaurateurs, swanning in every now and again to taste the menu and move the chairs around.'

Poppy was silent, then finally she giggled. 'Very well, Mister Big shot. Just remember . . . *I* am the only chef in your life.'

'You are much more than that, Poppy.' Chopra turned and walked onto the porch. He stopped beneath the gable. Poppy noticed that a rope was dangling down from one end of the triangular pediment. Her eyes moved up, and saw that the rope was connected to the cloth draped over the restaurant's nameboard. Chopra turned to her and grinned. With a theatrical flourish he tugged on the rope, pulling away the covering cloth and revealing the restaurant's name:

POPPY'S

Policemen's Bar and Restaurant

EPILOGUE

Rain thudded on the windows of Inspector Chopra's bedroom once more.

Mumbai was deluged. The prediction of Homi Contractor had been correct: the monsoons, now that they were here, were turning out to be the wettest in living memory. The city was in a constant state of alert at the prospect of repeated flooding. Where only a month before, everyone had deplored the drought-like heat, now everyone was complaining bitterly about the horrendous waterlogging.

Chopra awoke, and sat bolt upright in bed. He was bathed in sweat. He could feel his heart hammering away in his chest. He had been dreaming, dreaming of his Uncle Bansi. The dream had been about something that he had forgotten, something about his uncle that had simply not occurred to him until now; a buried memory that had abruptly floated to the surface of his consciousness, like a weighted balloon released from its tether.

It had been a sweltering day and Bansi had taken the eight-year-old Chopra to the mela that was held after each harvest in the nearby village of Ramnagar. Chopra had loved everything about the mela: the colour, the noise, the travelling troupe that came each year to entertain the crowds.

Uncle Bansi had enjoyed the fair every bit as much as his nephew; many people had actually assumed that he was part of the entertainment, and he and Chopra had been continually stopped by those wishing to have their fortunes told.

Towards the end of the day one of these well-wishers had repaid Bansi's agreeable prognostication by handing him a treat. Bansi had shared it with Chopra. He had never forgotten the look of utter pleasure that had passed over his uncle's face as he had consumed his half of the treat. 'If I had known they tasted this good, I would have had one every single day!' he had exclaimed.

And as far as Chopra knew that is exactly what he had done. Every day that his uncle had remained in the village he had gone to Hari's provisions store and purchased the same thing. How could he have forgotten? How could he have forgotten that his Uncle Bansi had adored Cadbury's Dairy Milk?

ACKNOWLEDGEMENTS

No book can be published without the help, advice and good wishes of a great number of people. In this lean age for the first-time author I am forever indebted to my agent Euan Thorneycroft at A.M. Heath and to my editor Ruth Tross at Mulholland. Their confidence is the reason you have just finished reading this novel.

I am grateful too to all those who helped incrementally improve upon the original manuscript. Thomas Abraham and Poulomi Chatterjee at Hachette India; Amber Burlinson, copy-editor, and Zoë Carroll, eagle-eyed proofreader. To this I add Euan whose insightful first comments helped me to tighten up the sense of place in the novel and to round out the characters. A special thank you to Ruth whose constant enthusiasm, relentless attention to plot detail, and gentle manner of persuasion elevated many aspects of this work. Who says editors have to be tyrannical?

I would also like to thank Ruth's team at Mulholland: Naomi Berwin in marketing, Kerry Hood in publicity, Laura

Del Vescovo in production, and Ruth's assistant Sharan Matharu. Similar thanks go to Euan's assistant Pippa McCarthy.

Another special thank you to Anna Woodbine who designed and illustrated the novel's cover, perfectly bringing together the colour and exuberance of India with the beating heart of the novel: one man and his elephant.

My brother-in-law Ashwin Chopra deserves an honourable mention for permitting me to borrow his name. His integrity is as unimpeachable as Inspector Chopra's.

Lastly, I'd like to thank those who have helped me in researching this work. My wife Nirupama Khan, my great friends from Mumbai, and my colleague at UCL and former Indian police officer Dr Jyoti Belur. A mention too for Terry Brewer who first took me to the subcontinent and in a very real sense placed my feet on the long road to publication.

MEET THE AUTHOR

Photo Credit: Nirupama Khan

Vaseem Khan first saw an elephant lumbering down the middle of the road in 1997 when he arrived in India to work as a management consultant. It was the most unusual thing he had ever encountered and served as the inspiration for the Baby Ganesh Agency series.

He returned to the UK in 2006 and now works at University College London for the Department of Security and Crime Science where he is astonished on a daily basis by the way modern science is being employed to tackle crime. Elephants are third on his list of passions, first and second being great literature and cricket, not always in that order.

introducing

If you enjoyed
THE UNEXPECTED INHERITANCE OF INSPECTOR CHOPRA,
don't miss the next Baby Ganesh Agency Investigation

THE PERPLEXING THEFT OF THE JEWEL IN THE CROWN

by Vaseem Khan

A TRIP TO THE MUSEUM

'Arise, Sir Chopra.'

As the gleaming blade touched gently down upon his shoulder Inspector Ashwin Chopra (Retd) found himself overcome by a jumble of conflicting emotions. Pride, undoubtedly, at this supreme moment in his life. But with pride came a boundless sense of humility. That he, the son of a schoolmaster from a poor village in the state of

Maharashtra, India, could be thus honoured seemed altogether improbable.

After all, what had he really achieved?

He was an honest man who had worn the uniform of the Brihanmumbai Police with an unblemished record for over thirty years – before a traitorous heart had forced him into early retirement – and in the India of today that was something to be proud of indeed. And yet was integrity enough of a virtue to warrant such accolade?

Surely there were more deserving candidates?

What about his old friend Assistant Commissioner of Police Ajit Shinde who even now was fighting Naxalite bandits in far-off Gadchiroli and had already lost the tip of his right ear to a sniper's bullet? Or Inspector Gopi Moolchand who had lost a great deal more when he had selflessly dived into Vihar Lake on the outskirts of Mumbai to rescue a stricken drunk and been attacked by not one but three opportunistic crocodiles?

Chopra was overcome by a sudden overwhelming sense of pathos, as if this singular occasion marked a peak in his life from which there could now only be a perilous and unwelcome descent.

He stumbled to his feet from the knighting stool and cast around at the circle of gathered luminaries in search of Poppy. He saw that his wife, radiant in a powder-pink silk sari, was engaged in conversation with a haughty-looking white woman, a peer of the realm whose name Chopra could not recall. Standing in the lee of the old dowager was his old sub-inspector, Rangwalla, fingering the collar of his ill-fitting suit . . . and next to Rangwalla, Ganesha, the baby elephant that Chopra's mysterious uncle Bansi had sent to him seven months previously with the intriguing missive stating that 'this is no ordinary elephant'...

He frowned. How did Ganesha get here? Or, for that matter, Rangwalla? ... And did they *really* allow elephants inside Buckingham Palace?

Chopra turned back to the supreme monarch.

He looked down at The Queen and realised, for the first time, that she bore an uncanny resemblance to his mother-in-law, the widow Poornima Devi, right down to the black eyepatch and the expression of intense dislike that Poppy's mother had reserved for him ever since she had first set eyes on him all those years ago.

The royal monarch's mouth opened into a yawning black hole... *BAAAAAARRRRRRPPPPP!*

Chopra jerked out of his daydream and looked around wildly. He realised that he was still sitting in the gridlocked traffic around Horniman Circle in south Mumbai.

The violent chorus around him testified to the increasing sense of desperation of his fellow motorists. A quick glance in the wing mirror informed him that the bright red sports Mercedes that had been bumper-to-bumper behind him was now attempting to ooze past by climbing onto the concrete verge of the Horniman Circle Gardens that lay at the centre of the roundabout.

As the Mercedes pulled alongside, the young man behind

the wheel barped his horn again. 'Excuse me, Gandhiji, you are not driving a tractor! This is Mumbai, my friend!' Loud foreign music blared from the vehicle and a chorus of laughter spilled forth from the youth's companions seated in the rear.

Chopra reddened.

He had half a mind to climb out of the van and give the obnoxious youth a piece of his mind. But then he noticed that a grey-furred macaque was watching him intently from the branches of an ancient banyan tree growing on the edge of the Gardens and he recalled the recent reports in the *Times of India* about the Horniman macaque attacks.

The gardens, once a favoured haunt of Mumbai's wealthy Parsee community, had recently been colonised by a troupe of bonnet macaques, displaced from their ancient mangrove home by the city's relentless urbanisation. The macaques had caused a stir by viciously assaulting a passing MLA – Member of the Legislative Assembly – much to the delight of the MLA's fellow Mumbaikers. The Member in question was embroiled in a bribery scandal and had three criminal cases lodged against him in the High Court. Far from disqualifying a man from running for office, it seemed to Chopra that a criminal record was almost a requirement for most political aspirants in his country.

'We're going to be late.'

Chopra glanced at his wife, Archana, known to all as

Poppy. Chopra loved his wife dearly, but at this precise instant he was struggling to recall why.

It had been upon Poppy's insistence that they were here now, on their way to the Grand Exhibition of the Crown Jewels of the United Kingdom at the Prince of Wales Museum in Fort. Chopra had known that traffic at this hour would be horrendous, but Poppy had been hounding him for days, ever since the exhibition had arrived in Mumbai two weeks ago, a full ten days before Her Majesty, The Queen made her historic visit to the city.

It was the first time that The Queen had ever visited Mumbai, the first time in two decades that she had set foot on Indian soil. The newspapers had been full of little else.

Poppy, like most in the city, had quickly succumbed to the 'royal malaria' as it had been dubbed. Chopra, however, had remained aloof.

As a closet Anglophile he was secretly delighted that The Queen had chosen to visit Mumbai. But Chopra was a sober and rational man. From his father – the late Shree Premkumar Chopra – he had inherited both an admiration for the British and the progress they had brought to the subcontinent, and a healthy perspective for all that the Raj had taken from Indians. He did not see the need to gush just because Her Majesty had come calling.

Naturally, Poppy did not agree.

All her friends had already been to see the exhibit, she had complained. They talked of nothing else.

Chopra's eventual surrender was inevitable. He had rarely refused his wife in the twenty-four years of their marriage. Poppy was a force of nature, flighty, romantic and a devil when aroused. It was far easier to acquiesce to her occasional whims than to act the curmudgeon. And besides, he knew, instinctively, that in the perennial war between the sexes it behooved a husband to surrender the occasional battle. The trick was to pick the right battles to lose.

He glanced again at his wife.

A slavish follower of fashion, Poppy had styled her long, dark hair into a beehive, which seemed to be all the rage following the release of a new Bollywood movie set in the Sixties. Her fair cheeks glowed with rouge and her slender figure was encased in a bottle-green silk sari with gold-flecked trim.

Chopra himself was dressed, at Poppy's insistence, in his best – and only – suit, a dark affair that his wife complained made him look like an undertaker. But he had not seen the need to purchase a new suit for a simple visit to the museum. The suit had served him well for the past fifteen years; it would serve him well for a few more.

As a concession to his wife he had made an effort with the rest of his appearance. His thick black hair – greying at the temples – was neatly combed and his brisk moustache was immaculately groomed. His deep brown eyes sat above a Roman nose. Nothing could be done about the frown lines, however, that had recently taken up residence on his walnut-brown forehead.

Supressing a sigh, Chopra looked back out at the Circle where a hapless constable was attempting to herd the gridlocked panorama of cars, trucks, motorbikes, bicycles, rickshaws, handcarts, pedestrians and stray animals.

If there *is* a hell, he thought, then it cannot be worse than this.

The queue at the ticket window stretched around the stylish new stainless-steel-plated Visitors' Centre. For once the usually riotous mob was being kept in check by the presence of the severe-looking commandoes patrolling the grounds. A line of these commandoes was stationed all the way around the museum adding an air of intrigue to the picturesque formal gardens in which the museum sat.

Chopra knew that the commandoes, in their black military fatigues, were from the elite Force One Unit, a special anti-terrorist squad that had been set up amidst a blaze of publicity following the 2008 Mumbai terror attacks. What the newspapers didn't know – but which Chopra had heard on the police grapevine – was that the Chief Minister, having achieved his self-aggrandising news splash, had subsequently slashed the unit's funding. The savings had disappeared into that strange place where percentages vanished on the subcontinent. The handful of commandoes to survive the cull now spent their days sitting in their Goregaon HQ idly polishing the M4 assault rifles they were wielding so impressively today.

As the queue inched forward he took the opportunity to once again admire the recently renamed museum. It was now called the Chhatrapati Shivaji Maharaj Vastu Sangrahalaya after the warrior-king, Shivaji, founder of the

Maratha Empire. But to Chopra it would always be the Prince of Wales Museum. As he looked up once again at its three-storied façade, clad in kurla stone and topped by its Mughal dome, he felt a gladness knocking on his heart. This feeling overcame him each time he thought of the treasure trove of ancient relics housed inside those enigmatic walls, going back as far as the Indus Valley civilisation, which scholars now claimed might be the oldest of them all.

He had been coming here for nearly three decades, ever since he had first arrived in the megalopolis as a freshly minted constable from his native village in the Maharashtrian interior, a bright-eyed seventeen-year-old with Bombay dreams in his eyes. Since then he had learned a great many lessons, the most painful of which was that all that glittered was not necessarily gold.

The relentless pace of change in the big city often dismayed him. The constant striving for the future, as if the past was a yoke that had to be cast off and trampled into the dust of history. He had found the museum to be a refuge from this headlong rush into the unknown, a balm for the affliction of nostalgia from which he suffered.

Chopra considered himself a historian, a guardian of the legacy of ancient India, one of a dwindling number. He knew that his country was now intoxicated by progress and the prospect of becoming a superpower. But for Chopra there was still much to be gleaned from the traditions of a culture that had persisted for more than seven thousand years. Modernity was not everything. Technology was not the answer to all problems.

They purchased their tickets and then waited patiently as they were both frisked, Poppy by a female officer inside the Visitors' Centre. They were asked to deposit their phones and cameras – which were not permitted inside the exhibition – before being herded towards the museum's main entrance where they queued up to pass through a metal scanner. Ahead of Chopra a woman refused to give up her gold wedding necklace. The guards inspected it and allowed her to keep it. A tall, broad-shouldered Sikh man set off the scanner and pointed to the thick steel bracelet on his wrist, a core article of his faith. Again the guards permitted him to pass. Another man argued to be allowed to take in his asthma inhaler. The guards examined the object, turning it this way and that in their calloused hands, then exchanged mystified glances. Eventually, they shrugged and handed it back.

Chopra frowned.

If this was what passed for top security, then it left much to be desired, in his humble opinion.

They stepped through the entrance and into the Central Gallery.

Chopra was intrigued to note that the usual exhibits had been replaced by a collection of objects from the days of the Raj. Ordinarily, the Gallery housed pieces from all eras of India's past – a jewelled dagger from the court of Shah Jahan; a terracotta lion from the empire of Asoka the

Great; a clay seal from the Harappan civilisation inscribed with that enigmatic and as yet undeciphered Indus Valley script.

A frown appeared on his brow as his eyes came to rest on the tacky waxwork models of the British Royal Family that now took pride of place in the gallery. A plump, middle-aged man with sunglasses parked in his heavily oiled hair had his arm slung cosily around 'The Queen's' waist whilst his wife took a photograph of him.

Chopra would have liked to linger over the Raj exhibits but Poppy was already urging him onwards and upwards.

They followed the herd as everyone jostled their way up the marble staircase, past Miniature Paintings and Himalayan Arts, to the second floor where the Sir Ratan Tata Gallery had been commandeered for the Crown Jewels exhibit. Four more Force One guards were stationed outside the newly installed reinforced steel doors that now fronted the gallery. The guards straightened to attention as the visitors arrived, their fingers involuntarily flickering to the triggers of their assault rifles.

Chopra knew that security had been a principal concern as soon as it was announced that – for the first time in their history – the Crown Jewels would leave their native shores and travel abroad with The Queen. He remembered the fuss in the UK earlier in the year when the press had gotten wind of the plan. An ancient law had had to be amended just to permit the jewels to be moved.

It was still unclear exactly *why* Her Majesty had agreed to the Indian government's request for the jewels to be exhibited on the subcontinent. The Queen herself had remained tight-lipped on the matter. Chopra, for his part, had always held the monarch in high regard and considered her adherence to traditions emblematic of a bygone age, a time when discretion and good manners were paramount.

Only twenty visitors were permitted inside the Tata Gallery at any one time. They waited impatiently as the previous group filed out, buzzing with excitement.

Chopra shuffled in with the others into the air-conditioned sanctum of the gallery where they were immediately greeted by the sight of two tall, broadly built white gentlemen wielding ceremonial halberds and wearing the ruffed, red-and-black uniform of the Tower of London guardians. He had read that they were called Beefeaters, a term which had caused some consternation in India, where the bulk of the population considered the cow to be an avatar of God.

The guards stepped aside to reveal a portly Indian in an ill-fitting Nehru jacket, Nehru cap and round-framed spectacles. To Chopra the man looked like a plumper version of the freedom fighter Subhash Chandra Bose.

The man welcomed the newcomers with a beaming white smile and spread his arms as if he meant to sweep them all up in an enormous embrace. 'Welcome to the Crown Jewels exhibition!'

Chopra squinted at the tour guide's name-tag: ATUL KOCHAR.

Kochar was an enthusiastic man. He might have been an

actor in his spare time, Chopra reflected, such was the animation with which he narrated the tour of the exhibits.

Chopra listened with only half an ear. Like most of the others in the red-carpeted room his attention was instantly drawn to the Crown Jewels securely ensconced behind various glass display cases stationed around the gallery.

He plucked his reading spectacles from his pocket and pushed them self-consciously onto his nose. From his other pocket he removed his copy of the *Ultimate Guidebook to the Crown Jewels*, which Poppy had insisted they purchase from the Visitors' Centre for an extortionate sum. As Kochar continued to speak, Chopra peered at the nearest display cases then leafed through the guidebook for the corresponding entries. His keen gaze picked out particularly fine pieces. Here, for instance, was the Imperial State Crown, the crown the current Queen had worn on her coronation, studded (according to the Guidebook) with 2868 diamonds, 270 pearls, 17 sapphires, 11 emeralds and 5 rubies. And over here lay the Sceptre of the Cross in which was embedded the Cullinan diamond, the world's largest white diamond, known as the 'Great Star of Africa'. He found himself entranced by the magnificent jewelled sword made for the coronation of King George IV, fashioned from the finest Damascus steel and inlaid (the Guide said) with a 'king's ransom in jewels'.

'But how much is it all worth?'

Chopra looked up to see the plump man who had photographed himself with his arm around the waxwork Queen accosting the tour guide with a belligerent expression.

Kochar gave a somewhat strained smile. 'No value can

be placed on the Crown Jewels, sir. They are the very definition of priceless.'

'Nonsense,' barked the man bombastically. 'My family are Marwari. We are in the jewel business. There is always a price. Come now, don't be coy. Let us have it, sir.'

A chorus of agreement washed over Kochar. As he looked on Chopra felt a twinge of sadness strike his heart. Was this all these people saw? A dragon's hoard of treasure to be weighed in dollars and rupees? What about the weight of history that lay behind each one of these magnificent creations? Or the skill that had been employed to manufacture them?

'Stop your yapping, man. Did you come here to appreciate the jewels or buy them?'

Chopra turned to see the tall Sikh man he had queued behind at the metal detector glaring at the Marwari. The Sikh was a big, muscular gentleman with a fine beard, fierce, bushy eyebrows and a stupendous yellow turban. The retort that had sprung to the Marwari's lips died a quiet death. His face coloured but he said nothing.

The Sikh pointed at a magnificent, eight-foot-high sandstone carving of the goddess Kali, which had been left inside the gallery due to the fact that its rear was affixed to the gallery wall. 'You are probably the sort of fool who does not appreciate even our own history.'

Chopra felt an instant liking for the irate Sikh.

'Yes,' agreed a pretty young woman in a bright blue sari and red spectacles. 'We should all learn to appreciate our own heritage. Only then can we truly appreciate someone else's.'

The crowd swiftly saw which way the wind was blowing and galloped towards the moral high ground. There was a sudden chorus of agreement with the big Sikh. 'Indian culture is the best, no doubt about it!'; 'You can keep your Crown Jewels, sir. The Mughals threw away more magnificent treasures when giving alms to the poor!' A circle widened around the Marwari who blushed furiously.

Kochar spared the hapless man further embarrassment by smoothly drawing everyone's attention to the centrepiece of the exhibit – the Crown of Queen Elizabeth, The Queen Mother, in which was set the Kohinoor diamond.

Chopra knew that the presence of the Kohinoor on Indian soil had caused quite a stir. Ever since the legendary diamond had been 'presented' to Queen Victoria more than one hundred and fifty years earlier it had been the subject of controversy. Many in India felt that the Kohinoor had been stolen by the British and it was high time those great colonial thieves were forced to rectify the matter. The news channels had been awash with talk of demonstrations and civic protest, particularly from the India First lobby. In an attempt to ward off potential embarrassment for the government, Mumbai's Commissioner of Police had ordered a clampdown on protests during the royal visit, an act which itself had courted controversy as it was deemed inherently unconstitutional.

Chopra listened now as Kochar narrated what he called 'the mysterious and bloody history of the Kohinoor'...

The first historically verifiable record of the Kohinoor came from the memoirs of Mohammed Babur, descendant of Tamerlane and Genghis Khan, and founder of the

Mughal Empire. Babur claimed the diamond had been gifted to him by the Pashtun sultan Ibrahim Lodi, though the truth was far bloodier. Lodi had perished to Babur's invading army and the Kohinoor had been part of the plunder claimed by the new ruler of the subcontinent.

It was at this time that the curse became widely known.

Discovered in an ancient and enigmatic Sanskrit document the curse stated: *'He who owns this diamond will own the world, but will also know all its misfortunes. Only God, or a woman, may wear it with impunity.'*

Over the coming centuries the curse had proved alarmingly accurate in its dire prediction . . .

The run of ill fortune commenced with Babur's son, Humayun, whose empire was overrun by the great general Sher Khan. A broken man, Humayun would later die in a freak fall from the stone steps of his court library. Sher Khan's victory was short-lived, however – the general soon perished when a cannon packed with gunpowder exploded on him during the siege of Kalinjar Fort in Uttar Pradesh.

Next came Humayan's grandson, Shah Jahan, the visionary behind the Taj Mahal, who installed the Kohinoor in his magnificent Peacock Throne, and paid the price for tempting fate when he was subsequently imprisoned by his son Aurangzeb. Legend had it that in order to torment his father Aurangzeb had the Kohinoor set outside the window of Shah Jahan's cell so that he could see the Taj only by looking at its reflection in the great stone.

In 1739, Nadir Shah, the Shah of Iran, sacked Agra and Delhi and carried off the Peacock Throne to Persia not realising the ill fortune he was bringing upon himself. Shah was assassinated shortly thereafter and the Kohinoor subsequently passed through a number of hands before ending up in the treasury of Maharaja Ranjit Singh, ruling prince of the Punjab.

In 1839, following the death of Ranjit Singh, the British claimed the Punjab for the Empire, and the Kohinoor was surrendered – through the machinations of the British East India Company – to Queen Victoria. Transported to England in 1850, it was duly presented to Her Majesty as a tribute from her 'loyal' subjects on the subcontinent. A line of British female Queens had safeguarded the great jewel ever since. In this way the prophecy was said to have been fulfilled.

Kochar beamed at his rapt audience and then abruptly announced that they had a further fifteen minutes to view the Crown Jewels before they would be requested to make way for the next party.

The crowd dispersed around the room.

Chopra bent down to take a closer look at the Kohinoor.

'Careful, sir. Don't get too close or the sensors will go off. They are very sensitive.'

He looked up to see Kochar smiling wearily at him. He realised that another man, late-middle-aged, with greying hair and a noticeable paunch, was staring down at the crown from the opposite side of the display case. The man's brow was furrowed in consternation and Chopra could make out that he was sweating heavily even though the room was air-conditioned. The man seemed to notice his scrutiny and looked up with a guilty start.

Chopra's own brow furrowed.

It seemed to him that he had seen this gentleman before, but before he could place him the man turned and shuffled quickly away towards one of the exhibits lining the walls of the gallery.

Chopra looked back at the crown, resplendent on its velvet cushion. His eyes were automatically drawn, once again, to the Kohinoor. The display lighting had been set up so that it accentuated the legendary diamond's beauty. Truly, he thought, it deserves its name: Koh-i-Noor – 'mountain of light'.

And suddenly there was a feeling inside him, like a whispering in his blood. Here was a living tie to the ancient India that he so cherished. He wondered what it would feel like to hold that enormous jewel in his fist, just as the greatest monarchs of the subcontinent had once done. Would he sense the ghost of Babur hovering on his shoulder? Would he know Shah Jahan's misery as he looked longingly at that which had been taken from him by his own flesh and blood? . . . The Kohinoor, which, for centuries, had set man against man, king against king, legion against legion.

A loud bang jerked him from his reverie. Instinctively, he turned and looked for the source of the noise . . . He heard another bang, then another . . . Alarm tore through him as he saw a dense cloud of smoke swiftly expanding around the room, engulfing everything in a choking miasma of white . . . The world began to spin around him, the room sliding away into a gentle, soughing darkness . . . Another noise now, just on the edge of hearing, a thin high-pitched whine that he couldn't place.

As he slumped to the floor and into unconsciousness, the last image that came to Inspector Chopra (Retd) was of the Kohinoor diamond, spinning in the heart of a white cloud, rays of light shooting from it in all directions, incinerating everything in their path.